DINING WITH PRINCES

John Sligo was born in New Zealand in 1944. After completing his university education at St John's College, Cambridge, he worked for the Food and Agriculture Organisation (United Nations) in Rome, where he lived for thirteen years, travelling often to Greece and India. In 1982 he made his home in Australia and now lives at Bondi Beach.

John Sligo has been a film and television journalist, and his articles have appeared in Italy, Australia, New Zealand and Canada. His works of fiction include *The Cave*, winner of the New Zealand PEN Award for best first novel, *Final Things,* winner of the New South Wales Premier's Prize for fiction in 1988, and *The Faces of Sappho* (1990). *Pasta, Rices and Other Vices* (1993) was his first recipe and travel book, based on his love of central Italian cookery.

DINING WITH PRINCES

JOHN SLIGO

Angus&Robertson
An imprint of HarperCollins*Publishers*

Angus&Robertson
An imprint of HarperCollins*Publishers*, Australia

First published in Australia in 1995

HarperCollins*Publishers*
25 Ryde Road, Pymble, Sydney NSW 2073, Australia
31 View Road, Glenfield, Auckland 10, New Zealand
77–85 Fulham Palace Road, London W6 8JB, United Kingdom
Hazelton Lanes, 55 Avenue Road, Suite 2900, Toronto, Ontario, M5R 3L2
and 1995 Markham Road, Scarborough, Ontario M1B 5M8, Canada
10 East 53rd Street, New York NY 10032, USA

National Library of Australia
Cataloguing-in-publication data:

Sligo, John
Dining with Princes

ISBN 0 207 18755X
I. Title
A823.3

Cover design by Katie Ravich.
Internal illustrations by Wendy Littlewood.
Printed in Australia by Griffin Paperbacks, Adelaide

8 7 6 5 4 3 2 1
99 98 97 96 95

Contents

For Nora Anna de Tersztyanszky
and for Sheila DeCaul Stone,
who will be kicking up her heels
somewhere to the 'Hallelujah Chorus'

I

ROMAN FOLLIES

Slaughter at DEAR Studios — *Caligula*

I looked in the kitchen mirror and wondered if I might be movie-star material. The beard might limit my roles, but since I'd given up smoking and gone to many a banquet I looked quite Neronian, and that might improve my chances for *Caligula*.

Outside on the Penitence Alley it was winter and too early for the old ladies with their hand-knitted shawls to be sitting against the stone wall sunbathing, knitting and nattering and, like the Fates, keeping an eye open for misdemeanours. Down the road they were still in sleep behind the high umber walls of the Queen of Heaven gaol and, down at Augusto's, the grocery doors were opening. It was six-thirty in the morning.

I made my caffe latte and munched bread and honey at the marble-top table, then took a shower, and went to the lavatory. Wandering along to the bedroom I got dressed in casual jeans, a smart brown shirt and sports coat. The air was warm from the terracotta stove, whose pipe ran through to the kitchen chimney flue, the smoke almost asphyxiating the two old women two storeys up when the *tramontana* blew from the alps. I was quite selfish about this and told them they should open the kitchen window and air the house, and that anyway they were just a couple of old witches looking to make trouble for me. Does my comfort mean nothing, I would ask them. Apparently it did not.

I sat on the double bed — it was a *letto matrimoniale*, suitable for two or three couples if need be — and looked over the photos my Swedish friend, Ben, had taken of me. Myself, in a dinner jacket, hair mussed, myself in a frilly shirt, rings on the fingers and hand placed against the left cheek, eyes sombre with that eighteenth-century hooded look of sensuality defined and

satisfied — *Les Liaisons Dangereuses.* This look was not familiar to me until I remembered that Ben had taken the shots while I had a monumental hangover; if they wanted that look in the film, I'd have to be drunk every night. I shuffled through the photos again as the street came awake. I'd tell the production he'd photographed Liza Minelli, I decided.

I selected five photos and went down the marble stairs.

I got to my latest car, a large old German Opel, and drove off down Penitence Street, leaving the alley to get on with the day.

DEAR studios were across town and the appointment was at nine. I drove towards them with that casual recklessness of Italians — weaving, hooting, screaming, abusing and never looking at the traffic behind. In Italy, the rear vision mirror doesn't exist.

I parked the car and went in for my interview — with one of the assistant directors. We sat in an office with venetian blinds and a Rousseauesque potplant, and the assistant director looked at my photos. He picked out one of me wearing a dinner jacket and holding a large Venetian crystal glass. The photo was cut off at the waist and below the jacket I wasn't wearing anything, but this the assistant director didn't know. He looked at me looking like a Harvard or Cambridge graduate and said, 'I think I saw you in that film.' I looked bored, as if I couldn't recall which film it was.

'Now,' said the assistant director, 'do you mind doing nude scenes?' I had nothing against nakedness as such, in fact I relished the role of summer satyr, naked down by the waterfall at Mercedes' farm. I loved the freezing cold water, the green trees locked into a canopy, the moss on the rocks, the Etruscan feel. I decided I wouldn't mind if it were absolutely part of the artistic purpose of the scene. But somehow this wasn't said. 'Certainly not,' I snapped back in my persona of the upper class slumming it with Hollywood on the Tiber.

The young man looked around the office. 'Well, you see, it is *Caligula*, and what we had in mind is not nudity as such. It is a dawn scene with Malcolm McDowell. You will be playing a speaking slave, under bedclothes of course. The scene, it is very opulent. They'll be using something like tiger skins.'

I felt a small surge of star quality. 'Oh well,' I said, 'I suppose, as long as it's something like that.'

'Of course,' said the assistant director, keen and upwardly mobile, handing me my lines, 'you'll be the one who speaks to Malcolm.'

That night I played bridge with friends, and Susan, who worked with Gore Vidal, thought she might be working on the film.

'On *Caligula*?' I asked as we cleaned up on four hearts, which always happened as long as we were sitting parallel to the bath in Francesca's apartment.

'It's Gore's *Caligula*,' explained American Susan, who had short hair and a businesslike East Coast approach to life. 'He is not at all pleased. In fact, I think he may sue Guccione if they use his name in the title. They've turned his script into something else and just want his name to sell it.'

Francesca's boyfriend, Jos, smirked. '*Penthouse* is putting up the money. Christ, I can imagine what Bob Guccione will be looking for.'

Susan also looked smirky. 'I may get a job as production assistant,' she said, 'but you won't see *me* acting.'

'Why not?' I demanded, hackles rising. 'I can't imagine for a moment that a film starring Sir John Gielgud, Malcolm McDowell, Peter O'Toole and Maria Schneider won't be something worth acting in.'

'And what did *she* get up to with Marlon Brando in *Last Tango in Paris*?' asked Susan.

'What?' I asked. It seemed best to pretend I hadn't seen it.

'We went to it,' said Jos. 'Remember the butter?'

'Three spades,' said Francesca tactfully.

'And,' I went on over a spaghetti supper, 'eight and a half million dollars will produce something great. It's a huge budget. As for the press releases! They claim it might gross more than *Gone with the Wind*.'

'Who knows,' said Jos, 'you might become famous or — '

'Or,' added Susan with a smirk, 'something else.'

I had, of course, heard the rumour that Gore Vidal's *Caligula* was likely to degenerate into some sort of spectacle, but I decided to put such thoughts out of my mind.

The next Sunday morning I found myself at the Piazza Santa Maria bar, looking up, now and then, to the frescos of the wise and foolish virgins painted on the facade of Santa Maria in Trastevere.

I was reading *Panorama* and there was an article in it about *Caligula*. The set was being constructed entirely in DEAR studios — they were copying Fellini. *The film-going public*, I read, *will never have seen a Rome like this . . . the opulence and the splendour, yes, but also the barbarism and cruelty and*, I read on, startled, *over one thousand pounds of human hair have been used for the wigs*. This, it seemed, had all come from Sicilian women, their hair being the toughest and most durable. Were the ladies of Sicily now bald?

Susan arrived yawning, with Sammy her dachshund on a lead. The regular thugs were arriving, too. Fat Marco, the bulldog, was already slouched in the sun beside his favourite thug, the espresso machine was going full bore; a bike revved up in Piazza San Egidio; the clock chimed ten.

'My God,' said Susan, reading the article, 'they're importing pythons!'

'I wonder what they'd want pythons for?' I asked, taking the article back to read further. 'And why goats, Himalayan goats, leopards, swans, mastiffs, pigs, eels, oxen, and all in specially built cages which will be air-conditioned as necessary. Isn't that amazing! Though I suppose the eels will come in fresh from Lake

Bracciano, or maybe the Tiber. Plenty down there.'

The church bells began clanging for the first mass of the day and the vast steel-barred doors of Santa Maria in Trastevere were opened.

I arrived on the set at five-thirty the following day. The call was for six. I'd given a lift to Roger, a Bostonian whose marriage had failed and whose mother had moved in and was paying his rent and much else besides. Roger had got the job through someone high up in the production, which was now barred to everyone — no press, no friends or friends of friends. Susan had got the assistant's job and was starting that day too.

We hung about smoking cigarettes and looking for coffee in what appeared to be a vast warehouse.

Scattered around were human-size crosses, wreaths of plastic flowers, acres of tulle and chiffon, spikes, wheels and spears. Roger, who had a lean face that once had been youthfully good-looking but had deteriorated in divorce and the freezing winds of the late forties, stared at the concrete expanse. 'I wonder what they want the crosses for?' he asked, shifting around on the chair.

The coffee lady arrived and filled up two white plastic cups. It seemed that an error must have been made and the call should have been for later than six. Maybe it should have been eight.

A young guy arrived fashionably late. '*Ciao*,' he said. '*Sono* Gianni.' He had curly hair and was wearing an old leather jacket, dilapidated jeans, and sneakers. Gianni was, so he told us, a film-maker; he had won a prize at the Berlin Film Festival.

I was wearing smart jeans, a checked shirt and a jersey hung around my neck. Roger looked as if he'd just come out of a lecture at some Ivy League school where the quadrangles forever rang to the sound of youthful voices on the edge of life. It occurred to me that Roger was still back there, on the edge of life. Gianni, however, was right in the middle.

'*Allora*,' said Gianni, with a rich Tuscan accent, '*cosa facciamo, oggi?*'

'Are you,' I responded, 'one of the slaves?'

'*Mi pare di si*.' Gianni switched into English since Roger was looking uncomprehending. 'Yess, I theenk so, and we speek together about somzing. I get it from my friend who is assistant director. They are having nice times interviewings girls for these film. They must do for them — '

'How many did they interview?' cut in Roger, leaving me wondering what the girls had to do.

'Five hundred ladies and five hundred gentleman from poor places. You know, from *borgata*, from slums,' Gianni said for Roger's benefit. 'Must all be vigorous and look ancient Roman. Kind of like types Pasolini use all the time.'

'For what?' asked Roger.

'Why,' said Gianni, 'to make real things. So that everything look real. In demand great deal of natural talents.' He grinned. 'And we are the privileged ones. We do not do such interview.'

'What *is* to happen?' asked Roger at nine-thirty, getting petulant.

The make-up ladies had arrived, the hair ladies had arrived, the props men had arrived and things were moving. It was almost time, so Ricardo, Gianni's friend the assistant director told us, to go into make-up.

Around us, a few of the Roman youths and girls were already being fitted for size to crosses, or finding themselves in tulle and wreathed in plastic flowers. Blood was oozing from gaping wounds which in the ladies seemed to be around the breasts or, poignantly, just above the mound of Venus.

'What were the *borgata* girls doing in those interviews with the assistant directors?' I asked Gianni. We were now both sitting in what looked like barbers' chairs and our hair had been washed. The lights were white but the mirrors were peachy in colour, which hid wrinkles and gave kindness to the reflection.

Gianni smirked, fingers to his lips, indicating he would tell me later the nature of the ladies' audition, for three strong Roman women — who might have once come from the *borgata* — now started to put our hair in curlers. They blow-dried, they adjusted, they gelled, they blow-dried again. My curly bouffant hairdo was not exactly in keeping with my idea of an aristocratic slave at Caligula's villa on Capri, who would make comments on the political situation in Rome. Nor did it suggest, as I had imagined for myself, a slave Celt, undoubtedly son of a high chieftan and an adept in druidic practice.

The hairdressers were around forty-five or more, had raddled olive skins and merry sexual eyes and were filled with the kind of life force that made them ever ready to straddle men and play them for the silly innocents they were. They curled and puffed and played and my fantasies vanished as I was transformed into a male bacchante, hair rising and curling and twisting and turning. I looked at Roger and he too had become a wild unrecognisable being.

Now the make-up ladies were working on me and Gianni. Gianni was turning into a Caravaggio boy, and I began to feel anxious and depressed as my face altered and I suddenly realised that I was already in costume. This, too, was not what I had expected: a white tulle nightdress, rather décolleté, emphasising my hairy chest, and a groin-length tutu, the white chiffon jockstrap hardly concealing what it ought to. And my face? Why hadn't I realised it before? I was powdered white, with rouged cheeks and dark blue eye-liner, while Roger was getting contrasting shades of green eye-liner and pink lipstick. Gianni was lush-lipped with pale grey eyelids.

'What are they paying you?' I asked Gianni. He was, it turned out, getting less than me. Roger was coy about his fee, since he knew someone high up in the production company and wasn't saying who. I felt mildly annoyed at this lack of class

consciousness; after all, a slave is a slave is a slave is . . .

'*Allora*,' said the hairdresser, smirking at my image and full of savage female glee. 'You look a real little *putto*, OK?' She stood back to admire the effect and the three ladies lavish raised eyebrows at each other. Gianni smiled back and so did I as we were herded out of make-up and onto the concrete tarmac floor where we stood huddled together, nervously smoking. I was wondering what a *putto* was, but didn't dare ask Gianni. It might be a he-whore, or it might be one of those little god sprites that pose harmoniously around Victory, popes or Roman ladies pretending to be Our Lady.

We had more coffee and sat down on some bales of chiffon as around the corner came a troupe which must have come from some demented production of *A Midsummer Night's Eve*. Behind them slouched two mastiffs, sizing up the victims for Day One. The troupe gathered around us chattering and smiling and time was subtly altering. Enclosed in the chiffon jockstrap, frizzed hair like a crazed harpie after a day on meths, I could feel modern Rome disappearing. Gianni noticed my expressions and shrugged a Tuscan shrug, which is less common than the Roman male shrug. It doesn't indicate that world-weary feel — the Roman male who has seen everything and is for sale and has been since the Empire went decadent — rather, it is the sturdy ploughman's reaction.

So time passed and I became a *putto* in tulle.

At midday we got our call to go on set.

We wound up stairs of concrete and arrived at the exterior of Caligula's villa on Capri. I looked around. In the annexes, protected by gauze curtains, were various slaves in a state of tulle and pain. One girl, white and bloodless apart from her wounds, was tied in chains; another was preparing to be whipped for offending the emperor. There was a huge, round, shallow, empty copper bowl. I stopped looking.

The cameras moved up the ramp with Tinto Brass behind them. He was wearing a blue shirt and had a soft belly that flopped into it.

'What did they get the girls to do in the auditions?' I pressed Gianni again as we huddled together near the first annexe, furnished with a golden phallus below the head of the emperor. Gianni had no time to reply as silence was called for. A procession formed at the bottom of the ramp and the cameras moved to take one. Charging towards us came the mastiffs, followed by scantily clad nymphs and shepherds bearing food for the kitchens. The boys were half-naked and so were the girls. The camera purred.

'Smile, smile,' shouted Tinto Brass. 'More animation, more vivacity!'

The procession reformed and take two bounced forward. I gaped. Tiberius was obviously being catered for by a particularly deranged delicatessen — a horse's head, blood fresh and eyes glazed came by, carried on a platter by two game young ladies with a bit of blood splashed on them. Behind them a deliquescent octopus slouched with gelatine arms, blobbing along in deathly displeasure. And now, guts on trays, cuts of meat; a shark? Yes, and it smelt. On and on came the procession, *galante*, high-stepping, with the horse's head and deliquescent octopus and meats and guts wobbling on platters.

Now, around the corner, from one of the annexes commanded by the camera, out came the first victim, held high above their heads, like a trophy, by two young men. She was naked, of course, and had been tortured to death. Her head flopped listlessly, but then angled for the camera and she smiled. 'Cut,' said Tinto. 'No smiling. You are dead so no smiling. You are not Elizabeth Taylor.'

Again they did it, the boys prancing out now like the procession before them, their long black locks and their lean muscular bodies animated, one now displaying an erection as innocent as that of a dog after a bitch. This seemed to please Tinto Brass. Both boys grinned cheerily as they passed us with their burden, and disappeared down the ramp, locks still waving.

Behind me, in the vast copper bowl, powdered mud was being

mixed with water and some colouring. It was stirred until it became a rich volcanic red. An assistant director came over and smiled at us. 'Now, would you three just step close to the bowl?' Roger went first, followed by Gianni and then me. We clutched our tutus and adjusted our chiffon jockstraps.

The assistant director went into conference with a lackey and returned with Tinto Brass. 'I think he will do,' said Tinto Brass, looking at Roger, whose body was quite lean with the belly skin becoming elastic. 'Yes, he will do.' Tinto pointed to the wall behind. On it was a kind of mini-cross which I had not noticed before. 'Yes, he will do. Now,' he addressed Roger, 'we want you up there. You will be naked and what has happened, but will not really happen, is that you are like St Sebastian on this cross except you are impaled through the *culo* . . . the anus. Yes, and much blood. You must writhe and moan and blood will pour down your legs.'

'No, no,' said Roger, his face registering yuppie horror and memories of a prostate examination.

Now firmly in the world and mind of Tinto Brass, I wondered if Roger would be forced to the cross and impaled as punishment.

'No, no,' insisted Roger. 'I was not employed on this film to be impaled through the anus.'

The young assistant director shrugged and a tall Italian youth, with long hair cut into a fringe and long ringlets, shrugged and agreed. He climbed up and his arms were tied to the cross tree, anus carefully missing the spike. He complained; his arms were untied. It was agreed that he would simply put them behind his back when it was time for his scene. He rearranged himself away from the spike, then relaxed and smoked a cigarette, framed by the marble wall. 'I want more money,' he called out.

Now it was the turn of the three speaking slaves. (I looked around for tiger skins.) 'Please everyone step into the mud bath,' said the assistant director. I found myself following Roger and Gianni into the copper bowl. We stood huddling together, looking at the mud. There seemed no point in bringing up the tiger skins, we simply being poor slaves, and the camera anyway ignored us. It was eyeing a naked girl who was clasping the emperor's marble head and simulating love with his golden phallus which stuck out of the wall below the head. She was not enthusiastic enough and Tinto Brass grew impatient. He growled at an assistant, who ran over to the girl and pushed her buttocks upwards to get them moving rhythmically. Of course, blood was dribbling down her legs.

In the bath, the three slaves were told to take off their chiffon and tulle, while the young girl caught Tinto Brass's mood, threw her head back and arched towards the emperor's dick. Really, it was too high on the wall to allow intimate connection, but her buttocks thrust gamely towards it and her legs tensed and curved in desire. Tinto Brass shot her a lot and afterwards his tummy flopped, satisfied. By now I was naked and was lowering myself into the mud, as were Roger and Gianni.

Sir John Gielgud stood on the ramp smoking a cigarette, face impassive, dressed in planter's white shorts and shirt and white socks pulled up high. The boys and girls frolicked by him and in the mud bath the three slaves shivered.

The camera moved to the male slave impaled through the anus . . . someone removed his cigarette and fresh blood was poured down his legs. He moaned; his teeth grimaced, but he didn't move up and down. Again Tinto's belly tightened and the camera surveyed and the motor purred and Tinto's belly flopped.

'I am sick of this.' My temper was rising. I got out of the mud bath and for the first time saw Susan, who looked discretely the other way. Neither of us had any intention of acknowledging the other. 'OK,' I said to the assistant director, who was called Carlo, 'I was employed — '

'And me too,' said Gianni, 'for a nice scene with tiger skins.'

'And,' I said 'we walk off unless you pay us double.'

'Double pay,' shouted Gianni, 'and brandies. We want brandies or we walk out and we fuck up your first day's shooting.'

The assistant director, faced by this class revolt, retreated towards the door, through which, somewhere, were accountants and money men. Maybe Bob Guccione was through there, checking up on the film and considering the exciting days to follow.

The assistant director returned and we were promised more money if we agreed to stay in the bath. Brandies were brought. Roger took one but refused to ask for more money. He, after all, was an Amherst boy, part of Wall Street and part of the superior breed who do not bargain. Gianni and I formed an alliance, rageful and working-class, drinking brandies and waving our dicks at the camera. 'How they use them,' I muttered to Gianni, 'how they use these kids. Bloody cannon fodder for their sick middle-class minds.' We demanded another brandy and it arrived. We were warming up and Gianni's dick started to swell, with rage, with sensual pleasure in opposing the master class and with plain biological reaction to booze. He was concentrating so hard so as not to shame himself that he seemed in meditation. Why, I wondered, now also concentrating hard, do men tend to get erect by numbers? Beside us was Roger glancing here and there, as if seeking out a friendly face at some Manhattan cocktail party where there was much talk of the latest Man Ray retrospective. It didn't look as if Roger's dick had done much since his marriage and, I thought scornfully, probably little or nothing during it either.

Sir John Gielgud left, face still impassive. Now Gianni and I were quite drunk and Roger was standing defeated in the mud. I looked scornfully at him again . . . how lacking in slavehood he was. He had so deeply coated his genitals that they were practically invisible! Was he ashamed of them? Gianni and I poured more mud over our heads and across our bellies with deliberate glee. You want us slaves, we are slaves; but just remember, Tinto Brass, slaves have a habit of ripping their masters to pieces. Would the camera film that — Tinto Brass ripped to pieces by the two slaves, Gianni and John, while Roger looked around, now desperate for a conversation on the Man Ray exhibition?

The moment of affirmation arrived. Caligula was almost on us. He glided to us from on high, dressed also in chiffon, with a wreath around his head. He came close and stood and chatted to himself. He gazed schizily at the air and killed a mosquito, and finally invited the slaves into conversation. I began in English and Gianni replied, but Roger buggered up. We tried again and again Roger forgot what he was supposed to say. Tinto Brass screamed and Roger was tearful, cringing before his might. We did six takes and Malcolm McDowell was remarkably patient.

Day One ended back in tulle with blankets to warm us as we trailed down the ramp and out to the dressing-rooms.

There were showers in a vast expanse of empty shed. They could have been showers for players after a rugby game, except there were only three people to wash the mud from themselves.

'Well, there you are,' I reflected, thankful that gas didn't flow from the nozzles.

A few weeks later Susan and I had coffee with Teresa Ann Savoy, a plain young woman who I could not imagine as Salon Kitty, her last role, in the Tinto Brass spectacular of the same name. It was a cool day and at three in the afternoon the square was almost empty, except for a policeman awaiting the bag-snatchers he would never catch. But the fountains still played and the wise and foolish virgins still carried their lamps on the facade of Santa Maria in Trastevere, almost as old as Christ in this city of popes.

Teresa Ann Savoy, it seemed, was taking over from Maria Schneider in *Caligula*. (Weeks had passed; I did not go back to the set after Day One.) Maria Schneider as Drusilla had walked off the set; she couldn't take Tinto Brass looking at the world through a keyhole. She had done an interview in *Panorama* and said she was sick of sodomies, lesbian loves, masturbation, sadism, and relationships with animals which could fill a treatise on sexual pathology. She had taken the role, I read, because '*they paid me 120 million lire and because it was to be a work of "Kolossal" artistry. I didn't think that, in fact, I was being paid to prostitute myself.*'

I looked at Teresa Ann Savoy, whose real name could not have been Savoy. She was an English working-class girl, perhaps petit-bourgeois, and she had a small, innocent, tired face. It was hard to imagine her with Malcolm McDowell, but then, seeing Malcolm, it was hard to imagine anyone existed in him. Indeed it was hard to imagine anyone existed in Sir John Gielgud, Peter O'Toole or, looking at her, Teresa Ann Savoy. But it was not difficult to see that someone existed in Tinto Brass.

Susan and I and Jos and Francesca played bridge after the film was over. It was everything, said Susan, that the scandal magazines had described. As she made a four-diamonds bid, I wondered if Peter O'Toole had been there to observe the girls masturbating, the boys masturbating, the corpses, the dead sharks, the deliquescent octopus. No-one seemed to know. I asked Susan what the *borgata* Roman girls had had to do in their auditions, since I had forgotten to ask Gianni. 'Oh,' said Susan, laughing, grimacing, horrified and again almost laughing. 'The assistant directors told the girls they fancied they had to show if they could do a *pompino* — a blow job — and they filmed them on video. And, what is worse, some of them weren't even given a part.'

'Did they do that in the film?' asked Francesca, horrified.

'Oh yes,' said Susan, 'and a lot more. And the strange thing is that on the set it seemed logical. It was as if that was the only world that existed! Kind of like being in a concentration camp, I suppose.'

Lucy Plays Saint Joan

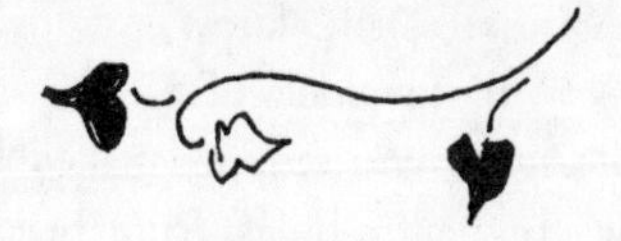

It was 1970 and I was working for the United Nations in Rome. I had just completed my Cambridge degree; the world was my oyster.

On any Sunday back in 1970, baroque Piazza Navona was not a busy place. None of that weekday blitzkrieg of Germans, gobbling up Rome as later they would gobble up Tuscany. No, not even the platoons of Americans, husbands in checked trousers and with beer-stained cheeks, making loud noises of approval to 'honey', she often boasting a blue rinse and standing manfully before a fountain so that male honey could snap her.

In Piazza Navona I made friends with a French Jesuit priest who smoked pot and seemed to have two girlfriends. I met Pierre, Marie and Claudette every Sunday morning for coffee around ten at the Kiosk bar.

That Sunday morning a young woman was sitting at the table with them. Pierre introduced us. She was in a healthy poplin, carried a Greek ethnic bag in blue and had a sturdy face and quite a large bosom. She came from downtown Oklahoma and was suffering angst. Her name was Lucy.

'Freddy says he can't keep me,' said Lucy, plunging everyone into the middle of her crisis while Claudette gave the waiter our orders. Pierre, saturnine of face with bee-stung lips and twinkling eyes, became sympathetic — it was the nearest any of his friends got to his priestly side. He patted Lucy's hand, then got back to reading *Messagero*.

Lucy pointed Freddy out to me, stationed mid-square, where some early Japanese tourists were gazing blankly at the facade of the baroque San Agnese. 'You know,' Lucy's eyes were on Freddy, a feral black with the look of a successful barracuda, 'at her martyrdom Saint Agnes was stripped naked by these real thug soldiers but her hair grew ultra-quick from her head and covered her vagina and her ass.' I saw Lucy at black Freddy's feet on some opulent Persian carpet and herself wearing some Desdemona-type nightdress and begging him to cut her head off. 'Yes,' sighed Lucy, 'after that, they tried to burn her; then that didn't work so they cut her head off and it talked and converted quite a few people.'

Oh la la! Priest Pierre put down his newspaper, 'How marvellous is our saint!'

'Now,' went on Lucy, 'I've got to get out of Freddy's flat since he doesn't want to sleep with me any more and I can't pay the rent and he has to get someone who can pay it. He says he'll take Rachel back now she's got money for the abortion he did for her.'

'*Cochon!*' spat out Claudette of the short black Piaf hairstyle. 'First he get Rachel pregnant and then he charge her for aborting his child and now he take her back because she pay the fee and the rent.'

Black Freddy was now at the far side of the Four Rivers Fountain and looked to be negotiating a deal with a blond Jugoslav I'd met around the traps.

'He has suffered terribly,' Lucy confided to me, 'being black and from the Bronx. He came here to study medicine and raise his political consciousness and become a doctor for his people. He swears James Baldwin really tried to make him and he's had contact with Cuba and all that revolutionary stuff.'

Marie lit a cigarette. 'Even a donkey can study medicine in Italy, that is why he come along with all those other dumb Americans! And how do he support himself?'

No-one answered since everyone suspected.

'Abortions, drugs, and if you ask him what is an artery he think it is a river in England. They do not even cut up a corpse. They see no patients, but very good for Freddy who make big play for himself as suffering black!'

'You see, don't you, John?' asked Lucy, searching for understanding of Freddy.

I guessed Freddy was a revelation and probably not many blacks had arrived in Oklahoma — at least there were none in the musical.

'*Cochon,*' spat Marie again, for the benefit of the French contingent.

I shrugged my shoulders and got on reading *The Daily American; Messagero* was still beyond me.

'You see,' said Lucy on the next Sunday morning, which was also sunny and eviction by Freddy was now certain, since Rachel had not only the abortion money but a month's rent from some unspecified business venture, 'Freddy really believes in the American dream and so do I. I know it'll be only a couple of hard years in New York before I get into off-Broadway and I'm gearing up for the audition already! I'll do it in October.'

'You recite *Saint Joan?*' asked Pierre, who was obviously nursing a hangover.

Lucy smiled at Pierre, then at me. 'You've got a great flat, John,' (she had been there for a drink) 'with all that antique stuff and I could easily just crash on the sofa. It won't be for long. I've got this really steady boyfriend, Bob. He's military in Germany and I've written to him to send me eight hundred dollars or maybe whatever he can rake up. I'll be helping Vocek sell his paintings from next weekend which will probably bring in some steady cash.'

The paintings were turned out by the barrow load in Dubrovnik for male and female honey and I didn't think much money would be coming Lucy's way.

'So you see, John, I really really need somewhere to crash till the money comes.'

Pierre observed the fountains playing, a whisp of cloud high above the cupola of San Agnese, then Lucy giving my lips a robust kiss and considering plans for dinner at my place that evening.

'I've been so lucky here,' said Lucy on the ninth day after moving in. 'Everyone has been so good to me. I mean, I have really experienced life in Rome and Freddy thinks he might even marry Rachel once he's through medicine. He really means to study hard this year.'

Lucy mixed a gin and tonic from the UN commissary stock and helped herself to a Benson and Hedges before dipping into the smoked salmon and black bread she'd prepared for our late afternoon snack. I half hoped today she'd ask how the office was. However Lucy was now back in some drugstore in downtown Oklahoma: outside were wheatfields and a haze of evening light laced with milkshakes while she told her dad she would be a great actress. Then I told her about my friend, New Zealand Sophia, who was arriving, and Lucy understood I would need some space, what with no door between the bedroom and sitting room, etc.

Sophia had been in Austria up to nine days ago with noble Ludwig and had learned to say '*Ach so, mein liebling*' while Ludwig solved Germany's problems in between introspective bouts of Hegel and Schopenhauer and hash.

Lucy understood arrangements would have to be made and smiled wistfully.

Sophia was probably smiling wistfully too, in London, thinking about noble Ludwig.

The next evening I arrived home to Via del Gesu to find Lucy had invited my neighbours, Maria and Sergio, over for a drink and was preparing smoked salmon on biscuits and some cheap caviar on black bread. They arrived at six and Lucy was the gracious hostess. Sergio was twenty-six, a Sicilian with the lean viperish good looks of the upper class: a mix of Arab, Norman, French, Greek and God knows what else. Maria was flaxen-haired from Poland and she had no residency papers and didn't speak Italian or English and probably found problems with Polish. Sergio didn't speak Polish at all and no-one was absolutely sure whether he'd smuggled her across a few borders or found her in a bar.

Lucy poured gin and tonics and soon Sergio, with limited English, just knew he had to invite Lucy over to stay on their sofa since the money was bound to come from Bob, and that way I would be free to be with Sophia.

Lucy sealed it with a kiss each for Sergio and Maria, and I stayed open-mouthed during the next round of drinks. Lucy would move out that night to give me a couple of days to get in the mood for the visit. But she'd be popping in for an evening drink, since she'd be just across the staircase.

Three days later I parked my Alfa Romeo sports car near Stazione Termini. Sophia was waiting in the station bar, as instructed, and looking frazzled; it had been a long trip from London, she'd been waiting for me for two hours and someone had put an acid tab in a glass of wine at a party in Clapham. In the middle of tripping she'd rung her mother in New Zealand and told her she was the incarnation of Helen of Troy. Her mother blamed the breakdown on Ludwig and Germany. Sophia had then rung Ludwig to tell him the good news but he was high on hash and his ambition to reunite Germany and get back his estates in Prussia.

We had a campari and soda while I admired Sophia's chestnut hair and electric blue eye-liner and hectic energies which boded well for the stay.

'It wasn't even as if he tried to seduce me on LSD. God, I

could really kill the guy.'

'I still could,' she said again as I ushered her through the *portone* of my palazzo with its medieval lock, broken sometime in the sixteenth century. She stopped to admire the marble steps. 'Do you know any Sicilians?' she asked. 'I wouldn't mind putting out a contract on that bastard.'

To Sergio's surprise, and Lucy's, the money arrived two days into Sophia's stay. Along with it was a train ticket for Berlin where the reunion would take place with soldier Bob. Lucy decided on drinks at my place since it would be good for Sophia to meet my neighbours. Lucy asked me to buy some good caviar from the UN commissary and to make sure I got more gin and also a bottle of whisky since Sergio liked whisky.

My neighbours arrived at six and Lucy made the conversation. 'And revolution', said Lucy, 'I never understood before about capitalism and how really violent revolution is the answer for lasting peace. Freddy has some fabulous new friends and they are all for violent revolution. But, I won't be here to help with that, and I guess there is no point talking to Bob about it since he's army.'

'Who do they want to kill?' asked Sophia.

'Oh, I think magistrates and politicians and judges and you know, all the guys who grind down the proletariat. And,' she added, pouring me another gin, 'since it's my last night in Rome, I'm taking the gang to Piazza Navona for dinner. *Da* Giovanni's. It's just off the square.' She finished her gin and picked up her Greek ethnic handbag. 'So I guess I'll leave you guys to the good life.'

'Who's going to dinner?' I asked, to make an easy exit for Lucy and half suggest that maybe we might be owed a little hospitality.

'Well, for starters, Freddy and Claudette. Claudette's left Pierre and had an abortion and I've got a feeling she and Freddie are really interested in each other. Then, there's Piero who's a definite revolutionary and Vocek and Simone — you don't know her but she's moved into the sitting room at Freddy's; and Lucio — his father is something bourgeois like mine — like, a bank manager. Anyway, enjoy yourselves.' Lucy was at the door.

'Don't take all that money Bob sent you,' persuaded Sergio. 'You shouldn't carry around dollars. Just take enough for dinner.'

'You don't understand, Sergio, my friends are really with it. You know, really anti-establishment.'

Sergio, dressed in a white shirt and blue jeans, shrugged.

Maria looked at Lucy with wide blue eyes.

Lucy left.

I returned from the opera at eleven-thirty with Sophia. Finally the mirror was reflecting two bodies on the bed and the arias of Cav and Pag were forgotten.

It did not occur to me to think about Lucy with her large breasts and wide open face from the prairies, only streets away, and giving her audition speech from *Saint Joan*. Nor did I think of the moon and the streets and Lucy leaving with Piero, who was really revolutionary, and admiring the Pantheon on the way home and Jesus Street where I lived and then the *portone* and no lock and Piero with his revolutionary eyes grabbing at Lucy. Not a good night kiss, since Lucy's plump body is rigid as if she were Saint Joan finally at the stake and waiting the cleansing fire, while Piero has her on the wall and is grabbing at her bag and smashing at her, and Lucy is down on the third marble stair, blood streaming from her cut lip and upper gum with one tooth loose and, while, through thick medieval walls Sophia and I are reaching our final aria, Piero, the hope of the terrorist left, is kicking Lucy in the stomach, unzipping his cock and trying to work out how to rape Lucy, grab the bag and masturbate, all at the same time.

Suddenly we heard a scream: an Oklahoma heifer being

branded. I bellowed back, bull to my heifer. I grabbed a towel; I ran down to the kitchen for a knife; I rushed for the door still bellowing.

Piero ran too, leaving only a dribble of sperm on Lucy's right thigh. He'd missed the money tucked into the bag since Lucy had rolled over and was clasping the four hundred dollars tight against her.

I looked down at Lucy, wondering if my face was as white as hers. I leaned over her but she didn't seem to see me. Then Sergio and Maria and Sophia arrived and Lucy said 'Piero' and Sergio was swearing in a mixture of English and French and Italian about knives up the anus and mothers treated to the horrors of hell and Piero fucked by goats and pigs and priests.

Sophia and Maria took charge, since Lucy's eyes were wide as death and as vacant and men could not help her stand.

'We must ring the police,' I said as we got her onto my sofa.

No-one spoke for five minutes and then finally, in the silence, Lucy began to weep, staring at the Spanish rustic cupboard.

I looked up *Pronto Soccorso* in the front of the telephone book.

Sergio shrugged. '*Noi andiamo*, John. Maria, she have no papers.'

Sophia had a bloody cloth against Lucy's face and Maria held her to her for a moment.

'Of course we must phone the police,' decided Sophia, rinsing the cloth and wrapping it in ice cubes from the fridge.

Sergio shrugged but agreed to make the call. Maria looked worried, trying to decipher his mood. Sergio put down the phone and his face became cool and closed. 'They will come,' he said, 'but now Lucy, she must be staying here otherwise they come to the door and make trouble for Maria. She have no papers to be in Italy. But it do no good if they do come. It do nothing at all.'

'I wonder what he meant?' Sophia was holding Lucy against her shoulder and gently rocking her.

'Oh,' I replied, staring down at the olive green floor tiles, 'it must be Sicily and the Mafia and all that. I mean, this *is* Rome.'

We sat on either side of Lucy while she had some brandy and talked obsessively about the evening and how they had eaten *aglio olio* pasta and the bread and salads and the *pollo arrosto* and the Frascati wine; she lingered over the moon shining down and the white papers used for the table cloth and how Rachel had found a job as assistant production assistant on the new Fellini movie and how possessive Freddie seemed to be of Claudette who had been looking a bit peaked . . .

The *carabinieri* arrived — one avuncular, the other lean, silent and watching and aged around thirty.

We went with them to the local hospital and Lucy was sewn up without anaesthetic.

We went to the police station and made the *denuncia* in Italian which took forever since I didn't have the verbs and Lucy had trouble talking.

Lucy left two days later to go to Bob in Berlin but was determined she would return for the trial, for everyone knew where Piero lived — with Vocek, the seller of paintings at Piazza Navona.

Sophia got me to propose the next day and then spent two days on the phone to fat Ludwig, who persuaded her that she must come back to him since their destinies were linked.

Sophia got on the train to Vienna where Ludwig would meet her and take her to the opera and not talk about Hegel, but only about his place in German destiny and poetry and perhaps marriage once both felt their love soar.

I went back to work and the place was quiet.

I started walking again in the evenings and looking in windows and watching people eat.

At night, in the bedroom, I looked at myself in the wardrobe mirrors and began going to sleep by eleven.

Sophia rang to say that Ludwig had proposed and arranged an

audition at the Vienna State for the chorus but she had decided against marriage for the moment. However, she was Ludwig's anchor in a difficult world and must make her sacrifices.

I continued to work for the Food and Agriculture Organisation. I read reports that meant nothing to me.

I wondered about Lucy and the case.

One evening, ten days after she'd left, Sophia rang to say she was staying on with Ludwig and as I hung up there was a knock on the front door. I opened it. It was a man of around thirty. Then I remembered: the other policeman; the one who had sat there and said nothing while the avuncular type had looked sympathetic and taken down notes. I undid my tie and asked him in and it turned out that his name was Sargente Fosso.

Sargente Fosso sat down in the most comfortable armchair, under the Spanish peasant cupboard that Vera, my landlady, had had picked up a couple of years before. He had a thin face and a dark five o'clock shadow and sweat marks under his armpits. I lit up a Benson and Hedges cigarette brought from the UN commissary along with the gin and whisky and smoked salmon and French wine and other duty free goodies. Sargente Fosso lit up a Nazionale Filtro which was a cheap Italian cigarette.

'So,' said Sargente Fosso, noting this blatant display of class difference and the gold carton of cigarettes on the antique peasant dining table, 'this woman? She still stay here?'

I thought into my Italian and the lessons I'd been having. 'No,' I replied, 'but she attends upon the pig to come towards trial. She will come back to the city for the trial. She is still in terror.'

Sargente Fosso carelessly flicked ash onto the green sitting-room tiles.

Pointedly I fetched an ash tray and placed it on the floor beside him.

'She has gone?' asked Sargente Fosso again in a bored voice.

'Yes,' I said gently.

'And,' said Sargente Fosso, 'she has no permission to be in

your apartment?'

'Oh, yes,' I smiled.

'You have no *permesso*,' said Sargente Fosso. 'You have made no *denuncia* to the police station.' He eyed my expensive suit.

I looked perplexed. I tried hard to understand. 'You mean that you not arrest that shit who try to robble Miss Lucy and drag out her dick and Miss Lucy beaten up?'

Sargente Fosso looked bored, I presumed, with my atrocious Italian and my uncertainty about male and female gender.

Sargente Fosso continued to look bored but at least used the ash tray.

'Where you come from?' I asked, suddenly suspicious.

'I come from Palermo in Sicilia.'

I stubbed out my cigarette. 'Me is waiting for arrest. When?'

Sargente Fosso stood up and walked around the room, he peered into the bedroom, he returned and looked downstairs to the kitchen; he left, shutting the door quietly.

I told people at work and they shrugged and got on with office gossip. I decided to forget about it. It was probably just that I hadn't understood. Yet, rumour had it that Piero was still in town and certainly not hiding. But new interests were on the horizon. Alicia, a bona fide student at the University of Rome, was willing to give me Italian lessons for English lessons from me. She had beautiful bronze hair and beautiful breasts and was a beauty.

I was starting to feel OK again and no longer found myself staring at myself naked and alone on the bed.

I was enjoying my day dreams of Alicia the next Friday, when there was a heavy knock at the door. I opened the door and cool air flowed in followed by Sargente Fosso who didn't seem to think that he needed an invitation from me. This time he tried out the rocking chair. That was my usual seat and my brown shoes were beside it. He stared at me patiently.

'Where do you work?' he asked.

I went to the drinks tray, poured myself a gin and tonic, put in some ice, descended to the kitchen, cut a lemon, returned, put it in my drink, sat down and lit a cigarette and gazed at Sargente Fosso, wearing an identical shirt with a new jacket in deep brown.

'I work for the United Nations.'

This definitely interested Sargente Fosso. He took out a notebook and wrote down the information, which, I was sure, had been given in the *denuncia* for the attempted rape and robbery of Lucy.

'You have a *permesso di lavoro?*'

I decided I needed another ice cube. I went over to the drinks table beside him, took another cube, sat down and put it in my glass.

'Yes, I have *permesso*, I have been permitted. I am diplomatic immunity.' I concentrated on the juniper flavour of the fine Tanqueray gin. Sargente Fosso seemed to be sneering, in doubt as to my credentials, and my mercury was rising by the second. Finally it shot beyond high fever. 'Why comes you here? Why makes you visiting my house when I don't ask you? You done nothing about the rapes and robberies and just come here and that man Piero who rapes and pulls his dick out and robs, you do nothing, even though he is living!'

Sargente Fosso openly sneered and I lost my cool. I got up, marched to the door and threw it open. Sargente Fosso stood too. He was foiled, enraged, engorged, his small reptilian brain boiling.

'Why you come to my palace? Why you bother me? What do you think you done?' I asked with transcendent simplicity.

'I tell you,' menaced Sargente Fosso — Sicily, I was sure, and first cousin marriages and Mafia behind every sibilant word — 'you come to the *questura* tomorrow at half past ten. There I will charge you with having Miss Lucy Schulz in your house and not reporting it to the *questura* as the law demands!'

I stood open-mouthed as Sargente Fosso departed down the marble steps, each footstep as precise as a *falanga* stroke.

I rang my friend Isabelle who worked at the New Zealand Embassy and was anyway the consul and had been with Sophia and I at the opera and knew all about the story. I explained what I thought Sargente Fosso had said and gave the time in Italian: *dieci e mezzo domani mattina*.

'You're making wonderful strides with your Italian,' she said, 'to even get an idea of what he was talking about. I'll meet you outside at ten twenty-five.'

I knew where the *questura* was, just around the corner, from my street, Via del Gesu.

I returned to my gin and tonic and stared at the dissolving ice.

'Now,' said Isabelle the next morning, outside the *questura*, 'don't tell the *sargente* I'm from the embassy, just say I'm a kind friend who's going to translate.' She straightened my blue tie like a fond mother seeing her son off to school, then slicked down my hair. I felt as if I were about to have an unpleasant interview with the headmaster. I whimpered to myself: why hadn't I offered Sargente Fosso a gin and tonic and a packet of Benson and Hedges? Why hadn't I . . . I knew there was something else I hadn't done but I couldn't think what.

Isabelle, in a smart spring suit and a crimson silk shirt and scarf, grasped her sensible Florentine shoulder bag and strode through the front door of the cop shop. I shuffled after her. Isabelle got the room number from the desk sergeant, a pleasant red-faced lad who, Isabelle informed me, from the accent, was probably from Trieste.

'It's an old facist law which is still on the books,' Isabelle, mountain goat, called down to me as I plodded after her up the stairs. I couldn't be bothered asking what law she was talking about.

We arrived, several stories later, and Isabelle knocked on the plywood door. Without waiting for a reply, she swept in, like

matron during the ward rounds. There was one chair in front of the desk in which she sat down and then looked around. 'A chair for the *signore*,' she told Sargente Fosso.

Sargente Fosso found himself picking up a chair from the corner before he realised, as he dusted it down, that the command had come from a woman and a foreigner. He reddened under his olive, roughly shaven skin. Isabelle looked him over like some piece of second-hand clothing she would not buy for her most indigent relative.

'And so?' she asked crisply. 'What is the problem? The *signore* does not speak much Italian. He has some absurd idea that you want to charge him for kindly having in his house a young American female who came to your attention after she was assaulted in the hallway of the *signore's* house.'

Sargente Fosso started to outline the charge.

Isabelle listened as he gathered steam. But she got bored and interrupted. 'And tell me, Sargente, when was the last time you notified the police when you had guests? Or, being the *carabiniere*, do you feel yourself above the law? Or, perhaps your house has never known a guest?' In other words, you are a piece of pig-shit whose mother would not grace the portals of your house in case she contracted one of the many unmentionable diseases from which you are suffering.

The *sargente* recognised the insults implied. He was ready, as a Sicilian rapist, son of a widowed mother and one hundred priests, to attack. He drew himself up behind his natural plywood desk which was pitted with cigarette burns. He was glittering with gold braid and wearing a uniform that made him at least an admiral of the fleet. Even I sensed the high operatic feeling and ignored the grubby fingernails and the shirt which had been washed and ironed once too often. He opened his mouth; he shouted sounds at Isabelle which became threats and insults and Isabelle threw caution to the winds and shouted back. They traded threats, Isabelle with relish and Sargente Fosso with growing rage, opera forgotten for vendetta. Indeed, I observed with fascination, Sargente Fosso was hooked and out of control, stabbing, writhing and running.

Isabelle took a small black notebook from her Florentine shoulder bag.

'I wonder what you want with the *signore*?' asked Isabelle, writing down Sargente Fosso's name. 'What are your intentions, apart from bullying him?'

'Who are you?' screamed Sargente Fosso, hook tearing against his stomach wall as the rod jerked back.

Isabelle slammed her card down on the desk and a cheap biro rolled off onto the linoleum floor. Words flowed around Sargente Fosso. Words like, 'The *signore* is a personal friend of the ambassador' (I didn't even know what his name was); 'He comes from a most prominent family' (I conceded with a small smirk that this might be true); 'The *signore* is a nephew of our prime minister' (was I understanding correctly? I'd rather have a leper for an uncle); 'A personal friend of myself, Miss Isabelle, Consul to the Embassy of New Zealand and Third Secretary to His Excellency, the Ambassador' (true). Then the words mounted: a complaint to the head of the *carabinieri*, a letter to the appropriate functionary in Foreign Affairs.

Isabelle stood.

Isabelle swept to the closed door.

Sargente Fosso executed a Nureyev leap, was at the door before her, holding it open, smiling and apologising.

'There has been an error,' said Sargente Fosso to Isabelle's departing back.

'That,' said Isabelle outside the *questura*, 'should fix that little shit!'

'Why did he do it?' I asked, wiping a thin film of sweat from my forehead and loosening my tie.

Isabelle glanced at her watch. 'I've got to fly.'

'Why?'

Isabelle shrugged. 'All he wanted from you was a *mancia* — a tip for the trouble he took for you in writing down that American kid's complaint. Maybe he wanted a few thousand lira. Maybe he couldn't work out why you didn't rape her too. But anyway, since you didn't give him some lira, you insulted him. You made him stand on his honour!'

Isabelle drove off in her smart cream Alfa Romeo saloon and I walked out to Via Nazionale and hailed a taxi to return to work. Mentally, I took Lucy's hand and together, from Oklahoma, USA, and Dundedin, New Zealand, we defiantly faced Mother Rome, city of whores and virgins and wives and mothers.

I changed my flat, moving from Jesus Street to Cedar Alley. I kept on the bedroom window ledge a postcard from Lucy which said that she really forgave Piero and could understand why he had tried to do all he did and that the experience was proving beneficial for the sort of plays she was auditioning for in New York and that she had exciting news: Bob was being posted to Vietnam, and although that was terrible it would also give him a real life experience and the war, anyway, probably wouldn't last much longer. She was hoping to take a holiday in Saigon to get some more real life experience.

I unclasped my hand from Lucy's and looked out sardonically at the high brick wall which kept my neighbours, the sensible Carmelites, from contact with the humdrum world.

A year later another postcard arrived. Lucy was back in Oklahoma and engaged to a wheat farmer and Bob had been killed in Vietnam. She didn't ask after Piero and Freddy and Claudette and Marie and Pierre and Vocek and the rest of the gang.

Dining with Princes

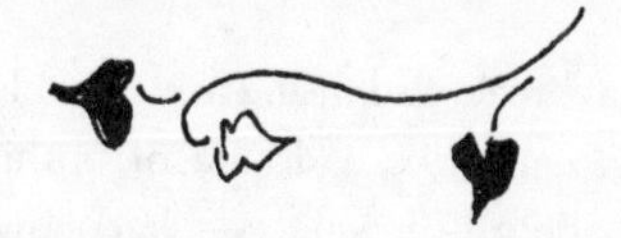

Enrique would be dressing in his deep green smoking jacket. In it he had the quality of a Velasquez noble, with his brown-black eyes, Moorish nose and slightly olive skin. Enrique radiated firm masculine virtues in philosophy and poetry and hospitality. And this evening he was entertaining his distant cousins.

Their Royal Highnesses the Prince Idris, and the Prince Cherif and the Prince Selim had only just discovered they were Enrique's cousins and this would add interest to the evening. Both families were, of course, related to the royal house of Morocco. 'We fled, you see,' Cherif told me, looking vague, 'and came with camels to Libya. We had a quarrel in our family.' I had relayed this news to Enrique and he decided to have a royal get-together. So an evening had been arranged.

But it hadn't been that light-hearted over the last few months. I had met Idris at a school I taught at, a very good international school called Saint Stephen's. Teachers wrote courses for groups of ten kids, and some of them went on to Yale and Columbia and Sarah Lawrence. Irene Alberti taught Russian before moving on to help Solzhenitsyn and she was almost par for the course in a civilised and actually educational process.

Idris was my student and friend and a lot had happened in his young life — to the extent of Black September sending a low-level hit squad into Rome of which he and his brothers were the target. The politics were complex but, because of the oil crises, Gadaffi had an open field in his very first assassination play into Europe, and the Italian Government which had given the kids diplomatic immunity had suddenly forgotten about their protection. No doubt that was just an oversight, considering the problems of an Italy without oil, but it had happened. However, others were acting for the kids, right up to the top, but no-one dared talk since that was very dangerous.

But tonight was a break and I and my friends intended to play it very, very light, really like a drama of nothing at all. I'd told Idris and Cherif about Enrique — nephew of Azana, last president of democratic Spain, before Franco seized power and knotted the garotte around the Spanish soul. Enrique knew about bad power — as a kid he'd seen it murder innocent people. His father had been under sentence of death, after Franco's victory, for being a theatre man, friend of Garcia Lorca, brother-in-law of the president. He'd seen fear and seen death and knew he and his brothers were just kids in a filthy power game coming out of Libya. So — why not a frivolous evening where they forgot that the bodyguards would be in a car at the entrance to the street with their guns, and we would forget what was happening behind the scenes. We would enjoy Enrique's story of how he had royal Moroccan blood, how he was a descendant of the Prophet, and the kids would like the rich setting of that apartment and the rich food. It was time to get into role for the evening since God knows what tomorrow would bring in this cat and mouse game. It was good of Enrique to give them an Arabian night's evening.

On Penitence Alley, I bustled around looking for something suitable to wear for this great occasion of infidel cousin meeting true believer. I selected smart dark brown trousers, a green roll-up jersey in fine wool and a waistcoat in velours. Then I changed my mind and decided on a silk shirt, a silk scarf at the neck, light fawn trousers and smart brown shoes. Maybe a ring in cornelian? Overdoing it a bit, I thought, mindful of my stubby fingers.

At Enrique's apartment on Vicolo del Fiumicino, Isabella, the maid, in her smart apron of white, wearing a sedate dark blue dress, her cheeks slightly reddened from rouge or booze, feet in sensible black, and black eyes like a cherry-picking French peasant, peered across the narrow, narrow street. Opposite was a palazzo which housed whores in one apartment. Isabella closed the shutters tight; she disapproved.

Isabella was the grand-daughter of the founder of the Liberal Party in Portugal, whose son got Isabella's mother pregnant in the house where she was a maid. Then Isabella went into service and got pregnant and had a child too. It was really a dynasty of illegitimacy. Now Isabella had become a Mormon and was tracing her ancestry and was in love with the Cuban Ambassador's butler. The Ambassador had been sent from Cuba by his revolutionary son to live out his life in accustomed bourgeois comfort.

Isabella also adored being a servant and waiting on Enrique, who had said to me about society's woes, 'The problem is this. All that has changed, John, is that no-one can afford servants now. Once servants go, entertainment goes, dinners go, leisure to read and think goes. It is all that has changed in Europe. No servants means no leisure!'

I agreed. I would have loved to be lying late in bed reading Verlaine and Baudelaire and Jung and Marx and Fanon, sipping hot chocolate and having a devoted Isabella draw a bath with essence of pine oil, then hot towels, pressed shirts, pressed trousers, breakfast prepared, while I poetically considered the fate of the oppressed in the Third World. I glanced distracted around the whitewashed study in my apartment. Oh Apollo, Apollo, when will you give your devoted servant money to enjoy himself? There was a slight jarring in the harmony of the spheres, followed by a peal of amused laughter.

I finished dressing, put on a coat, and opened the front door. To the immediate left the door was open. This was Signora Paula's apartment. I had been allowed in to see her great treasure, located in the bedroom, on the chest of drawers. '*Eccola*,' had said Signora Paula, a widow of many years. 'Sometimes, *caro* Giovanni, I cannot sleep at night and then I can sit up and look at her. What a lovely lady.' Signora Paula, as a special favour, turned off the bedroom lights and I sat on the bed as if for a home movie.

There she was, in white and blue, with a halo of small lights that twinkled on and off as she revolved around her base.

'That is a very beautiful statue of Our Lady, Signora Paula.'

'*Si*, Giovanni,' said Signora Paula, 'she keeps me company through the night when my arthritis won't let me sleep.'

I walked down the marble stairs, washed clean by Maria, the *portiera*, onto the damp ground floor where Maria and her brood roosted.

I passed another Virgin Mary with her son, Jesus. Jesus has a large flaming heart which he holds in his hand. His mum, with a resigned look of a Jewish mother, seems to be saying, 'OK Jesus, I known your heart is bigger and more compassionate than mine. I can see that. I'm holding mine in my hand, so you can make a comparison. And what joy it gives a Jewish mother to see you radiating with that heart. Really, really nice. But why, Jesus, my son, why did you not get married? Why did you break my heart and leave it here in my hand? Staying a bachelor, Jesus. Who knows, one of *nature's* bachelors?'

I had quite a snigger at my fantasy and dusted off the plastic flowers in a brief exorcism of blasphemy.

Over in Vicolo del Fiume, Enrique would be dressed by now; opposite the whores would be simulating their first orgasm of the evening (they were very select and screamed only for customers who paid over one hundred thousand lira), and the royals would be leaving their villa down the coast, bodyguards with submachine guns in trailing Mercedes. It was going to be a usual Roman evening.

I traced my steps down Penitence Alley, onto Via Penitenza and up the steps onto Lungotevere. For the moment the traffic was slight, held up, like a shoal of fishes, at the lights down by Via Conciliazone which leads to the Vatican.

I crossed the Vittoria bridge. The stone was white with

moonlight and down on the winter river the bats skimmed to and fro.

I adjusted my step like an animal: here I was not known, this was not my quarter. The alley leading to Enrique's was dark and closed, but I stopped to observe the fourteen or so alley felines who slouched, posed and purred around the *fontinella*, which grew like some iron vegetable out of the cobbles. The water in its lucid clear freshness poured through the tap and down the grill into a drain, from where it would go to the stinking Tiber.

I hurried to Enrique's door, glancing across to the house of the whores. I pressed the *citifono*. Enrique answered. I trudged up the clean marble stairs. I rang the apartment bell. The door was opened by Isabella, everything held in firmly, face dimpled and fat, and wearing the prim red lipstick that would go with a dark coat, a black handbag and mass on Sunday, Monday and Tuesday. But Isabella in that skull of hers was reaching towards special consummations, special Mormon rewards for servitude and her illegitimate dynasty. Isabella in no way felt shame — certainly not — for it was part of being a servant to experience furtive love from the master's son. If it had not happened, what sort of son would the master's son be? There she stood, resplendent, solid. I wouldn't have lasted two minutes with Isabella as my servant.

Isabella said, '*Buonasera, signor*.' She took my coat and left with it for a distant room and a distant courtyard where fig trees bore large ripening fruits, where porticos supported laburnum and wisteria, where pianos tinkled across the way as the girls got on with their accomplishments.

I smiled at the six-feet-long book-lined hall and smiled at Enrique in his green smoking jacket, dark trousers and soft white shirt. The books had been in storage since the Spanish Civil War, and in the adjacent small dining room they rose ceiling-high in their leather covers — brown, green like the smoking jacket, reds, dull vermilion, gold.

Old memories rested here. Enrique was a carrier — like

Typhoid Mary, he harboured germs of history and of democracy, and very large bacilli of memory. The books conjured up Garcia Lorca, a happy childhood in a large house during the republic; theatre; the works of his uncle Azana, banned in Franco's Spain.

With the second whisky we were both loosening up. Spain was now rocking to the irregular beat of Franco's heart, but what would follow? Juan Carlos was being groomed for the role, but Enrique, a republican, was sceptical. Mrs Franco, he said, visited antique shops and ordered what she liked; she never paid. 'Shops closed when they heard she was on her way for a shopping spree,' said Enrique, as he watched Isabella lighting the candles on the crystal candelabrum, its droplets of crystal now catching the light.

Mercedes arrived dressed in creams and gold.

The doorbell rang again and the young princes came in.

Cherif was lanced by emotion, his face, his eyes, his spirit, filled with poetry. It was a pity he admired Hitler.

Idris was lean, smiling with a vexed anger and hardness which might turn bad. The young one was like a blackbird.

The conversation began warmly. The first course was brought in. It was my favourite — a rich sponge dish through which fish and seafood swam in a sauce concocted out of a bechamel with added ingredients that Isabella would not divulge: she might give the recipe, but alter cooking times and leave out a couple of essential ingredients. The royals were impressed by the rich smell, the polite conversation, the wines, the brocade and the very uncomfortable sofas on which they had sat before dinner.

The fish course was carried out and Cherif was flushed and talking compulsively about Libya and what he would do when Gadaffi was ousted, but not, thank God, about Hitler. I supposed Hitler was someone out of a fairy-story, like Alexander the Great. Scorched like all my generation by the concentration camps, I tried to imagine someone seeing those events — the marching feet, the iron and steel, the discipline — as heroic fiction. Behind

Cherif stretched the desert, the camps, an old man, a patriarch with his sheep and goats who would not visit the accursed cities. Silence; the plates scraping now with emptiness. A rest and then some veal with a herb sauce; potatoes light as foam and drenched in cream, chives, butter, black pepper.

Isabella accepted compliments graciously.

More wine flowed and the candles were losing wax.

'And so,' said Enrique, whose second name was Cherif, 'the story? How is it that a Spaniard has Moorish blood of the Moroccan royal house?

'It happened like this,' he said, as everyone sipped brandy and coffee and Isabella could be heard far, far away in a distant kitchen, washing up. 'A Spanish gentlewoman left her home in Cadiz to sail to Rome. She was bound on a pilgrimage to the holy city.'

'This city?' asked young Selim. 'This Rome?'

'Yes, this Rome! And while on the sea, she was captured by pirates and sold into slavery in Morocco. In the marketplace, because she was fair-skinned and a virgin, they expected a high price.'

'Yes, that is important. To be a virgin. It increases the price,' said Cherif, with long tribal experience of such matters.

'Wouldn't get much for you, Mercedes,' I said, and the princes looked coy at the thought that this distinguished older woman, who had grown-up children, could be so considered. But Mercedes laughed and agreed that her price would be less than a virgin's of twenty or so.

'And so she was sold at the slave market at Marrakesh,' continued Enrique. 'She was well treated because she was a virgin, and then . . .'

'And then?' asked Selim. 'Who bought her and what was the price?'

'The price is lost to history but it is certain that it was high because a eunuch thought the harem of the emperor would benefit from such a one.'

'And so she is taken to the harem,' said young Selim, licking his chops in anticipation, 'and what happens?'

He reached for the wine. Cherif tapped him on the wrist and Selim became a shy young adolescent out on the town with his brothers. His bright blackbird eyes stopped shining for a moment.

'We can imagine,' said Enrique, his eyes blazing, with genes jostling to give paramountcy to himself as a royal descendent. 'Perhaps she is bathed in a marble bath and perfumes are added to it and she is dressed and — '

'And,' said Idris, 'she was in luck, the Spanish lady?'

'Yes,' said Enrique, sibilant. We were no longer in Rome and the princes, like cats, responded to the new vibration.

'And the eye of the emperor fell on her and she was married to him. She was made a wife, an empress of Morocco.

'And by him she had a son and this son grew up and was sent to Spain, by the emperor his father, and there in Madrid, his mother's plan came to fruition, for her son had been reared by her as a Christian!'

'Christian?' Eyes goggled, Selim rubbed the gold ring he was wearing to ward off the evil eye. 'A Christian?'

Idris looked embarrassed, as did Cherif, whose eyes sparkled for a moment with holy zeal.

'So,' said Enrique, 'he was baptised a Catholic by a bishop and he returned to Morocco. Then the eldest son, his brother, who had ascended the throne died and *he* succeeded him. And so, on the throne of Morocco, sat a Christian emperor for almost a year!'

'That is terrible,' said passionate Cherif. 'That is terrible.'

'And,' said Enrique, 'it became known the Emperor of Morocco was a Christian and in a palace revolt he was deposed by another brother and sent to Spain. There he lived in Madrid, with a small pension from the Spanish king and there he drank much wine.'

'Poor man,' said Cherif, eyes now tear-filled. 'To be the son of the king and then king and so to end life.'

Enrique shrugged. Arabic, mysterious, are the ways of Allah, he indicated, somehow including his new cousins and leaving the Christians at table plucking nervously at the edge of the lace tablecloth.

'And so, though a poor man in Spain, he married a Spanish gentlewoman and so I, his descendant, am the cousin of the Emperor of Morocco and my second name is Cherif, like yours.' He smiled at Prince Cherif.

'You go and stay with the Emperor of Morocco?' asked Selim. 'I hear he has real nice palace with lots of cars.'

The wine decanter we passed around, but Selim, with his bright little eyes, was excluded from partaking by another tap on the wrist.

Enrique answered Selim's question. 'In the days of the republic when the emperor made a state visit to Madrid, through emissaries, my father made it known of his existence and his hope of meeting the emperor.'

'What are emissaries?' asked Idris, and Cherif did a quick Arabic translation. 'Oh,' he said, 'your father send to the king his ambassadors?'

Enrique nodded sagely. 'Indeed he did and the Emperor of Morocco said he indeed knew of this branch of the family but the Emperor of Morocco did not deign to meet his infidel cousins.'

Cherif nodded curtly. The emperor had done the right thing; he had been hard and vigorous, but just in that he had acknowledged the blood relationship.

'We used to have a portrait of the emperor,' concluded Enrique, 'but it vanished during the civil war when our house was looted by the Fascists.'

The wine was passed again and Selim yawned.

'But,' said Cherif, eyes tubercular bright, an Arabic Chopin with a fast polonaise in his head, 'you are certainly our cousin!'

'Indeed?' said Enrique.

'Yes, yes,' said Idris. 'And although you are an infidel,' he sipped

delicately at his brandy, 'you are a descendant of the Prophet.'

Selim looked excited. 'You descendant of Prophet, too?'

Enrique nodded and a tapestry of genealogy unrolled. I had drunk too much wine, I had eaten too much; I got confused between the wives of the Prophet, the Prophet's son-in-law, the Prophet's daughter.

'So,' said the royal prince, Cherif, 'you too are our cousin for we are out of Morocco. And so, even now,' he waved the wine glass, 'though infidel you have the *baraka* of the Prophet.'

'Yes, yes,' said Selim, 'we all have *baraka*. It is like light. It always shine on us and protect us.'

'And so the Prophet smiles on you,' insisted Cherif, 'you are of him and one day he call you back to the true path. Maybe tomorrow! Who can know with the Prophet?'

I tried to picture Enrique being called in a vision by the Prophet.

'And when we return to Libya we will call you,' Cherif was blazing with enthusiasm. 'You will come to us. We will show you our palace. We will take you to those ruins you like with ancient things like Rome and Greece. You can take some back with you if you like, some statues and things. We don't like them much but you will enjoy them.'

I imagined ancient Greek or Roman temples and Enrique with a stone-cutting electric saw while he sized up the friezes and considered how they would fit into his Roman apartment.

'And, we will take you to the desert. We will take you where you like. We make sure you have wine and cigars and whatever else you like.'

Mercedes was smiling with sheer pleasure at this Isak Dinesen evening.

'And even though I am a Christian,' asked Enrique, 'I have *baraka*!'

'Yes, yes' said Cherif. 'The Prophet forgive you for error.'

'And you know,' he added, 'it is better to be Muslim. This

Pope Paul, he pays women to sleep with him.'

'Really?' said Enrique, presumably trying to envisage Pope Pauline (as some people called him, when not calling him the Hamlet of the Vatican) cruising in his large car around the city walls looking for a lady for the night.

'Yes, yes,' said Cherif, 'my father has seen a cheque he write out for a girl in Milan who was a lover of him before he becomes pope. And, too, I have heard he keeps woman in Vatican, but away in private rooms where no-one can find out.'

'Well, well,' I said, 'wonders will never cease.'

The evening ended and the royals vanished to their car, the bodyguards summoned by radio. Then, some weeks later, they left Rome in a private jet. President Sadat had offered them one of Farouk's palaces in Cairo; he had fallen out, yet again, with Gadaffi.

'You know,' said Enrique on the phone, voice plaintive as I gave him the news, 'I didn't really want decorations or palaces in Libya or even Greek friezes. I really only wanted one, just one tiny, tiny little oil well. Just one.'

POSTSCRIPT

8 October 1994

Years pass, the story is written, names are forgotten, changed, rechanged. Is Enrique de Rivas, Javier or Enrique? Our phone conversations confuse the story further. But at least in the letter from Mexico I have the real story of the Muslim rebel who became a Christian. And, I suddenly and smugly realise, all life is fiction anyway. At least when written about. What did Mercedes wear that evening? What did Enrique say about the Spanish gentlewoman who became the Emperor of Morocco's wife? I'm sure I got that right in the story if nothing else. But I'm equally

certain that he said his renegade ancestor reigned as Emperor or Morocco or did I, as novelist, just want that glorious shock in the royal princes? I'm sure he returned to Morocco, after his baptism which I'm sure was secret, or did he? I also cannot remember the name of the youngest prince and nor can Enrique.
Mexico, 16 September 1994

Dear John

How hilarious to write about that character who says he is the pretender to the throne of Magreb! But his name should not be Javier nor Enrique, but something very Spanish and Catholic, such as Jose-Maria, or Luis-Maria, or more visigothic, such as Teodoro, Doreteo, or plainly anarchist such as Germinal, but not Javier nor Enrique, certainly. On the other hand I cannot remember Idris' brother's name, but if you call him Ahmed, you cannot be very far from the truth, since 90 % of the Moslems are called Ahmed, including the Profet (On Him Peace). Remember the important name there is Muley Ishmail, Sultan of Marocco from the seventeenth century till the middle of the eighteenth. We are all his descendants. My forefather (that is my great-great-great-great grandfather seven generations back) was a grand-son of Muley Ishmail. He was known for having had five hundred children, of which only eight legitimate, and of these eight only four reigned, among which the father of one who became a Catholic in the Church of San Gines in Madrid, where he was baptised at the age of 28 on December 23, 1770. While this letter reaches you I shall probably be trying to find in Marchena, the town near Servilla where he lived and probably died, some more traces of his life. Do not forget to record that he participated in a siege of Gibraltar (which must have taken place around the end of the eighteen century,) where it seems he was seriously wounded 'in his parts', namely his balls. I suppose this must have happened after he had generated his five or six children, of which one became a friar in

Granada.

That's all the news. This city is grim and boring and unlivable, so I subsist with painting and some reading. Next Saturday I am flying to Spain with a nephew and his wife and we shall be, we hope, in Cordoba, Granada, Sevilla, Caceres, Salamanca and Leon. Rome on October 20.

Sorry this letter is not more entertaining, and I hope the next one will be a little more spicey. (Oh, the Renegade, after he became Catholic, he was appointed by the King of Spain, Charles III, head of a Royal Regiment. Then he left pregnant a young lady in Cadiz, was forced by her parents to marry her in a hurry, so he did not, as he should have, ask His Majesty's permission. He was punished for this. One of his sons was a hero at the battle of Balien against the French of Napoleon. So much glory!)

As ever,

Enrique

The Transit of Venus

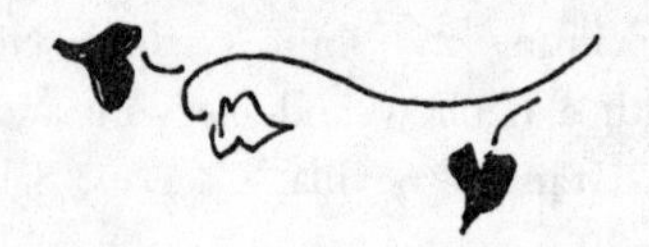

I had told Mercedes that I thought I would spend some time in India in an ashram. I also wanted to indulge myself by seeing what astrology had to say about the year. Now, spread about the round oak table in her apartment were astrological books and the ephermerides which give the position of the planets, the sun and the moon. Mercedes put on her tortoiseshell reading glasses. While she completed her rough calculations I looked at the large painting by her son-in-law of the summer plain and hills of Cortona. It was 30 March, early spring, and madness was in the air as almond trees burst into blossom around Rome.

Mercedes began a technical description of the horoscope which I took very little notice of, simply waiting to be told plenty of positive things. Jupiter would be in a good conjunction with the moon which boded well for August. Saturn would be doing something irritating in November, but no doubt could be cowed into behaving itself, while Pisces promised artistic success in February.

I went through to the kitchen to collect the lunch things.

'Well,' said Mercedes finally, 'from what I can see it should be a good year.' She patted her greying hair and looked fond. 'But in early June there may be three or four days of difficulty as Mercury transits . . . so I would put off India until later that month.' I didn't hear the rest. As I put down the tray the cutlery fell off.

'I'm never sure about the accuracy of these yearly readings.' Mercedes took off her glasses as I fetched the cauliflower cheese and baked potatoes from the kitchen.

'Why?' I asked.

Mercedes began serving. 'Could you fetch the butter?' she asked.

By the time I had returned from the kitchen we had both forgotten about astrology. Mercedes began talking about her book on Francis Bacon, whose good reputation she was thereby to reinstate.

After lunch I visited Sheila. Her apartment was on Piazza Santa Maria. We sat in her bedroom with the *bombola* gas heater on. She was reading Henry Miller's *The Colossus of Maroussi* in preparation for her yearly summer holiday in Greece. Upstairs Mirella, her daughter, practised her violin scales. 'She's been at it for an hour,' observed Sheila. 'We had a fight and now she'll practise until she's sure she's half destroyed me.' She sighed. 'I can't wait for summer.'

We crouched closer to the gas fire. When the *tramontana* blew even lightly, her place became a fridge.

'Where's Saul?' I asked. Saul was Sheila's fourteen-year-old son.

'Upstairs in his room reading comics.' She reached down for the pot of tea which was drawing in front of the heat. 'And probably masturbating. I keep finding these sperm-covered towels.' She poured the tea. 'I ever so delicately *placed* a box of Kleenex in his room, on the bedside table, but do you think he will use them?' She sighed again. 'If only they could grow up faster and behave like mature people.'

Across the lower terrace, in the other bedroom Mike, her eldest son, lounging back on his bed had just turned Bruce Springsteen to full volume. Mike was wearing his jock's tracksuit with a jersey over the top. Sheila opened her terrace door. 'Will you *please* consider other people for once in your life?' Mike didn't hear her but Bruce, the farting boxer chewing on his tennis ball by the trough of geraniums, gambled over and licked her hands profusely. Sheila knocked on Mike's terrace door. Mike turned a bemused face towards her and smiled and yawned. Sheila entered. I gathered from her gestures that the room smelt and that Mike was a great lazy hulk who ate his mother out of house and home and would be the cause of her selling her last mink. Mike got off the bed, shuffled, flexed his biceps, yawned again, picked up a large number of socks from the floor and threw them into a cupboard, the door of which couldn't shut from overflow. Sheila returned. Her idea, anyway, was that when a cat has kittens, the kittens take nourishment for a short while, then become fully mobile in their own interests.

'And he seems,' said Sheila, 'to spend half his time dreaming about girls and the other half eating. Here am I, penny pinching to get us all to the island again and will they take jobs? No!'

'What sort of jobs?' I poured another cup of tea.

'Chopping firewood, paper runs!'

'In Rome?'

'I'll have to ring Price Waterhouse and get them to sell some more shares.' Sheila rubbed her feet together and pulled up her thick red woollen socks. 'I really envy you, off to India and that guru. Not that I would *think* of wasting *my* time on some Indian quack, but at least you'll be enjoying yourself.'

'Mercedes is thinking of coming too,' I mentioned.

'Wouldn't she,' snapped Sheila, then relented.

I closed the curtains as Mike killed Bruce Springsteen and headed for the front door.

'Well,' said Sheila, 'we can have some time to ourselves now.'

Spring burst into song and faded into early summer. I went for my inoculation shots — typhoid, paratyphoid, cholera and smallpox — and for one day lay on my *letto matrimoniale* projecting fever dreams from some deep swamp. Then I forgot about the inoculations, since I had met Mildred, an Englishwoman, and we were having a brief affair.

I didn't tell Sheila, of course, since our relationship was more like that of loving friends. Besides, what you don't know won't hurt you.

Mildred was a biology teacher, and with late spring in the air biology was *de rigeur* as everyone finalised their dates for fleeing the humid Roman summer.

Mildred was leaving at the end of June for England and Sheila on the twelfth of June for Naxos. Mercedes was going to India and the ashram to be triumphantly in residence by the time I arrived around June 20.

'It's not likely,' I told Mildred, 'that I'll get cholera or any of those diseases.'

We finished our coffee in Bar Domiziano.

Mildred admired the photos of old-time boxers on the walls, brandishing fists with Italian panache.

Outside on the footpath looking at the old city gate, Porta Settiminiano, she told me she was back again with her married boyfriend, Tiberio. Neither of us felt any deep regret. We kissed on each cheek, Italian fashion, and I waved her off in her blue Mini Minor.

I walked down to Vicolo del Cinque, stopped at the fruiterer and then continued upstream to Signora Rossi's shop. It was in a *cantina* filled with unopened boxes, dresses hanging on rails, and a huge armchair favoured and occupied by the *signora* with five or six of her ten cats in residence on her lap. She wheezed out greetings and we got stuck into our usual discussion on opera.

The smell of cat pee blended with the coffee grounds I spooned into the percolator. I put it on the ring and lit the gas. We finished reliving Signora Rossi's starring role as the countess in *Figaro* at the San Remo Opera House, while she dug around in a huge plastic bag at her feet. She surfaced with four nineteenth-century Venetian crystal wine glasses. I took one and admired it. The others she placed on her lap between two sleeping cats. The glasses were probably being fenced, and we agreed on a low price. The *signora* got up to pour the coffee, spooning in almost as much sugar as coffee to warm us both up.

'I give the glasses to you as a special favour. All artists like us must have beautiful things to make up for what we suffer in life.' She smirked conspiratorially and lost facial shape. I paid over the few thousand lira asked. Definitely fenced goods.

There probably isn't any connection between buying fenced goods and deciding on a test for syphilis. At least, none that is obvious. Yet, as the planet Mercury that Saturday crossed Saturn in bad conjunction with the house of health and well-being, I decided to walk to Santa Maria and pick up a newspaper, then, for some reason, decided to go to San Gallicano, the VD hospital, and have a test. I didn't have any reason to suppose I had syphilis. But I was a great fan of Isak Dinesen and she'd had syphilis, and anyway I'd heard San Gallicano was worth a visit — a medieval pesthouse.

At the newspaper shop on Piazza Santa Maria certainly I had felt no vibration to indicate that a short-lived astrological square had come into operation and that all over Rome people with the same horoscope, or close to it, would be falling out of buildings, finding lifts breaking and eating poisoned mushrooms.

It was a gentle two-hundred-yard saunter to the clinic.

I walked into Via San Francesco a Ripa and saw on my left the long low barracks hospital, squatting against the high umber wall like a diseased beggar.

I took a smart left turn into the street and through a small door which opened onto the waiting-room. There were two long wooden forms and on one of them a woman of dingy aspect with her arm about a cretinous-looking child eating pumpkin seeds. Straight ahead was the counter.

A male nurse with a white pimply face handed me a biro. I filled in the form, then walked through a door and into the surgery where a doctor, harassed like a waiter with a fractious clientele, grabbed an ancient syringe from the rusting steriliser as the nurse fitted on the rubber bandage. My vein stuck out; the needle went in.

'I've just had my inoculations. I'm going to India. Will that make any difference?'

The doctor shrugged, drew blood back into the glass cartridge.

'Come back in three days,' the male nurse told me. He lit a new cigarette from the doctor's, sat down at a plywood desk and got back to his crossword puzzle.

'So, inoculations make no difference?' I asked the male nurse, since the doctor had walked off down the passage.

The male nurse filled in five across and shrugged.

I returned three days later, before work, to get the results. I went to the counter and gave the false name I'd used. 'Is the test for Marlon Bramble ready?'

It was a new male nurse who'd had a few days at the beach.

'Would you mind stepping inside?' he requested.

Five or six peroxided ladies who'd seen better days sat and buffed their nails, smoked Nazionale filtro and observed.

I walked into the surgery and saw my face reflected in the office mirror.

It was pasty.

The nurse sat down at the plywood desk. As if telepathically summoned a young doctor came along the passage. He had long greasy hair and his white jacket had yellow stains on it. He was smoking a Nazionale filtro too. I dug in my pocket for my own packet. 'So,' said the young doctor, 'have you had a test before?' I shook my head and lit up, my hand artificially firm.

'*Mi dispiace,*' said the doctor, 'your Wassermann has come back positive.'

I sat down. Isak Dinesen had had syphilis. So had Schumann or Schubert. And Guy de Maupassant? 'Holy shit,' I heard myself mutter.

'Now, have you been with any prostitutes?'

I shook my head, then remembered. I nodded. 'A year ago, in Bali. With a — but she — I haven't seen any signs. I mean, it was only . . .'

The young doctor took an ancient needle from the steriliser. 'We now take blood and do the Nelson test. It is absolute. Sometimes there can be an error with the Wassermann.'

'Does it happen often? An error?' I allowed myself to be helped into a chair. The rubber bandage went around my arm, the needle stabbed in, the blood flowed back into the cartridge.

'Now,' said the doctor, 'no sex with your girlfriend.'

I recalled that I had been gabbling on about Sheila.

'Not even with a condom,' continued the doctor.

'But,' I croaked, 'I'm going to India, to a guru!'

The doctor ignored the obvious pathos of my situation.

The needle was withdrawn and a small piece of sticking plaster was slapped on the wound. It looked like it came from a consignment meant for the sick and dying of the Third World.

'We will give you pills to take when you are in India. The course lasts a few months. Then we retest you.'

'And?' I asked, imagining years of tests coming back negative, then positive.

'The prognosis is good.'

I looked at the three dirty coffee cups on the plywood desk and then down the passage to the glass door through which, I supposed, went the doctor to tend those riddled with terminal syphilis and associated diseases. All, no doubt, lying together in promiscuous squalor. 'I suppose I'll have to tell my girlfriend,' I muttered. The nurse shrugged, picked up a magazine, turned to the crossword and started filling in ten down. I walked back through the waiting-room and one of the syphilitic whores yawned, showing a fine set of amalgam fillings.

Outside in the summer sunshine I remembered that I would have to call in to work sick. I went back to Piazza Santa Maria in Trastevere, walking across cobbles filthy with the dirt of

centuries. I sat down at a table under an umbrella, ordered a cappuccino with some brandy in it, then used the bar phone. I said I had developed a sudden fever and that my temperature was high; I hung up to condolences. I returned to my table and sipped the cappuccino. From there I could see the green-painted *portone* of Sheila's apartment building. Soon Mike and Saul came down on their way to school, followed by Mirella in a blue dress, her violin under her arm.

I sipped slowly. Fat Marco, the bar bulldog, shambled over to slouch down beside me to be scratched behind the ears. A moped cruised through the square and the policeman watched it — Italian kids were now on hard drugs. The boy and his mate on the moped were on the look-out for some early tourists. Snatch a bag and pay for the fix. It happened ten minutes later. A middle-aged Scandinavian woman screamed and hit the cobbles before letting go. The moped vanished with a burst down the alley by San Gallicano. The policeman watched.

I got up and left money for the cappuccino. Rome was rotten with the poison of the centuries, her veins were drying up. 'Terminal cultural and religious syphilis,' I muttered to Marco the bulldog. Marco yawned. The waiter checked the amount on the plate.

I shuffled along the square to the green door, rang Sheila's bell and waited. She answered, sunshine-bright, the buzzer went and the door opened. I decided to climb up the stairs, which might give me time to become certain, proud and romantic. I pulled in my belt one notch and loosened my tie. Inside the lift cage the steel ropes started untwining and moving like metallic snakes. I walked more briskly as the lift came by with Sheila's neighbour, Contessa Fiorelli.

In the apartment below Sheila, the family had already left for Sperlonga, where they went every year. The husband, however, stayed at home for the first month. And there he was: this was *his* holiday — across, just inside the small kitchen balcony, was the protruding bare bum of Signor Albano, who usually wore a blue

suit, was the proud father of three girls and worked in a bank. The bottom was pushed discreetly out the open, green slat doors, the buttocks large and white and soft. I lit a cigarette and stared mournfully at them. What went on inside Signor Albano's head? No-one would ever know, since the head was never visible. But the plan was obviously this. Signor Albano, feeling the heat while washing the floor like some poor, downtrodden maid, overworked and abused by the mistress of the house, had taken off his clothes to work more comfortably and *was not aware* that his posterior was on full view. I was tempted to lean across and ask Signor Albano how he saw the world.

Three years ago, when Sheila moved in and summer had come and the Albano family had moved *en masse* down to Sperlonga, she had had her first experience of Signor Albano's posterior. She had screeched and gone into a Jewish American princess high kick of nerves. But the next year she had said, 'My, my! That floor is getting a good wash this year.' And sometimes, 'What a lovely bottom, I wonder, *I really wonder* who it belongs to.' Her sons would just snigger and plan things like heating up a long poker to red-hot and causing Signor Albano considerable pain and shock. Or using a slingshot with staples in it to ruin the sheen of those white cheeks. But Sheila had decided Signor Albano's summer holiday must never be ruined.

I arrived at Sheila's door and pressed the bell. She opened, smiling. 'Resting, are we? Well, everyone has gone to school. Just three more days for them. I've got the same house on Naxos. The *kyria's* finally gotten around to writing to me.' She let me in. 'I'll put on the coffee. Mirella actually volunteered this morning to go down for the *cornetti* and you can share mine.'

I stood in the small kitchen and told Sheila that Signor Albano was out early. Sheila went onto her balcony to check. She came in again and made up a breakfast tray. 'He's early this year, in the day, I mean. It used to be from eleven until three, but it's only nine o'clock.' She clicked her fingers. 'Of course, he'll be on overtime today. They only left yesterday for Sperlonga.'

We took the coffee through to the bedroom and sat and looked at the geraniums that Sheila had remembered this year to keep watering. The flowers were bright pillar-box red and soft pink. 'We could sunbathe later or go down to Ostia for lunch.' She placed a kiss lightly on my cheek and surveyed fondly the unmade bed. I lit another cigarette. How do you say what has to be said? I sipped the coffee; I withdrew and brooded; I looked at myself in the mirror to see what I was conveying. As usual, nothing much. I'd never have made an Italian.

'I've got something that I must tell you.' I stubbed out the cigarette and held Sheila's hand. 'It's highly unlikely anything will have happened to you.'

'Your hand's sweaty,' she remarked.

We both stared at our reflections in the mirror.

'Your eye's got a tic,' Sheila said.

'So would yours if you'd just heard what I've heard,' I snapped back.

'What is it?' Sheila put on her minorly concerned look.

'A year ago,' I began to confess, 'well, we'll leave that out. But, as it happens, I've had a Wassermann test.'

Sheila knew about those. In America, when she was getting engaged, they were compulsory.

'And?'

'And they say it may be positive!'

'May? It is or it isn't.'

'It is. But they are doing a Nelson. It takes around ten days. And you'll be gone to Greece soon afterwards. You'll have to get tested too. In case. But — I'm sure it's only mild syphilis and maybe it isn't.'

Sheila's eyes went into an owl stare. She clutched her grey shirt. She looked in the mirror at herself, she stared at the reflection of her fine hands, and her hands went to cover her small breasts. 'Oh! Oh! Oh!' she wailed. 'What have you done to me? *What have you done?*'

Sheila buried her face in her hands. Outside, on his terrace, Bruce the farting boxer chewed on his tennis ball. Sheila lay back on the bed and stared at the ceiling. 'I think,' I said, 'I'll get the gin.'

I returned with the gin and tonic and we got into bed both wearing our underpants. 'We mustn't touch each other,' commanded Sheila. 'Oh God, my poor children with a syphilitic mother!' I poured two large gins. 'Doesn't it go to the brain early?' Sheila demanded. 'It might explain why I've been feeling so erratic lately.'

I didn't mention that Sheila was only noticing what everyone had always known.

'It's worse for a woman being syphilitic. It makes her into a kind of Typhoid Mary! And the children! Can they get it by kissing me?'

I didn't know.

Sheila fetched her medical dictionary and we read aloud to each other about syphilis. At the end, I shakily got out of bed and poured another gin and tonic each and put in lemon and ice. I took a glass to Sheila.

'I've never drunk gin at ten past nine in the morning before,' she said, grabbing at it.

'I have. After a Cambridge May Ball. After breakfast at Grantchester.'

Sheila, now permanently owl-eyed, stared at Bruce the farting boxer, who was dismembering one of Mike's tennis shoes. 'Bruce has a terrible oral complex.' Sheila propped herself up on cushions. 'Once I found him in the cellar of a friend's place. There was an open bag of grain and he was eating non-stop and it was coming out the other end undigested! He would have died from it, if we'd given him water.'

'I've forgotten to water the geraniums.' Sheila got unsteadily to her feet. 'At least the flowers must stay healthy.' She arrived at

the open terrace door and glided out like a sleepwalking Lady Macbeth. I followed. The hose was turned towards the geraniums and Bruce, who loathed water, rolled on his back as an act of submission. Sheila gently kicked him in the ribs. She aimed the hose as I found the tap and turned it on. We had forgotten Mike's open door. The water arched out violently and cascaded onto his bed. Sheila wiped her brow and concentrated on the geranium troughs.

'What if,' she said, after flooding the terrace, 'I have given it to you?' She squinted with the sunlight. 'I must admit, well, it is possible I have, well, that I have made one or two small concessions here and there.'

I sniffed a coming confession, which would make my other admission of infidelity easier. I went in for the gin and we stood for a time observing the flooded terrace and bed. 'That will teach Mike,' said Sheila, 'for not appreciating me.'

We returned to her bedroom and sat on the edge of the bed.

'It might be me?' Sheila sipped delicately as if the gin were cough medicine. 'I might have gotten it from my husband.'

I could feel the confession slipping away. 'Hardly,' I said. 'You both had to have Wassermann tests. Everyone did in the States.'

'He was a stockbroker,' said Sheila, 'in the futures market. He had nothing. He made all his money on my father's advice. He might well have given it to me. He never gave me proper maintenance. It's I who pays for the kids. Not that I would let that man near them. And God! I sell share after share. I'm going to be a poor woman in a few years, cleaning the houses of the rich.'

She glanced around the huge bedroom and through another glass door to the huge marble fireplace of the living area. 'And, I have to confess something.'

'Yes?' I gently stroked her leg.

'But first,' Sheila glanced at the gin bottle, 'I need some reinforcement.' I topped up for both of us.

'Just imagine,' said Sheila. 'It's only quarter to ten in the morning.'

I gazed at the fine bones of her hands and her buffed nails.

'We must seek advice on how to handle our tragedy.' She reached for the phone.

'First,' I said gently, 'you have something to tell me?'

Sheila looked at me defiantly. 'You know Pino? Well, he has a rock band as well as being the postman. And after my party which Pino's band played at . . . Well, the next day when he came to deliver the post, a small event took place and I must confess, continued to take place, *ogni tanto*.'

Pino was a good-looking Sicilian who, according to my friend Piero, had three women on his rounds, including a correspondent for a famous American newspaper. I simply had not suspected Sheila. I had thought it was . . .

'So,' said Sheila, 'and how did you come to get syphilis?'

I shrugged. 'It was just a small thing. Last year in Bali. At Poppies. At the club I was offered a tryst.' She sniffed. 'And she was said to be one of the finest. Well, the problem with men is that they can't resist the opportunity of a highly trained courtesan and . . .'

Sheila picked up the phone. 'I will ignore what you've said and ring the children's therapist. She will know what to do. What precautions to take. What we might expect if we are both diseased.'

'It'll be the end of my sex life,' I informed her.

Sheila ignored me and dialled. Then she took my hand and lowered herself back onto the pillows, then demanded one of mine so she could sit semi-upright. She held my hand to steady herself for the long wail of horror, pain, fear and loathing.

She got off to a flying start and it took the therapist five minutes to find out what the matter was.

'What test did they give you?' Sheila asked, pausing for a moment.

'Wassermann,' I told her.

Sheila handed on the information.

'Where do you think you got it from?' she asked a moment later.

'Bali,' I replayed, 'from a woman who was reputed to be the second best courtesan on Bali.'

Sheila raised her hand to stem the flow of reminiscence. 'He probably got it from some two-bit Balinese whore.'

Sheila raised an eyebrow and informed the therapist again in weary tones, in case she hadn't heard the first time.

'How long ago?' asked Sheila for the therapist.

'It was last summer, in June.'

'It was last summer in June and to think,' wailed Sheila to the therapist, 'he came back here and straight away' — this time the therapist cut in and Sheila listened respectfully. It seemed that the therapist was agreeing that Sheila had been given a rough ride in this one. Sheila put her hand over the receiver and told me the therapist felt for her. Then she told the therapist she had told me that the therapist was on her side and launched into a comprehensive history of her sexual misdemeanours since the age of eleven and her relationship with her parents, who were probably to blame. This went on for a long time and I topped up our gins.

'She says,' Sheila again put her hand over the receiver, 'that we can be cured of syphilis and since they are giving you the Nelson test, it means the Wassermann is not one hundred per cent accurate.'

I refused to grasp at straws. I knew I was fated to this disease — madness even. Perhaps some great writing would come out of it. I stared blearily out at the terrace which was still flooded. Sheila had been on the phone for forty minutes and now I wanted to tell the therapist my feelings.

'I want to talk to her,' I said. Sheila raised an eyebrow and condescended to ask *her* therapist if she would listen to *John*. I also had a lengthy list of sexual confrontations, starting at the age of nine (which beats Sheila, I thought in a moment of satisfaction, by two years).

'She says she cannot speak to you since she is my and my children's therapist.'

'She means,' I snarled, 'she's not going to be able to clock me and send in the bill.'

'Are you sending me in a bill for this?' demanded Sheila. 'Are you so mercenary?' Sheila put her hand over the receiver. 'She is not charging me, so there!'

I lay back on the one pillow left to me, feeling deep loathing and self-pity. I knew the therapist would find some other way to bill Sheila.

'Thank you so much, Dorothy,' said Sheila, in deep gratitude. She began writing on the bedside pad. I supposed this was a list of sedatives Sheila should begin taking.

'I have written down the name of a good private clinic which will test me,' she told me.

'I'll be tested too,' I decided. 'To be triple-sure.'

Sheila remembered the receiver and replaced it. 'We will ring them up and ask them when they will take our blood.'

She did so, but it grew complicated since they thought Sheila wanted to donate blood. I intervened and it was established that at eight the next morning they would take blood for tests.

'No need to tell the receptionist what test,' whispered Sheila.

Sheila wanted a description of the VD clinic, whose roof could be seen from her top terrace. For some reason we both climbed the stairs to look at it. 'Imagine,' Sheila swayed and leant against the wall, 'that just across from me is that plague hole. It's a wonder they don't escape and come biting us.'

We carefully descended the staircase, returned to the bedroom without intending to, went to sleep. We woke up with headaches at two-thirty in the afternoon. The room was hot from the heater and Bruce was asleep on our feet, snoring loudly. 'God, Bruce needs a bath,' I whispered. I wandered out to the kitchen, fetched mineral water and then went to the bathroom for disprins. We swallowed the mineral water and looked out at the terrace.

'You may stay the night,' Sheila decided. 'But I will have to sterilise everything you've used. Glassware, cutlery, probably the sheets too.'

She got out of bed and drew all the drapes and Bruce sighed with pleasure as the fan was turned on.

'We will leave a note for the children to get themselves pizza and to bring one for us too. After that we will listen to some Mahler and then we'll take some sleeping pills so we can get a good night's rest. I don't think we're allowed to eat in the morning. No breakfast.'

Some time later the children came in, read the note and went for pizzas. Some time afterwards there was a knock at the door. Sheila went, with a towel draped around her. Some time after that Mirella began practising her violin and Mike, who hadn't noticed his soaking bed, turned on Bruce Springsteen. Saul, presumably, was, as usual in his bedroom, masturbating. The house didn't seem to notice our presence at all. The pizza was half-cold, since Mike had stopped off to yarn to a friend. It was pizza Napolitana with *alici*. Sheila, who hated anchovies, spent precious seconds digging them out and putting them on my portion. Mike discovered his wet bed and blamed Saul. Sheila raised an eyebrow at the language.

'Now,' she said, some time later, 'I think we should take a sleeping pill. We'll have to be up at the crack of dawn. I want to sneak out of the house before the children are awake. They can get their own breakfasts.'

We took two sleeping pills each, remembered to turn off the gas heater and dozed off with the dusk creeping into the room and a breeze off the Tiber from the reopened terrace window.

We woke at four-thirty the next morning. A bird had started to sing in a dippy rhythm of warbles followed by two atonal coughs. We went through to the bathroom and Sheila gave me an old towel which she could, if necessary, burn, and an old toothbrush which she threw in the waste bin as soon as I had used it.

The birds were all now singing as Sheila dressed formally in a long rust brown skirt and a saffron coloured shirt. She spent twenty-five minutes making up her face and choosing a perfume. I then climbed back into yesterday's sweaty underpants and crumpled jeans. I put on my blue shirt and, on Sheila's insistence, did it up to the neck and put on my blue tie.

Sheila decided that her colour combination was a disaster and we needed every possible good omen this morning. She selected a long, creamy gold skirt and a blue shirt; she then decided she must iron the blue shirt. I sat down on the bed as she plugged in the iron and set up the ironing board.

We left the house at around six. Mike was already up, body-building on the terrace.

'Hi Mom,' he said, 'where you goin'?'

'Out for an early morning walk,' Sheila replied, austerely.

'Since when?' asked Mike, beginning press-ups.

'Since this morning!'

We marched firmly to the door.

'See ya, John,' called out Mike.

Sheila meanwhile, in panic, put on her sunglasses.

Sheila's Fiat was parked around the corner near the *fontana*. She took the keys from her bag and opened the door.

I tried the other door; as usual, she'd forgotten to secure it.

We drove carefully through Piazza Santa Maria. This was illegal, but no police would be around at that hour to supervise the handbag robberies. We turned right into Piazza San Egidio and along towards Via della Lungara. Everything here was saturated in a renaissance, while we were driving towards confirmation of the original fall.

Fifteen minutes later we parked, on the opposite side of the road from the clinic, under a plane tree. We looked at each other; I looked, finally, at my watch. An hour later a male arrived in a grey suit and carrying a briefcase. He went in. A woman arrived and a moment later a couple, then the door was opened and a woman peered out.

Sheila took my hand. 'Imagine,' she whispered, 'we have to tell them what it's for.' We walked across the road and pushed through the glass door. Sheila raised her chin and with a gracious smile sailed straight to the counter, like a Catholic mother of four whose son was standing that year for parliament. 'We have come for a compulsory blood test,' she announced regally. The bleached-haired girl was bleary. She handed over a form. Sheila glanced down it and nervously took her pen and ticked. I took a form, located Wassermann and did the same. The girl went away buttoning up her white uniform and could be seen handing over our forms to a young doctor who was smoking a cigarette and drinking coffee out of a plastic mini-cup.

I realised Sheila was pretending that, as a Catholic with four children (one of whom was standing for parliament as a Christian Democrat) and about to remarry, she couldn't, as a virtuous widow, possibly have syphilis. I felt a desire to negate this image and tried a macho shuffle, hands in jeans, sneering at the receptionist. It was a lamentable performance and Sheila gave me the eye. The eye said *dignified middle-class abhorrence for such matters that the state demands of us who will soon be joined, by the Church, in holy matrimony*. As far as I knew, Italians weren't required by law to have a Wassermann.

We went back to the wooden form and leant against the white tiles. 'Thank God no-one else is here waiting,' Sheila whispered.

It was, I realised, like being in church just before the priest enters for mass. There is a sacred hush as the congregation faces infinity and the sacrament of life.

'Just imagine a whole row of syphilitics sitting here and waiting for blood tests. Imagine the scenes!' whispered Sheila.

I imagined a shy couple approaching the alter, arms taut, rubber bandages in place and veins bulging, waiting to give the blood of life to the needle.

'*Allora, numero uno*.' The white-faced nurse had powdered over her acne but it showed through in pink blotches.

Sheila stood up and raised her chin and walked forward slowly, as if about to attend a reception. She disappeared through a door which swung shut behind her. I lit a cigarette. A moment later she reappeared and walked slowly back to her seat. 'It doesn't hurt at all,' she whispered. 'And they just draw the blood. They ask no details *at all*.'

I followed the beckoning finger as *numero due*. Half a minute later my arm was swabbed, the bandage in place, the vein protruding and the needle sliding into it. I left the cubicle. Sheila took my cigarette from me — I had profaned a holy place — and placed it delicately in the tin cigarette container on the floor. We walked silently together over to the car.

At her door, Sheila offered a chaste cheek for a light kiss. As we parted, the children came through the *portone* on the way to school. Mirella said nothing to us; she was looking severe. Saul, in his tracksuit, ran out, intent on getting somewhere fast. Mike loafed by and flexed his muscles and smiled and sauntered. Sheila looked graciously at them, as if they were her audience at some gallery opening.

I went to the bar, bought a *gettone*, and called into the office, saying the fever was still there and I had developed stomach problems as well. It was agreed that it must be some kind of food poisoning. I walked back through the square and along past Bar Domiziano, where I stopped off for a coffee. I didn't meet anyone I knew. I continued along the Via della Lungara and since the Farnesina was open I walked up the gravel path and through the open door, turned right and right again, sat on an ancient carved chair and stared at the Raphael fresco — Tritons, sea gods, dolphins and exuberant life. Raphael died young; I decided I would put some spring flowers on his grave in the Pantheon. I left the painting and stayed for a time in the gracious gardens.

Back at home on Penitence Alley I put a call through to Mildred, the school teacher. She agreed to see me, at morning interval, in her study. That meant around quarter to eleven. I set off in my car along the road that led out of Rome. I arrived early and sat in the bar opposite the school and sipped a cappuccino and then another. I managed to smoke four cigarettes in succession, then I had another cappuccino. I was dying for a pee, but the bar's lavatory was broken. I glanced at my watch, went to the *trattoria* next door and explained I must go to the lavatory.

Across in the school, the classes ended. I walked up the drive and went into the main building. I climbed the marble staircase and found myself on the second floor. I knocked on a door and went in to be met by the smell of acids brightly consuming the air. I looked around the shelves littered with apparatus: tripods, machines for holding test tubes, which could be instruments for torture if you were ten inches high, which was what I was feeling.

On cue fresh-cheeked Mildred, wearing a sensible blue blouse and a dark blue skirt, opened another door.

'Oh, there you are,' she said. 'Come on in, I'm just making coffee. My God, you're not looking wonderful. What have you been up to?'

I shrugged.

The jug boiled and I watched the steam. Mildred poured the coffee and handed it over with milk and one sugar. We'd got to know each other well enough to know what we both took in our coffee. She looked me over for signs of a nervous breakdown. I put the coffee down, since my hands were shaking.

'You see, Mildred,' I said, lighting up a cigarette.

Mildred said not to smoke, then said, 'Smoke, it doesn't matter.'

'You see,' I tried again, 'last year when I was in Bali . . .' I shook. Why should this have happened to me when I was only being romantically licentious? Did it happen to Conrad? To Baudelaire? 'Well, I've had a Wassermann,' I said, 'and they say it is positive. I have to have a Nelson.' Mildred, busty and warm, came over, sat down and drew me to her bosom.

'Well?' she said.

'I had to let you know — ' I tried for the heroically moral stance and failed lamentably, 'since you will be going to England.'

Mildred remained calm, like a proficient ward sister. 'I see,' she said. 'Well, as you know, apart from our small fling, I have been having a relationship with Tiberio. He's married and, of course, has no intention of leaving his wife. Not that you would expect an Italian to give up on the mother he's married to. She irons his shirts, washes, cleans, makes children and food.' For a moment Mildred looked close to losing her English cool. 'And I have had an occasional little fling with Tim, after you and I broke up.'

'My God,' I said, 'it's like dropping a stone in water. Sheila may have it and Pino the postman. He may have handed it on to Bernice Seitz of *The New York Times*, since he was philandering with her. Then his wife. And, for all I know, his wife is having it off with some Sicilian. And then,' I gulped at my coffee, 'Tiberio gets it and gives it to his wife and she has a lunchtime lover. And he probably has a wife. My God, I might have infected half of Rome by now!'

Mildred started laughing and so did I. Soon we were weeping tears and gasping for breath in that acid-smelling room.

I stopped and gaped at jars full of dead lizards and snakes and pink and grey foetuses of small animals.

For reasons known only to the gods, Sheila's test was ready the day before mine. For this meeting with destiny, Sheila had slept alone in her large bed and at Vicolo della Penitenza I had slept alone in mine. At ten that night we had phoned each other and said that we were now going to bed.

There was no early morning rising; the result of the test would be ready at ten or maybe nine-thirty. I had already explained I could not be at work until around eleven and that the same would be true the following day. I made no excuses about my illness, my stomach or my nerves.

I woke at seven and went for a run up to Doria Park. In the early morning the sun was hitting through the pine trees and on the lake some swans were looking with arched necks at a horseman on a grey gelding.

I arrived at Sheila's at nine and rang the bell. She came down wearing severe grey, a grey silk shirt and a red coral necklace to define the neck where the axe was about to fall. We had a cappuccino in Piazza Santa Maria; we drove to the clinic; we parked; Sheila glanced at her watch. 'The test could have been back by nine-thirty. It is now ten past ten.'

She go out of the car and walked across the road. She motioned to me to wait outside and went through the door which swung shut behind her. A minute later she came out with a plain white envelope in her hand. She stood alone, face severe, serene even. She opened the envelope. She stared at the paper with great dignity. Then her face broke into an incredulous smile. She did three can-can kicks and threw herself into my arms. 'I am not syphilitic.'

'I am not syphilitic!' she screeched at the surprised faces of three passing nuns.

Then, choosing my moment well, I confessed to my dalliance with Mildred.

We went to bed early that night. We both knew I had syphilis and that the delay in my result was simply for clinical retesting. Sheila was in her heroic mother mode. She was supportive. She held my hand. I got drunk. I wondered whether, before going mad, I would write some wonderful poetry that would be dedicated to her, who would spend her life, after I had blown my brains out, worshipping at the shrine of my poetry and giving elevated interviews on the tragedy.

Sheila made herself a new pot of tea.

As morning broke, Sheila arose from her bed, virginal in her movements, face serene as alabaster and went to make coffee. She returned with a caffe latte, sweetened with honey. She sat on the edge of the bed as I took it and sipped. She placed her hand on my forehead to check for fever. (She then washed her hands.) Then she fetched for me two disprins and one valium, and instructed me to go to the lavatory and to shower and wash my hair. As we left the building she took my arm. We arrived at the clinic and Sheila, as noble Jewish mother with errant son (a son is loved whatever he does), took my arm and pushed me forward to the door. It was now obvious that we were not coming this time for the blood test which would allow us to marry, but that rather I was the son who had got himself involved with some trollop.

On Sheila's arm I went to the counter and gave my name. Sheila gave a gracious, if distant smile to the receptionist nurse, whose acne, I noted, seemed no better. I took the envelope and turned and walked slowly through the door. I heard a bird singing in the tree; I denied the fumes from the passing cars — the world was of pure crystalline clarity. I opened the envelope. I stared at it, not comprehending. I handed it to Sheila.

She read it and shrugged. 'Well,' she said, 'what would you expect from the attendants at that plague pit? They probably mislaid the labels and you became someone else.'

Later, I went for the Nelson result. It was negative.

I asked the male nurse why the Wassermann was positive. He shrugged.

I told him about the inoculations.

The male nurse shrugged again and said, '*Forse.*'

'He said, "Maybe",' I said to Mildred over the telephone. I was now in a state of rage. 'I *told* them I'd had cholera, typhoid, paratyphoid, tetanus, smallpox.'

I met Mildred for coffee.

'I didn't tell anyone,' said calm Mildred. 'I thought I would wait. And,' she finished her cappuccino, 'I checked up in the books. The cholera spirochete looks very much like syphilis spirochete.' She went into a technical description and I got lost. Perhaps it was the cholera something else which was like the syphilis spirochete.

'It must be that,' decided Mildred. 'Well, all's well that ends well.'

I went to see Mercedes. Sheila had been on the phone telling her the whole story. Mercedes welcomed me. She had had the maid prepare a celebratory roast chicken and potatoes and salad. She had her astrology books out again. 'Isn't it all marvellous,' she said, as we sat having a glass of wine. 'I was right to the day. Right to the day!' She went into a technical description of Mercury transiting something or other.

All I knew was that there had been a difficult transit of Venus and that Sheila had decided, as penance, that we would not be lovers until after the summer holidays.

Schulski and the Messiah

It's winter and the small fire in the long antique grate hisses and spits. It hardly warms the air above it, let alone the huge room whose windows look over to the Gianicolo and the floodlit Spanish Academy.

The dining table is further down the room and Sheila, the hostess has lit near it a small *bombola* gas heater. Its heat too is absorbed two feet away, in chill. Everyone is rugged up. I in grey rolltop, Sheila in a crimson cardigan, Schulski, Sheila's sculptor friend, in a blue rolltop with a hole in the sleeve and Pamela, his girlfriend in a cerise jersey which fluffs up around her white neck.

We've mostly finished eating the pasta I've cooked. I've made the *sugo* from bacon and mushrooms and cream with a few green capers and cracked black pepper. I pass to strong Schulski the carafe of dark wine. He and Sheila had bought a demijohn the week before in a village of the mountainous Abruzzi. It's now in bottles and sealed with olive oil. A few specks float in the glasses. Soaking it up with cotton wool, followed by a swift decant into the sink, never gets it all.

Schulski breaks off a piece of bread and moves with his wine down the room and stands in front of the fire. In the thirties, he ran guns for the Hagganah into Palestine. He was then, and still is, a sculptor and his style is one that Sheila mimics, she being one of the group who sit at Schulski's feet. The difference between the group and Schulski is his great passion and a great and terrible memory. The holocaust forms his structures and generates sharp curves, metallic wheels and rigid shapes screaming into the void.

But tonight Schulski is not the great sculptor. He is picking up

from the chair he'd been sitting in the latest draft of his novella. It is his first prose work and probable he will want to read aloud from the masterpiece. Sheila and I raise eyebrows at each other and Pamela allows a furtive giggle as Schulski shuffles it into page order. No-one dares tell Schulski the truth — that it's awful — in case he falls on them and rends them limb from limb. 'He is so threatening when he reads it,' whispers Sheila, pleased by Schulski's artistic violence.

By now, everyone had heard it so often they could probably write it down with hardly an error. It is about a Lolita who is living with a sculptor like Schulski in a huge studio in Rome. The hero builds a special small room high up in the studio and there the heroine gets up to unmentionable things with herself while the hero looks on tenderly. Later Lolita is abducted by a gang of bikies who then get up to unmentionable things with her which makes the hero very annoyed.

Looking at Schulski's taut frame and passionate clear eyes, I decide Freud has something in his theories about repressed material.

Pamela goes to the fire to join Schulski. She is dark haired and looks around fifteen instead of twenty-five. Schulski sits down and Pamela sits on Schulski's lap and kisses him fondly.

Sheila for a moment looks furious that Schulski loves Pamela more than her. I squeeze her arm and tell her that her soup (which was in fact watery) was great. That falls on deaf ears since Sheila couldn't care less about food.

'Well,' says Schulski, looking down at the new draft which is full of cross-outs in red pen, and about to read the revised first ten pages.

'Oh, listen,' says Sheila, ignoring Schulski ready, ready to read. She gets up from the table, swinging a red shawl around her thin shoulders. Her husky voice holds Schulski. 'What is it?' she asks.

I get up too as the high reed notes come to us, in small bursts of sound, now present, now lost, as the *tramontana*, that bright

clear wind from the alps, surges and falls across Rome.

'The pipers from the Abruzzi.' Sheila smiles and puts her arms around me. 'They've come down from the mountains to make their Christmas music.'

'It's "He Came Down from the Stars".' Schulski, a passionate Zionist, has moisture in his eyes. He reaches in his pocket and gives Pamela some loose coins. Pamela runs away like an excited little girl, away up the stairs that lead to the roof terrace. The door bangs shut behind her.

She comes back, cheeks red, a few minutes later. 'There are two of them with bagpipes and a little girl who's picking up the coins. They're standing beside the fountain and there's not a soul in sight.'

Sheila and I walk with her to the fire.

'You know,' says Schulski, 'once I sang in *The Messiah*, the bass solos.'

'Wonderful,' Sheila sees a way of distracting Schulski. 'Why don't you show us, Schulski? How are we to believe you if you won't demonstrate your skills?'

Schulski accepts a fill-up from me of Abruzzi wine and launches into 'Why Do the Nations'. Schulski pounds through and starts to lose key, descending by half tones. It is rather unnerving in this large room. When he finishes 'and imagine a vain thing', the Abruzzi bagpipers, far below, have moved on from our square.

'Let's put on the record,' I say. I've studied voice and feel like competing with Schulski. I'm also a bass.

'Yes, yes.' Pamela strokes Schulski's ragged blue jersey.

Sheila rushes for the pile of records and Schulski's belly, which has been pumping energetically in and out, relaxes under the jumper.

Sheila finds the record and puts it on. The orchestra begins 'O Thou That Tellest Good Tiding to Zion'.

'Where *is* Zion?' asks Sheila, the liberated Jewish American princess.

'I don't know,' replies Pamela.

'Israel,' answers Schulski.

'Well, it sure as hell is not Chicago.' Sheila throws on to the fire some pieces of an old chair I had chopped up that evening. We'd found it at the *fontanella*, around the corner from Piazza Santa Maria where everyone dumped their rubbish.

'And now,' says Sheila, rubbing her thin hands, 'why don't Pamela and I warm up for you boys?'

'For what?' I ask, smirking to myself. Ready, anyway, to outsing Schulski any day of the week. The only problem is, will my ego go to my throat and weaken the vocal chords?

The bass aria, 'Why Do the Nations', begins. And Schulski and I stand together in front of the fire to sing. Schulski roars it out like a young bull and I find it hard work cutting through that big wide sound. No edge to that voice at all. But, Lord, what an *effort* it is, this competition in male strut. Who could guess Schulski is a grandfather?

Sheila taps her feet and soon she and Pamela try out some go-go steps as they pick up the strut and the orchestra goes into a *da capo* with the trumpets blaring. Sheila hustles to front stage, holding Pamela by the hand and faces down the room to the dining table and a vast audience of fans.

Sheila and Pamela do warming up exercises for the coming 'Hallelujah Chorus'.

It begins and Schulski and I sing, arms around each other's necks.

Sheila and Pamela throw their arms wide to the glory and kick their heels in a go-go soft shoe shuffle.

'Hallelujah, hallelujah,' bellow I and Schulski as we ride triumphant into heaven with banners flying.

Sheila's lean body and small breasts are now taut, her Russian Tartar face raised to the ceiling in an ecstasy of go-go.

Pamela makes soft petal movements, like a soft sea creature, then both kick and prance as the trumpets scream out the war cry of the Jewish saviour.

And he shall reign forever and ever.

Sheila does a high kick, twirls and wiggles her bottom.

Pamela flips her hips.

Hallelujah, hallelujah, hallelujah, bursts from my and Schulski's throats, at last our voices blending and riding the chorus into a crescendo while Pamela and Sheila fling heavenwards loud throaty cries.

'Well, well,' says Sheila a moment later, picking up her glass of wine, breathing heavily, 'I wonder if the New York Phil-harmonic would like to buy our act.'

'Let's do it again,' I say. I'm a sucker for heaven, and besides, Schulski has sat down and picked up the new draft of his masterpiece.

II

ROMAN TRUTHS

Resisting Andreas

Some time in the night I threw off the peasant Abruzzi cover, and when I woke up at quarter to five the next morning my skin felt greasy, as if I had been sweating. I lay for a moment staring up at the white ceiling, then got to my feet and padded over the terazzo floor to the sitting room. I stopped and stared at the silver-painted candlestick on the floor, then I went to the window and looked down onto Vicolo del Cedro, and shivered. I leaned against the window sill. Below, a carriage went by, its wheels rattling over the cobbles. The driver was bleary with sleep and the horse had fresh ribbons in its bridle, with a posy of yellow roses pinned to its straw hat. But it was too early to go to Piazza Venezia. There were no tourists at this hour of the summer of 1972.

As the wheels echoed against the umber walls of Piazza San Egidio, I walked through to the kitchen and put on the percolator. The kitchen had too much undefined space; an old wooden table and a telephone attached to the wall, and formica chairs with tubular steel struts. I considered it, but couldn't think how to fill it up with myself and my possessions. I drank perked coffee with two teaspoons of honey and some cold milk, and returned to the sitting-room window. Shit was stirring in my bowels but I held it in while I remember the exact spot where the girl had stood.

She had been older than me, around twenty-seven. She had black hair and a long, withdrawn look, and she had said almost nothing. All that Andreas had said was to memorise her face and ask no questions about who she was or what she did. And so, looking at her framed by the window, I had been polite, offered coffee and talked about what was on in Rome that week. Then

she had left with Andreas and I hadn't seen her again. I wondered if I would see her today or tomorrow. I could still remember the blue dress, like one a Greek peasant woman would wear, but I had forgotten what she looked like right away. It was as if I feared retaining her image; my excuse was the light that shone on to her through the window, dazzling me, and made her an anonymous citizen of Athens visiting Rome.

A week after that meeting Andreas had told me I must have arms training. Andreas had said it in a low intense voice as soon as we met, by appointment, outside the *bombola* shop on the corner of Vicolo del Cedro. Inside the shop the dull-faced wife had been screaming at her husband over the stocking of pots and pans. I had half listened to the argument while Andreas continued to talk about the secret range where he was to have arms training and learn about explosives. Andreas, as he spoke of the coming events, clenched his fist in the pockets of his navy blue sailor's jacket. He was about my height, but the horn-rimmed glasses defined an older face, the face of a man in his late thirties. Andreas did not hear the woman's shrill voice as he adumbrated images of firing guns, but I did and the argument became the brutal cries of training warriors. As I looked to my right the familiar landscape of Piazza San Egidio became a strange and frightening place.

Why had the carriage gone by so early this morning? The question grew dull as, across from my sitting-room window, in the Carmelite convent, the nuns began to sing lauds. Their chanting echoed through a small barred window high up in the convent walls. It pierced through my hesitation about myself, like the wings of larks speeding from the darkness of this old earth, speeding straight into the turquoise sky; I was sure of myself. I stood there, my guts no longer churning.

I walked back through the apartment to my bathroom, stood under the shower and turned it on. It spouted a tired flow under which I huddled as I soaped.

After I had towelled myself I drank more coffee with honey,

returned to my bedroom and looked down on the empty mattress bed on the floor. Yesterday morning I had told Alicia, my girlfriend, that I was going to Florence for three days to visit friends. Alicia had turned to me as the nuns were singing lauds and she had already been wet. I moved hard in her and she loved me in the same way as the nuns sang for the clear light of early morning.

I yawned and got into my jeans, washed and pressed by Delphina downstairs. I put on an Italian linen shirt, then changed it for a loose blue cotton one. It was going to be hot and I would be sweating by ten or eleven. The other shirt would do for the return journey.

I sat on the bed and tried to meditate; my breath kept coming in shallow gasps. 'I'm scared,' I told myself. I wondered where I was going. Was it to Greece? Andreas had not said where, only that I must be ready at six. I lit my first cigarette of the day and viewed the overnight bag I had packed. I had forgotten to put in a change of underwear. I rummaged in a pile of unironed shirts and found two more pairs. That should do.

I stubbed out the cigarette. I had holidayed in Greece in 1968, staying in Piraeus with a Greek friend, George, whom I'd met when teaching at a language school in Oxford. His house faced a dusty street with huge potholes in it, mortar craters from the days of the civil war . . . I remembered the donkeys carrying panniers of vegetables; the tableau of women in black scarves, watching the street; the priests in their black robes. They had taken me back to a landscape which was somehow familiar, deep in my being. But modern Greece I could not get a grip on. I could not register the meaning of the military coup and 'Papa Dop' who ruled the country.

Now, years later, I understood about concentration camps and about Bouboulinas Street, where men and women were tortured with the *falanga* and electric shock. I knew that Janis Ritsos, the poet, was in the hands of the junta; as was Alekos Panagoulis, who attempted to assassinate Papadopoulos. And I knew now that my friend George had used the fascist regime; he was just a poor boy on the make. But then, back in Piraeus, having no history, I could only see the regime as a documentary film that I was watching in some cinema in New Zealand.

George had taken me to visit Archbishop Jacobus, who seemed to be one of George's successful social acquisitions. The archbishop had the high-pitched female whine of an old eunuch and had gazed at handsome red-lipped George with red-rimmed eyes while he fondled his yellow agate worry beads. We had eaten dreadful sweetmeats while I stared around me at the paintings and pastels of former archbishops, who all looked like hags out of hell. The large crosses on their breasts seemed ready to swell and straddle them.

And later I came to know the cause of my ignorance. My own country had given me no earth in my belly, and that was why I was making this journey today: to find out if I had courage and could act to honour my ideals. I went back into the sitting-room, sat for a moment, then walked fast into the bedroom, picked up my overnight bag and took it to the front door. I clicked my fingers, poured the rest of the coffee into a saucepan, added some milk and heated it. It was twenty past six. I doubted my watch and rang to confirm. *L'ora e sei and ventuno*. I put my watch forward one minute, then took my coffee into the sitting room and drank it looking down again into the street. I wiped my damp hands on my jeans and felt again in my shirt pocket for the passport. I took out my wallet and checked my driving licence and UN diplomatic card. I looked down the street again and kept looking down until Andreas arrived at a quarter to seven.

I waved to Andreas, who nodded, picked up my bag and opened the front door. On the open landing some tomcat had peed overnight and at the next level Delphina had hung out an early wash of grey nappies. They ate mostly pasta and the older daughter, Claudia, had too white a face.

At my knock, Dephina came to the door in an old cotton nightdress. She was only in her thirties, but the mound of her grey-looking breasts was beginning to flop and her peasant face, which should have been brown, was white and half-defeated. I handed in my key so she could clean my place the next day, which was Sunday. I told her I would probably be back late Monday evening, and went down the worn stone stairs.

As I came through the *portone*, Andreas finished his Gitane. 'What kept you?' he asked brusquely.

I looked at him, puzzled.

'Never mind,' said Andreas. 'But we are late. We must make time up. We must be out of Rome before the traffic blocks Lungotevere.'

Andreas took my keys and opened the door to the driver's seat while I put our bags in the boot. Its lock was broken and I had forgotten this.

I got into the driving seat of the Alfa and turned on the ignition as Andreas lit another Gitane.

'Has the car been checked?'

'Yes, it has been checked.' I let out the clutch and pulled carefully away from the sloping convent wall, manoeuvring past a battered Fiat van. We left my street and glided along Vicolo del Cinque, not even disturbing the cats rooting in the garbage by the *fontanella*. We passed Bar Domiziano, turning onto Via della Lungara and then out onto Lungotevere. There was no traffic, so I made an illegal crossing onto Ponte Vittorio and then across to the eastwards-moving lane. Soon we passed Castel San Angelo, where Tosca threw herself over the battlements to her death.

'What did you tell your friends?' asked Andreas, breaking into my thoughts.

I repeated what I had already told Andreas, that everyone thought I was going to Florence for a few days. Some people thought I had a new girlfriend there; others thought I was going to see some frescos; I had been talking a lot about Lippi and della Francesca . . .

Andreas asked more details of responses, as if this was very

important and, engrossed in this interrogation, I made the correct turn only at the last moment. Having crossed over to the Foro Italico, we were on the road which would lead, in about half an hour or less, to the north-bound autostrada. Andreas tapped his fingers on his jeans and I noticed that the jeans needed a wash.

'I have not been to bed,' commented Andreas, half turning so I could see the bags under his eyes and the uncooked pastry-white skin of his cheeks. It highlighted his black eyes which were hard and glaring.

'Slow down,' said Andreas.

I wondered whether he was carrying his Beretta, since Andreas was sure he was a likely target for assassins. It was now, apparently, like this in Rome: trucks moved up the Autostrada del Sol from Greece with arms for the neo-Nazis in Bavaria, while the Greek secret police had free access to Italy. We reached the autostrada, the oleanders screaming in pink and red. The sun was well up, losing its orange tones and settling into June whiteness. I took the autostrada ticket, gave it to Andreas to put in the glove box and settled back. I began to ask Andreas where we were going, at which he snapped at me again to drive slower.

'Drive slower,' he said again, and then, 'Have you had the car serviced?'

In the haze beginning to envelop me, I forgot he had asked me this already. It was as if the two of us would always be driving somewhere, to some important destination which would always be in front of us and he would always ask the same questions which I would forget he had asked.

'I told you to stop,' snapped Andreas as we passed a service station and shops. I switched off the car radio and Andreas leaned forward and switched it on. He readjusted his dark glasses.

'Stop,' said Andreas, another half an hour later. I turned into the petrol station, with its restaurant and coffee shop. Andreas got out. 'I must telephone,' he said. 'Check the oil and petrol.'

I backed out to the solitude of the black tarmac and directed the attendant to check the oil, water and tyre pressure. The tank anyway was nearly full. I looked for the sign to the lavatories and as I went in, Andreas was leaving a cubicle.

I peed, and left without washing my hands. In the bar, near the telephone, Andreas was sitting with a double black coffee. I ordered a cappuccino and a cornetto. 'This is your training run,' Andreas said quietly. 'Soon, I may use you in Greece.'

I considered the white froth in my cup. What about the firing range, and the woman from Athens? All that was fading away into a blur. I wanted to ask Andreas why he hadn't made his phone call. 'I have not telephoned,' he said with quiet intensity, seizing on my thoughts, 'because there are people around. I cannot use our phone in Rome, nor yours, for it will have been noted that you know me and it is probably tapped. I will wait until later. I think we are fine; I do not think we are being followed.'

I put down my coffee slowly and tried to remember Alicia's face but couldn't . . .

'You stay here,' said Andreas, going to the cashier and paying. He returned, tucking his wallet away in his back pocket, picked up the car keys from the table and left. I sat where I was until Andreas returned ten minutes later. 'Have you not finished?' he asked. I nodded. 'Then we go.' He got behind the behind the wheel and paid the attendant with a five-thousand lire note.

'But,' I said, bewildered, 'we didn't need any servicing. It was done in Rome!'

'Just some oil,' said Andreas as he turned on the ignition. He engaged the gears, which crashed. 'Tell me the order of the gears,' he demanded. I did so, and we took off with a hop that settled into a glide as we moved down to the autostrada.

Andreas lapsed into silence. The apprentice looked out the open window. On the left we passed by Orvieto, with its Etruscan foundations. The apprentice mentioned this to Andreas, who didn't seem to hear. The apprentice closed his eyes and then an hour later, by instinct, opened them again as we were approaching the Camuccia turn-off, which led to my friend Mercedes' country house. I followed that route in my mind, pausing at Lake Trasimeno. A further half-hour on, the hill town of Cortona would be in view on the right, and the tower of the princely Passerini villa, to the right of which lay Mercedes' house. I could feel myself bumping down the rough track, across the torrent and up, with a burst of the accelerator, to the old stone farm house. On its walls the red and white roses would be in bloom, and in the lower fields the olives would be bearing small, hard green fruits. The car, like destiny, passed by the familiar place; and anyway, that weekend Mercedes was in Rome.

Soon we flashed by the Florence turn-off.

The heat was rising up, it seemed, through the floor boards.

There were swathes of dryness and brown grass.

'I have not slept,' said Andreas again.

Late that afternoon, beyond the Milan turn-off, we stopped to eat. Andreas took off his dark glasses. 'I will have the car checked.'

I walked across the tarmac into the air-conditioned cool and up some rustic wooden stairs. In the restaurant, with its plastic-wooden tables, I lined up and collected lasagne, an *insalata mista*, a glass of wine and one of chilled mineral water. Sitting down, I watched through the blue tinted windows the cars hurtling north for the border. I made myself eat, since my stomach was pressing against my rib cage.

Andreas came in, rubbing his eyes. He came over to the table and sat down. 'Why didn't you wait?'

'I didn't know how long you would be.'

He finished his cigarette, joined the small queue and returned with a greasy *saltimbocca*, fried potatoes, a tomato salad and a glass of red wine. He drank the wine and smoked another cigarette. 'There is no time for coffee,' he said. 'Go now to the toilet. I will be ready in five minutes.'

The lavatory, downstairs, was the best I had seen on the autostrada, with clean stainless steel urinals, clean lavatories and a long row of wash basins. An old woman in a pink smock pottered about with a mop and plastic bucket; on a table were bottles of disinfectant and clean rags. I gave her a hundred lira and walked out into the hot afternoon, its edges fraying as a breeze came in from the alps.

The car had been moved from the narrow shade of a poplar. I leaned against the bonnet and waited. After twenty minutes I retraced my steps to the restaurant. Andreas had moved seats so that he faced the south-coming traffic. He had ordered a coffee and cognac and a large slice of cake, but the *saltimbocca* had hardly been touched. The apprentice sat down and looked at the cake and Andreas looked at him. 'Now we will leave,' he said quietly. 'I have a phone call to make.' He ran his hand through his black, now greasy, hair.

Back in the car Andreas consulted his map. 'Soon you will drive. When we get close to the border — '

'Which border?'

'The Swiss border,' Andreas snapped. 'I told you we were going to Switzerland.'

We circled out, apparently heading for the border town of Chiasso and that valley which runs into Switzerland. The Engadine Valley? I closed my eyes tighter and dreamed of the wheat fields in Umbria where poppies were swathing bright scarlet carpets through the wheat and the blue cornflowers. When I opened my eyes, Andreas had left the motorway and was slowing down to enter a small village. It had a northern feel, with sloping roofs and the stone a grey granite from the not-distant Swiss mountains.

Andreas drove onto a curb of green grass and I realised I was meant to drive. I got out and moved around to the driver's seat.

Andreas now had a new map open in front of him. I was directed along secondary roads and through small villages, most of which had been modernised. Andreas started to talk. He smiled at me, and lit a cigarette for me and insisted I eat half a bar of chocolate. 'This is a trial run,' said Andreas. 'We can have the car altered. There is a place that does it just out of Rome. That way, when you go to Greece, we can hide something important.'

I munched on the chocolate I didn't really want. Chocolate made me liverish.

'There will be years of struggle.' Andreas lit a new Gitane. 'It may not end in my lifetime. The only solution is violence.

'I go into Greece,' he went on, 'I'm not caught. They are stupid, the Greek security police. I have had meetings with them in Rome, they threaten my family, I just laugh! Violence is the way.' He took off his dark glasses. 'We must learn from the Arabs — blow up planes, target military bases. And the IRA! You have an Irish name.' His voice grew insinuating. 'You should be concerned for Ireland.'

'No,' I said, 'I'm not Irish. Perhaps violence is right for Greece. Perhaps! But the people you should target are the torturers, like the people who torture Alekos Panagoulis. Yes, that would help. Kill one torturer and blanket Athens with leaflets saying that the others will be killed if they don't stop. But nothing else.'

Andreas smiled to himself, the smile of someone who knew a great deal, and withdrew inwards.

We came to the border.

At the train station we loaded the car aboard. 'We are taking the San Gottardo,' said Andreas needlessly and I bit back a retort.

'I'm just tired,' I told myself.

The train lurched off and Andreas shut his eyes, clasping the plastic cup with the coffee half drunk — always black and always a double.

Watching the evening light hitting the last granite face and the last patch of fir trees, I did up my suede jacket and realised I was feeling cold.

Off the train I drove again. Andreas told me we were going to Basel and then was silent, his eyes looking ahead into the tunnel of light cut by the headlights. In the darkness he began to talk. 'You know,' he said, 'I was a school teacher,' he laughed mirthlessly, 'in the provinces. But when the military staged their coup I knew I would fight and so I left and now I work at a man's work.'

Then he talked about torture. He dwelt on the bastinado and the electric shock, then discussed the rape of some men and women in interrogation sessions. 'You would have to watch out,' chuckled Andreas to himself, 'they like doing it to young men, those ESA soldiers.'

I risked a quick glance to the side — Andreas was smiling for the first time that day.

'Take this corner,' he said two hours later.

I gathered that this must be Basel, since I was being directed through dimly lit streets.

'Now stop,' said Andreas.

He got out, collected my overnight bag and went across the road into the hotel. An old man in concierge's uniform was resting in a chintz armchair. He woke up as Andreas addressed him in broken German. Andreas asked me for the car keys and I went to the hotel door with him. 'What are we doing here, Andreas?'

'I will see you at six,' he said, and strode across the road. He stepped into the Alfa as if he owned it and, with a sudden burst of throttle, turned and vanished up the street.

I took my bag to the lift. My room on the third floor was warm. The curtains were bright red with flecks of yellow and the windows were double-glazed. The walls were wallpapered, which seemed tacky after the whitewashed surfaces of Italy. I picked up the phone to ask for an early morning call and breakfast to be sent

to my room: milk, coffee and a bread roll with butter and jam.

I got into bed, pulled up the thick duvet and thought of Alicia with her long bronze hair. But she was far way, as if in some dream place visited in my sleep. I wondered where Andreas was — probably going to talk with his resistance friends. I still did not know what I was doing in Basel or why I had left Rome. A deep irritation half surfaced, then submerged again.

I was woken up by the telephone at ten past five and two minutes later breakfast arrived. I took the tray and looked for some change for a tip, but I hadn't any. I offered a few hundred lira and the night porter took it reluctantly. The jam was raspberry, the coffee tasted of chicory. I had my first cigarette for the day and went to the lavatory. I showered and dressed in clean jeans and the Italian linen shirt. I put yesterday's blue shirt and underpants into a plastic bag. I glanced at my watch. Switzerland was presumably on the same time as Italy, so it was ten to six. It was better to be early for Andreas.

I went downstairs and paid the bill. The night porter had left and a young, fresh-faced woman took my American dollars and gave me change in Swiss francs. Turning, I caught sight of Andreas in one of the chintz armchairs. 'Where have you been?' he asked. I glanced at my watch.

'It is five to six and you asked me to be here at six.' Andreas smiled to himself.

'I have not been to bed at all,' he said when we were safely out on the footpath and getting into the car parked directly in front.

We drove off fast, passing a garbage truck and another one that sluiced the immaculate streets.

'Mercedes says that in Switzerland there is a lack of shit. She always says that in French,' I observed. Andreas shrugged. He drove as if he now owned the car. I was beginning to feel more in focus.

We hit the highway which would take us, I assumed, back to

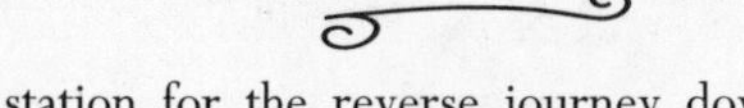

the railway station for the reverse journey down on the train to Italy. I asked Andreas, who ignored me as he again accelerated and the speedometer climbed up to one hundred and forty-five.

'Andreas,' I said, 'the Swiss have speed traps everywhere. They're not like the Italians. It's all law and order here, and fines for missing a lavatory bowl.'

'It's early,' he snapped and the car continued at the same pace.

I considered how I would behave in Andreas's position. I would have to give support and courage to my apprentice, I would talk about human rights, I would explain what was happening, since that establishes confidence. I would tell the person I was travelling with exactly what my purpose was, and where I couldn't be explicit I would explain that certain things had to be left out. Andreas broke into my thought.

'We will stop soon for breakfast.' Andreas lit a cigarette, holding the wheel with one hand.

He left me to fill up the tank and check the oil and tyres and water, but insisted on paying.

'So,' I asked, 'where are we going?'

'You'll find out.' He half smirked, as if this was the ace he was holding.

We ate breakfast and again were on the road. Then again we stopped at a service station. 'I have not shaved.' Andreas took his toilet bag from the glovebox and vanished around the side of the bar to the restroom. I pocketed the keys and followed him. 'What do you want?' asked Andreas, catching sight of my reflection in the mirror. I shrugged, and went to pee.

He pulled out again onto the motorway.

We reached a tunnel and Andreas tried out the horn. It was an antique one with a great rich raspberry sound that farted and mocked. The echoes bounced back in a dozen different distortions. Andreas's caffeine-induced laughter stayed into the bright Swiss

morning sunshine. Ahead was another tunnel. Andreas accelerated past a truck. Again he laughed and the horn farted and belched. 'I'll bet your girl Alicia is good in bed,' said Andreas. 'You can tell. She has that kind of walk. Once we're back in Italy, we'll stop for the night in Milan to rest. I have a friend there, her name is Sylvia; she is very left-wing and she has an apartment. She will make dinner for us and then later we will both take her to bed. We will both fuck her and the next day we will return to Rome.'

I risked a glance at his face.

The car accelerated again. Andreas talked about fucking the girl in Milan and the food she would cook; and there was a note of contempt in his voice. 'They are all the same,' he said. 'It is all they want. She likes to do it for me and my friends; she feels she is serving the resistance.'

'What are we doing?' I asked. 'Is this just a practice run?' My voice was too loud, as if that would hide my fear and repulsion.

Andreas roared with laughter. 'Did I tell you,' he said, 'that when I was last in Greece . . .' Then he changed his mind. We were suddenly on a roller-coaster road, with the small Swiss railway station at the bottom.

'The girl in Milan likes it,' said Andreas, 'when two men do it together to her.'

I thought of my friend, an Australian woman Andreas lived with.

He was always driving her sports car. I wondered now, what in her wanted Andreas, and what in me had wanted him.

But something else in me did not want what he was.

Now Andreas gave me the wheel, for the difficult manoeuvre of driving onto the open rail wagon.

We had ten minutes to wait.

Andreas opened the door and walked back down the ramp and along to a trolley serving coffee. He returned, sipped, and lit a cigarette. Suddenly the train hooted and belched diesel smoke as the carriage lurched towards the tunnel. In a moment we were in semi-blackness and Andreas felt behind the driver's seat.

'I have been up all night sewing,' he said and there was, for the first time, a strange pride in his voice. 'While you slept I was sewing.' He fondled the white soft material which was bulging with what could have been large batteries.

'Take off your shirt,' ordered Andreas in a quiet cool voice.

I obeyed. A car, three wagons back, switched on its headlights and the reflection created a halo around Andreas's head.

'They will not be able to see,' he said. 'Or they may think we are making love.'

I struggled out of my shirt and Andreas, now almost tender, took it from me. Then I felt his large hands going around my waist and the row of explosives was on my belly. Andreas tied the flaps around me twice, but the weight caused a downwards pull.

'Keep still,' snapped Andreas, all softness gone. Again his large muscular hands circled my waist. 'I have been up all night,' he whispered in the dark, 'stitching this. Now, put on your shirt.' I did so. Andreas lit a cigarette and smiled to himself, his face once more soft. I sat beside him, feeling the explosives tight against my belly. I supposed I should put on something: perhaps my light summer sports coat, which was somewhere behind the bucket seat. We arrived at the station and drove downhill away from the granite and firs. I noticed the small streams beside the steep and winding road; the rocks; some goats nibbling at scrub. I found I was held in some energy which again stopped me thinking.

Andreas's mood had changed too. He was jovial. He smiled. 'Don't worry,' he said as we reached the flat and moved down towards Chiasso and the border. 'If you go to prison, it will only be for two or three years. And I will come and visit you with my woman. We will bring you chocolates and flowers. And you have your United Nations card.' He played softly with the idea of the ID card. 'And that will help you. Perhaps they will not want to even put you on trial.'

I had nothing to say. Two pregnancies were upon me. One in

me, forming into a shape which had a head and could speak and ask; the other, the explosives around my belly.

It was warm now. Cool Basel, with its clean streets, was a life away. It must be like this when they take you to a wall and shoot you, I thought. You would think nothing, since somehow you cannot react anymore.

Then we were down in the Swiss side of Chiasso and Andreas suddenly barked an order. 'Turn here,' he snapped. I did so. I noticed that the oleanders had returned and that they were flowering here in pink and red and one there, close to a bar, in white. We reached the end of the street and at the railway station Andreas ordered me to stop. He got out of the car without saying a word and went to the boot and got his airline bag. He returned to the driver's window. 'I am getting the train across. The border is up there. Turn to the right.' He walked away and suddenly the internal voice could speak. It was as if all those *Boy's Own* heroic ideals had retreated into their dusty print. You are jealous of me, I thought. You are jealous of me because of my work and the university I went to. And, you are a coward. You half hope I'll be caught: that's why you arranged it so I'd be off-balance.

I stared at the yellow-painted station. It could have been a station in rural Tuscany. There was, I knew, nothing to do but go through the border to Italy. I had to return home.

I turned in the bucket seat and saw that the cars were queuing. I glanced at the station entrance Andreas had walked through and turned my car around and drove down to the queue I had not accepted the meaning of. I knew I had to create a mood for myself — a young man on holiday in a smart white sports car. I leaned forward to tune the radio into Monte Carlo and, as I did so, one of the battery things fell out, pristine in its white swaddling cloths. I reached down to grab it. As I did so, another fell out beside it and rolled close to the accelerator. I clutched at myself as if I had been stabbed, reached for them and picked them both up and placed them in the plastic bag behind the bucket seat which contained yesterday's sweaty underpants and blue shirt. Monte Carlo was broadcasting some French hits and I was a young man in a linen summer shirt in a white Alfa Romeo.

In the now trifurcated queue I moved on the extreme right. Beside me was a Fiat Cinquecento with a young woman in it. I looked at her in the Italian style and was rewarded with a covert appraisal. I smiled; she smiled; I lit a cigarette. Slowly, slowly, the queue moved forward. My mind had gone into overdrive; I was seeing everything and making equations which never registered as words. I took in the verandah at which a customs official stood, looking down. I took in the young customs guard, red cheeks, olive skin, who bent down to my window and asked what I had been doing in Switzerland. In deliberately atrocious Italian I explained that I had been on holiday. I showed my passport, I mentioned the United Nations, I turned down the radio. The guard looked to the official on the verandah and received a nod from him. The guard asked me to open the boot and I smiled and said the lock was *guasta* (broken) and would open without a key. As I spoke I felt the pregnancy slip down; it was ready to abort; it was flopping listless against my shirt; it had lost contact with my belly.

I heard the boot come up and then fall back and heard the returning footsteps of the guard. I looked out the window and raised an eyebrow at the girl in the Cinquecento. She smiled with me at the customs' antics.

The guard now wanted to check the engine. I reached down and pulled the bonnet release. The guard had trouble with the bonnet catch; he asked me to get out and release it. I picked up my green sports coat and climbed out with it across my belly. I could feel that another two of the cylinders were loose, inside my shirt. I started generating an energy I didn't know I possessed, a protective field that would blind the young guard. He would not find it peculiar that I was carrying a sports coat on a hot day. He would not see what he had to see — a man bent over and clutching a sports coat against his belly. He would see nothing. The watching official would also see nothing. Clutching my coat against my belly, I opened with one hand — somehow — the bonnet catch. The guard looked inside the engine and then I closed the bonnet and smiled. I returned to the car. The protective field was still generating. The guard saluted and waved me through.

I lit a cigarette. I now knew what else I had held away from myself about Andreas. Andreas resisted not because he wanted his people free and not even because he hated those who tortured. Like many others in such enterprises, he had crawled into resistance to live in his personal sewer, since that way he could find power in his dreams, could find a stage on which his deformities were concealed; it was dimly lit, and who could know what was real? He could exact his revenge on a world which could not love him — for what was there to love? Andreas hated the masters because he was not one, just as he had contempt for me for what he saw as my bright life.

And so, on the way up the hill and into Italy, I picked up two more cylinders as they fell from my shirt front and threw them into the back of the car. I sang *Bella Ciao*, the song of the Italian men and women who fought in the resistance against Fascism, who fought the Andreases of the day.

Questa mattina, mi son alzato, O bella ciao, bella ciao, bella ciao, ciao, ciao.

On the opposite footpath, as the car so slowly moved up the hill, I saw an old woman. She was trudging downhill towards the lower town. She was carrying a hand-woven willow basket and in it were bunches of red roses. All around, heaven was now dancing. The roses cast themselves in wild abandon across the willow lacings, and sparrows above shat everywhere, this good-luck portent allowed by celestial beneficence to land on every exposed head. Higher still swallows arched; in gardens cats slunk through undergrowth and, wearing a dowdy brown dress and brown sensible shoes, my lover caught my eye. We looked on each other with high regard in that moment, and both knew that

passion was imminent. She raised her hand as the cars again moved and she walked firm and high as a young girl.

Ahead was the sign for the railway station and the glow on the roses vanished.

I remembered now that Andreas had said that I must wait for him there.

I made the turn and a few minutes later was parking in a vast asphalt parking area. I took off the linen cummerbund and knew that I would not bother to ask Andreas for whom the explosives were destined.

I got out of the car, slammed the door and walked across the parking area to the station. To the right was the tunnel, the birth canal through which Andreas in the train would be pushed into Italy. On the platform I smoked a cigarette. I looked at the tunnel. I noted the dead rock. Then the train arrived and Andreas, like Napoleon returning to his troops, stepped down the three steel steps and looked around. I stayed where I was and Andreas walked down the platform towards me. I greeted him and then coldly pointed out to him that he did not know how to sew. Andreas went white. We returned to the car.

Andreas got into the driver's seat. I looked back at the tunnel. 'Your goods are behind the passenger seat and as far as I know this is my car.' Andreas got out without protest; he went around the car and got into the passenger seat. I got into the driver's seat and turned on the ignition.

'We will drive straight to Rome,' commanded Andreas, attempting reprise.

'Yes,' I said, 'we will not be visiting your friend in Milan. And you will not have the pleasure of watching me fuck or whatever else you'd planned.' Slowly and carefully I turned from the parking lot and moved down the road which led to Rome.

It turned out to be a long journey and Andreas did not speak one word in twelve hours. This did not bother me: after all, what was there to say?

Amalia Fleming

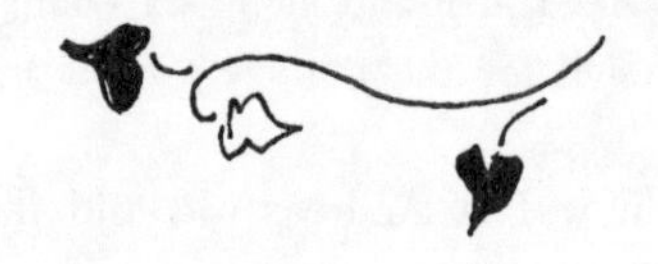

After I arrived in Sydney, a woman who was my friend died in Athens. When first I read the obituary notice, on the back page of the *Sydney Morning Herald*, all I could think was, 'Is that all she warrants here?' I knew that in London, Athens, Rome and other places, much would be written on her. As the day passed I found that I was recalling her face, her walk, her interior sense and then that I was mourning her. Not, I realised, because she was dead. She had lived richly and was old. But because someone had gone from my life who would never be replaced. She had earth in her belly and I'd known only a few like that. Then I drank some wine and found I was weeping. But it was not because she was dead but because this world produces few like her. Then I rang my parish priest, Father Austen Day, and asked him to say a requiem mass for her.

There were only a few regulars and the priest spoke little about her and the service was as it should have been: tender, but with the necessary abstraction which is one hallmark of the Anglican Catholic tradition. Afterwards, talking outside, I looked at the passing cars and thought, 'It was all I could do for you, Amalia. And it was the best thing. I doubt if anything said, whether by Prime Minister Papandreou, your colleagues in the European or Greek Parliament, or from Amnesty, will be more than what was quietly said for you on the other side of the world from your world, and in a world which knows little of what you knew.'

Then I was asked to give a talk about her for 'Insight', a 'religious' ABC programme. What *could* I say about her religious sense? I had no idea whether she was buried at one of those great secular funerals in which the Left specialises in mediterranean

Europe, or whether it had been in the cathedral with all the pomp of that religious tradition. I realised I had never spoken about religious things to her. We really hadn't had time in those days. Nor would it have mattered had we, since her being was doing. Then I thought of the obvious, simple statement, so much like that requiem which I knew she would have been pleased with, she herself being always without ostentation. It was made by a singular creature who lived before the time of the Christians. He had told a parable and it begins like this: 'A man went down from Jericho and fell among thieves . . .' As the story continues the high priest and other worthies, as usual, passed by on the other side of the road, but one person stopped and gave assistance. And I wondered then, in the actual realities of what we call the Light of God, what does count in this and other worlds. Christ had indicated in his parable he knew who it was who added to those energies. And I thought I knew too.

I sat at home and began resurrecting my memories, and they were inextricably bound up with the political events which had led my friend to enter again the public spotlight. And first I thought about when she and the democratic Greeks had finally triumphed in their fight against the dark shadow of man.

It had been in the summer of 1974. Brigadier Ionnides, the virtual dictator of Greece and head of ESA, the Greek military police, played his last card. To bolster up the toppling regime instituted by Papadopoulos, he embarked on the Cyprus affair. More accurately, the Cyprus rape. Had he been able to bring about *eonosis,* union with mainland Greece, the gratitude of the Greeks might have allowed them to forget that he was a murderer, a torturer and also a fool. But he *was* a fool and miscalculated. Turkey invaded the island and Greece, on the edge of war with her traditional foe, waited for a solution. And that came from the only source possible. The Greek military, pushed by Henry Kissinger, used their strength for the first time on the side of justice, forced Ionnides out and invited Mr Karamanlis in.

With him came the return of democracy and Amalia Fleming.

I was on holiday in Crete when the news came through that the hated regime had fallen. As soon as possible I set off by bus across the island to Rethymnon. I walked into the post office and said, 'I want to ring a house in Athens, but I don't have the phone number.' They asked me what the name was. I gave it. They looked stunned. The particular householder was a nationally proclaimed traitor to Greek culture and ideals, as the junta had conceived them. The resurgent Greek soul, symbolised in the ubiquitous symbol of the regime, the phoenix rising from the ashes of the coup of 21 April 1967, had taken on the Aryan sense and sensibility so carefully promoted in another time and place with equally disastrous results. Amalia was a traitor to all of that. On her file would be recorded earlier traitorous activities. Her work as a resistance militant in the Second World War, when she had sheltered New Zealand and Australian servicemen and risked the firing squad. She had found passports for Greek Jews. She had actively liaised with the resistance forces in the mountains. Then there were her current anti-national activities against the junta. The people in the telephone exchange looked at me peculiarly. Was I a police spy? An *agent provocateur*? Or simply some madman who did not know what had happened in Greece? I knew I was going to Athens to celebrate the fact that the colonels were back in hell where they belonged.

I first met Amalia Fleming in late '72 or early '73. Vassili, a former army officer and then an active resistance worker in Andreas Papandreou's Panhellenic Liberation Movement, gave me a call one morning. He wanted to know if I had some spare time. It seemed that Lady Fleming needed someone to help her with her work. I, of course, knew about her. When she arrived in Rome friends of mine had been bustling around looking for an apartment. Eventually one was found off Viale Trastevere, ten minutes from the historic centre where I lived. A student friend of mine had made her a bookcase. Irene Papas, the actress and anti-junta activist, donated some enormous Greek cushions; others supplied furniture.

I rang Lady Fleming, as she was then to me, and made an appointment. At least that was the intention. She said, her voice warm, 'Come around this afternoon. We will have afternoon tea.'

I got on the bus around four and as we wound our way through the siesta traffic I thought about her. On 28 September 1971, this woman who had met and married Sir Alexander Fleming, the discoverer of penicillin, and then had long been a widow, had been condemned by a military court to imprisonment. She would have preferred a life of peace and quiet surrounded by her flowers and her bevy of cats. Her crime, it seemed, had been that of compassion. The reason for her action was the regime's treatment of a particularly brave creature who had attempted tyrannicide.

Alekos Panagoulis, the would-be assassin of the tyrant Papadopoulos, had been, like many lovers of this earth, an amateur at nastiness. Alekos had mucked up: the explosive device had missed Papadop's car. Appeals, from amongst others, Pope Paul, had stayed the firing squad ready for Panagoulis but not the regime's torturers who, in leisure, perfected their craft on him. Athena Panagoulis, Alekos's mother, in her many appeals to the West, wrote in one of them: *There are thousands of prisoners and tortured souls in the gaols of Greece and they all need the respect and support of the free world. But there is one who has been tortured and is still being tortured more than the others, it is my son Alexandros Panagoulis!*

After describing the devastation wrought on this young man's body she asked the West to put pressure on the Greek Government so that she might take food to keep her child alive. So that she might *hold my son close up, embrace him and hold him tight in my arms.*

It was that knowledge which had set Amalia on the road to

what amounted to a court martial. She would have liked to free them all. She had already sold much of her silver to buy food for political prisoners. She fed the children of men and women who had been sent to concentration camp on charges of being communist. Some of them were, most were not. Their political views, anyway, were not her concern. She was only concerned with their children, whom intimidated neighbours dared not help nor intimidated friends give refuge to. She had entered the political arena because of her conscience. Her concern was the rights of humankind — whoever they were.

It was for these same rights that she had been arraigned and condemned. The nightmare of her interrogation I had read about in her book *A Piece of Truth*, published by Jonathon Cape in 1972. After some months she had been released from prison and placed under house arrest because of her heart trouble, her diabetes, her intestinal trouble, her glandular trouble. Then, early in the morning, the police had arrived, got her from her bed and onto a plane to England. On arrival she refused to disembark for forty-five minutes, and then swore to reporters she would take a short rest and walk back to Greece through Albania. After her anger cooled she settled into her exile and her work began as a focus for resistance and a public figure whom the junta no doubt wished they had kept in Athens.

I arrived at her apartment and rang her bell. It was answered by Amalia. We walked through to the sitting room, which was comfortable enough but thrown together for what surely could only be a short stay. She was then in her late fifties. She was no longer beautiful in the way our culture determines beauty. Men brought up in that tradition would simply see an older woman. Older women, used to the endless artifices of youth in concealed old age, would have found her unfashionable. Yet when she smiled something lit up within her. I looked again as we made small talk. She was, in fact, very beautiful. There was not a line on her face that expressed compromise or affectation. It was the face of someone who had lived by truth, as she saw it, and she lived for simple truths, I soon found out.

Our work ripened into friendship. Time passed and a melancholy was often upon her. The regime seemed secure, vulgarity triumphed at every level of society. And no matter how amusing it was to indulge in that wonderful and scathing Greek capacity for malice to one's foes, and some of Amalia's younger friends were experts at this, nothing could shake her out of her fear that the Greece she believed in was gone for good. The junta was not only the triumph of might, it was also the triumph of everything that lowered and confused the human soul. The endless list of those tortured, possibly murdered, sent to concentration camp, became as monotonous as the drone of the summer cicadas.

And then in November of 1973 came that most momentous of events, the revolt in the Athens Polytechnic. Those students, the *crème de la crème* of the education system, had demanded university reform and then, through a series of dramatic escalations, the fall of the regime. Then the tanks were at the barricaded gates and then through, and a dark madness seized the young conscript soldiers.

I was working with Amalia on a report to various human rights bodies the month it happened. Scores of people were probably murdered and many more tortured. Wounded were dragged from the ambulances and beaten. Soldiers burst into apartments and shot to death whoever they found there. In one case, a woman was murdered in front of her children.

And sitting there that day with Amalia, and the days which followed, the real horror was pursuing her as it was me. The atrocities were committed by young soldiers, hardly older than those they were set on, like dogs for the kill.

Until the revolt, Amalia had believed that only the professional monsters of the ESA, the Greek military police, unleashed by Brigadier Ionnides and his friends, had entered that hell catalogued so devastatingly by the Marquis de Sade. But now it was not that

ESA list of well-known names. Those butchers had been superseded. It was, as she said, children murdering and torturing other children.

Together we sat and listened to the last broadcast from the first free radio Athens had known since April 20, 1967. The Polytechnic was demanding the fall of the regime. We heard a young man intoning the Greek national anthem and breaking down in tears. And then another voice, that of a young woman, finishing the last verse for him. We heard the soldiers breaking into the studio and then, after a muffled gasp, silence.

Amalia sat where she was, her face drawn. Her heart was almost broken and you might have expected that her articles, published in *Expresso* and other newspapers, would have been devoted to the condemnation of those young soldier thugs. But, instead, it was a cry from her heart for their destroyed minds and hearts. Had Papadopoulos triumphed after all, was what she asked herself and me. She asked me what would happen to the young conscripts. How could they face their parents, their girlfriends, after sinking their boot into a young girl's genitals, or coldly murdering an already wounded boy. They were more terribly the victims of the regime than those 'brave children', as she called them, of the Polytechnic. But she would not hate. She did, however, tell all she knew and demanded in the name of humanity, judgement. But she wept too, for the waste of it all, for the terrible vicious waste. And for once history vindicated those 'brave children's' heroism, for their act was the last straw that broke the camel's back. Papadopoulos was replaced, logically enough, by the torturer Ionnides, and he was in other things an amateur, and lasted only a year. And then Amalia Fleming went home.

From the clear light of Amalia Fleming's country, where the shape and precision of things is visible, first came our knowledge of what constitutes human dignity. It is from her, a citizen of Greece, that we can learn to be counted one by one, if need be.

She did not speak with the rhetoric of the superpowers, loud in trumpetings of outrage at the nastiness of what the opposition gets up to and sure supporters of repression where it suits. She spoke with truth and with an uncomplicated knowledge of what keeps us human. Her ideals were realities; she possessed the knowledge and awareness given to those who have a compassionate heart. And when the blinding light of power politics has dimmed and we can see again the stage on which humanity plays its part, whom do we applaud?

After the fall of the junta I met Amalia a number of times, but the memory I wish to finish with was a meeting in December 1975, about fifteen months after the return of democracy to Greece. I was on my way to New Zealand and spent the night in Athens in order to see her. Katerina, her faithful factotum, had prepared dish after dish of delicious food. Katerina's cooking, like aged red wine, was definitely improving, I decided. Perhaps peace had got her hand in again.

Later we walked on the terrace, which looked across to the Acropolis. We discussed the trials of some of the torturers which were still going on and, most of all, the need through example and education to root deep in the Greek mind again human rights. And things were flourishing. The theatre, such a good barometer for Greece, was alive and well. Melina Mercouri was starring in a Brecht play, and satire, the joy of the Greek mind was sharpening and resharpening its darts in many cabarets.

That night she dressed elegantly and simply and went to a party for Andreas Papandreou. It was his name day. We went down in the lift together and she turned to me, sparkling, alert, full of that passionate life and sense not often found in the colder Anglo-Saxon soils. 'You know, John, I now want to live until I'm one hundred and twenty, but I fear I will not make it.' Then she laughed, since what did it matter, and was handed into the car.

Amalia, accept from me this small task of memory. I recall you well and always will. To you I owe a particular gift of life — an example — and you gave freely without even being aware it was yours to give. In time, you will be forgotten as we all are. Yet your sense will be reincarnated many times, for to those whose soul power is strong and vital, a hidden light is offered generation by generation. Those who possess it are those honoured by this universe which asks them to bear witness to humankind and tell it what compassion is. You were one of these and I thank God for your existence here, and now, elsewhere. We are not free, and never will be, of that dark shadow in man you took on, and so we need you. You, in your many faces. And I have spoken, in a way, not for you but for myself, so that I may remember, if things change in my world, that I once knew you, a great lady and a citizen of Athens.

Amalia, dear friend, may you rest in peace.

Aldo Moro

In 1969 coups were in the air. The Right ruled in Portugal with Salazar, and in Spain with Franco. In Greece a military regime had set up the first concentration camps known in Europe since the war. Explosives, guns and money flowed up from Greece to Germany and Italy. The Italian Right looked poised for a victory but it was balanced by a communist party which had the support of thirty-three per cent of the electorate. And in the universities in France and Italy, middle-class students went into revolution to clean up their nations, to reform, to introduce a radical state. They didn't succeed, but Left terrorism emerged from the ashes of their defeat.

By 1978 Greece was democratic, as were Spain and Portugal in their way of it. At least all three were on the way to freedom.

It was 16 March 1978, a fine morning in Rome — the *tramontana* blew across an eggshell blue sky and the willows greened down on Via della Penitenza, which my study window overlooked. At the street's end was the crumbling wall of the Chigi palace with some unlikely oranges hanging over it. Not edible but good to look at.

At six that morning I had been running in the Doria Park on the Gianicolo. In the early morning light and with the snappy air, the marble male statuary was flexing its muscles and the black-cloaked *carabinieri* were out exercising their horses. The horses, mainly greys, were inclined to a sprightly pace and an occasional festive breaking of wind. On the way home, I stopped off at the *panificio* on Via Garibaldi for my favourite wholemeal cowpat bread and then picked up a paper down at Ponte Sisto. I arrive at Vicolo della Penitenza just as Maria, the *portiera*, was checking out

the street, greeted her and ran up the marble stairs, which were still wet from the washing she'd given them. I got into the shower I'd rigged up in the kitchen and washed, while the coffee perked and the milk frothed up to the top of the saucepan.

I read *Messagero* as I ate breakfast. The main news was of the coming vote, that morning at Monte Citorio, which would bring the communists to government. That had been Aldo Moro's triumphant exercise in diplomacy: it was an acknowledgment that the Italian Communist Party was reformist — had been officially since 1976 when, at the communist summit at Hotel-Stadt in East Berlin, the principal western parties had laid claim to separate development from the Soviet Union. The thrust of the new programme had been outlined by the Italian Communist Party Secretary-General, Enrico Berlinguer, who described the qualities that the new communism would nourish: a democratic, secular, non-ideological state, affirming and guaranteeing individual and collective freedoms, the plurality of political parties and the possibility of alternating political majorities, the autonomy of trade unions. Arigo Levi of *La Stampa* christened the new movement 'Euro-communism'. It must have been some scene at Hotel-Stadt; Brezhnev was probably on Largactyl as a result. That was why Moro wanted Euro-communists in government in Italy. Not because Brezhnev was probably on Largactyl, but because the communists could take some of the responsibility for the economy.

Or was Moro being more clever? It was well known that part of the deal was Leone *out* as president — ideally not a forced resignation — for various Neopolitian practices too numerous to mention, and Moro *in*. The Vatican was all the way with the new policy, called by Moro 'convergent parallels', and by Enrico Berlinguer, not given to obfuscation, 'the historic compromise'. But what if part of the deal was the extraction of the Christian Democrats from the Mafia, the corrupt right-wing military cabals, the bankers, the industrialists? What if Moro was looking for a new broom?

But who was Aldo Moro? He was a religious man who believed in family values and had married a plain woman who had been a teacher. He was not of gentry or aristocratic stock; he had been involved as a kid in Catholic organisations which looked for Christian reform, as the Vatican saw it. He was a friend of Pope Paul who was from an upper middle-class family. Aldo Moro, unlike Giulio Andreotti, Mario Rumor and others, had never been suspected of Mafia links, of links with cabals and banks and corruption and the state terrorism which had begun with the Piazza Fontana massacre years before and provoked Dario Fo to write his play *Accidental Death of an Anarchist*. He was, to look at, a pleasant man who might have been a lawyer and he dressed well and conservatively. He was a family man, president of his party, had been prime minister or had he been . . . they came and went so often.

But if Aldo Moro was a decent man how did he go to bed with his party? It was a mystery, an Italian mystery. The only non-mystery was they he prayed in church almost every day, went to mass on Sunday, didn't have too many children, had no armour-plated car though Berlinguer of the communists did, and he always followed the same route to parliament, day in and day out. This was so well known it was part of a satire presented in a smart cabaret. All that could be laughed at were his routines, his decency, his kindly face, his piety and now this extraordinary revolution he proposed — a practising Catholic offering the communists a share in government. Was he showing his face, the face of a man who could no longer live with the way things were and saw the communists as the way of making sure Italy would get a huge house cleaning? I really didn't have a clue who Aldo Moro was. He was just a face seen on TV or peering out from a newspaper. With all the comments and statements on policy I still couldn't get a handle on him. I couldn't even suspect him of evil!

I wandered through the railway-carriage apartment to my study at the end. The *stufa di coccio* was still warm; I patted its terracotta

flank and settled down to work. Outside on the street, Piero the mechanic was whistling and Rosalba, his ten-ton wife, was seeing her boys Sandro and Romolo off to school. '*Mortacci tua,*' screamed Rosa, which means 'Death to your parents that I piss on amongst other more unspeakable things.' In Sicily that oath would get you a knife in the ribs or up the *culo*, but from Rosa it merely expressed ordinary maternal fury.

Rosa had been to hospital a year ago, where she had eaten only steak, had injections in the bum every day and had lost seven or eight stone; had arrived home and coupled with lean Piero. Then the jewel, Adele, arrived in the world nine months later, and Rosa was mountainous as before. 'Back to the trapeze for Piero,' I grunted to myself and leaned out the window to chat with him.

As I was doing so, Aldo Moro was thinking about going down to the car waiting to drive him to parliament and the St George's school bus was trundling into Via Mario Fani. I knew that street, since I sometimes took the bus out and did a day's teaching at St George's to keep some money in the pot. And I remember it particularly because, in that so-proper middle-class world, there was a flower-seller, near the corner of Via Strega, his three-wheeled *furgone* parked half up on the pavement. Around him were plastic buckets filled with the early spring flowers — daffs, jonquils, narcissi, violets, hyacinths and maybe some early lilac and some almond blossom.

That morning the kids on the school bus noticed that the flower-seller wasn't there; his truck tyres had been slashed overnight. But they didn't notice the restaurant across the way, with its potted shrubbery, or the four Alitalia pilots loitering there. And no-one on that street or in the entire quarter thought it strange that their phones were out of order. Nothing new about that — the telephone company wasn't noted for its efficiency, but in the Italian way of things, if you had a friend on the international exchange, it balanced the inefficiency and kept the phone bill down. Certainly the Red Brigades must have had a very efficient friend in the local exchange.

As I sat at my desk wondering how to make some money from writing — a thriller maybe? — Aldo Moro was in his car, the escort vehicle behind him. And driving down Via Trionfale, passing and settling ahead of Moro's car, was a white sedan with diplomatic plates, which seemed to be following the same route.

Around three minutes to nine, the three cars were in Via Mario Fani and beginning to slow for the turn into Via Strega. At the corner the white sedan suddenly changed gears and the foot that came down on the accelerator was that of a trained professional. Reversing at ferocious speed, the white sedan smashed into Moro's car in a kind of forced copulation of steel, bumper bars and radiators. The killers, in their pilot uniforms, leapt from the restaurant greenery and two drivers, two guards and one male secretary were pumped full of lead. The guards' hopes of promotion, of favours from Moro (a great *seigneur*), were now an eternal dream. Their blood dripped from the half-open car doors, staining the tarmac surface, and the seats were pitted with bullet holes and glass; two hundred rounds had been fired in just under two minutes. At that moment Moro was wrenched from the car and hustled to another vehicle.

Some heads poked out from the apartment buildings and then as rapidly disappeared when short bursts of machine-gun fire were aimed at them. Those who tried their telephones to ring the police found the lines were out of order. Perhaps then, for a few, the penny dropped.

No-one knew that from that morning, one of the most efficient campaigns Europe had ever seen would be launched. Its purpose? To split the Christian Democratic Party, discredit Moro and shunt 'the historic compromise' into a siding where, within a year, it would turn permanently to rust. The primitive brain power of the

CIA might have managed it, or maybe the CIA and the KGB — Russia didn't want a successful Italian communist party anywhere but in hell. Or had the extreme Left provided the gunpower, maybe the hideaway, and the extreme Right the tactics and the money? No-one would ever know, although everyone did know that the dark side of Italy was the empire of the Mafia, the cabals, the P2 Lodge, the Vatican Bank. They had access, institutions and means; the Left did not.

As day followed day, the drama reached operatic proportions. The Secretary-General of the UN appealed on Italian TV for Moro's life. Amnesty International offered its services. Yasser Arafat convoked a meeting of the directors of the Palestinian liberation movement. And the game of cat and mouse continued. One escape car from the kidnapping was found the same day in nearby Via Licinio Calvi, the second the day after and the third on 19 March. Someone was playing the police for fools, hoping to get their dander up.

On 18 April in Via Gradoli, close to Via Mario Fani, an apartment flooded and an irate woman below called the fire brigade. When they forced the door and checked the bathroom, they found the shower blocked and the water on full. They also found four Alitalia pilot uniforms, false document and registration papers, genuine letterhead from the central police headquarters in Rome, a radio receiver, and grenades stolen two months before from a Swiss armoury. The apartment building had been searched twice by the police but that apartment had never been entered.

On 20 April there was a note from the Red Brigades claiming that Moro's body was under ice in mountainous Lake Duchessa. It wasn't. Then another communique arrived, purportedly again from the Red Brigades demanding that terrorists up and down the country be released, particularly those presently on trial in Turin; if not, Moro would be shot. The terrorist prisoners were all labelled 'communists', yet the Red Brigades were known to consider the Italian Communist Party a revisionist bourgeois dishcloth, not fit even to wipe up the vomit of the righteous extreme Left.

And Aldo Moro wrote letters to his family, letters to his party. He told his party that his blood would be on their heads. But the trial promised by the Red Brigades, with Moro confessing his party's malfeasance and worse, was never published in the underground press as the Red Brigades had promised. No confessions arrived anywhere.

All that was still in the mind of the gods on that morning, at around ten past nine on 16 March, when I heard the sirens and went to the window to look down Via della Penitenza to the wall of the Farnesina, the former Chigi palace. Piero, below doing something to the guts of a Fiat 500, looked up. The three old tabbies, seated against the wall to soak up the sun, stopped knitting. Faint, far away across the city, and near at hand just down at Largo Cristina di Svezzia, the sirens rose and fell. They seemed to come from every possible direction. It was like the sound of many beehives, far and near, being stirred with a stick and the bees flying with harsh dissonance after whoever had done it, swarming for the kill in a Rome-wide whine of outrage.

The white-haired old Rossana and her two companions stood up and Piero put down the spanner. I stood taller at the window. One swarm of *carabinieri* screamed out of Largo Cristina di Svezzia, where a *caserma* was located, lights flashing, sirens howling into the void as they hurtled along Via della Lungara.

I waited, charting their progress and, in seconds, they were onto Lungotevere, heading east.

Piero shrugged, old Rossana looked at her knitting and sat back on her chair in the sun; I left the window and wandered through the apartment. Then the telephone rang. It was Sheila. 'What on earth's going on?' she asked. I could never be sure with Sheila whether it was a dream she had had, some misdemeanour of one of her children, or the world and heaven colluding to deprive her of some peace and quiet. 'The *carabinieri* are going mad,' she elucidated, sounding peeved that her early morning reveries on whichever large terrace should have been interrupted and that she might, with another jump of Jewish American princess logic, decide it was all my fault.

I made soothing noises and could feel Sheila *en brosse* becoming Sheila ready to purr. I made more soothing noises and suggested lunch. Sheila decided she would make a descent to the underworld from her large apartment overlooking Santa Maria in Trastevere, which looked along to an apartment Burt Lancaster once had owned. On the way to me, since now she was feeling creative, she would visit Schulski's studio and work on her piece of sculpture. To me the piece looked like Schulski at his most depressed and uninspired — a kind of neurosis in clay — but I didn't tell Sheila that. I told her that I was sure she would make great progress this morning on *her major work* and be feeling ready for *lunch* and *other things* by around one.

'There they go again,' she said, enunciating each word as if I didn't speak English. I opened the sitting-room window.

'They've already left from our *caserma*,' I told her.

'Maybe the Pope's dead,' Sheila suggested, 'or someone's been assassinated. The law courts are down that way. But,' she added, 'it's too early in the day for a riot.'

We decided on a good salad, some ham and *panini* and a glass of wine. Maybe an onion omelette, maybe a walk, after lunch and other things, in the garden of Queen Christina of Sweden who'd lived around the corner a few centuries before. We hung up.

All over Rome people must have been ringing their friends and lovers and asking what the hell was going on. Even Mrs Moro, for around half an hour, must have been wondering what the hell was going on. No-one ever thinks that when the sirens shriek they're shrieking for you.

It was around four, walking Sheila home, that we got our answer. The newspaper kiosk in Piazza Santa Maria had special editions out. We bought a *Messagero* and there was the face of

Aldo Moro — not the stunned face that the Red Brigades would photograph, but the face of the statesman Aldo Moro. The drama was under way.

All around Rome road blocks were set up, apartment buildings were searched, friends with expired residents' permits were on the train for Switzerland to wait two days and come back through another border crossing. It was very irritating, particularly for those who owned cats. Yet, people were also vitalised and clear-headed. Good and Bad were revealing their natures, the gods would speak and there would be a catharsis. Or, maybe there would. Maybe this would force the Christian Democrats into real reforms, *being* the party which was locked into the Mafia, the Church and all other earthly corruptions that gave funds to the believers — all that made a maggot fat and ready for its apotheosis into a shining bright blowfly, ready to lay eggs in whoever offered their soul — that is, if the money and the deal were right.

On May 2 — the day after May Day, the forty-seventh day of Moro's captivity, when the people carried banners demanding the State did not give in, that terrorists be punished, that the communists be included in the ruling party — Sheila and I and Schulski decided to go to Lake Bracciano. High on the gossip agenda was the probability of low-level taps on the phones and I had perforce been sounding like a fascist since the old whirrs and clicks were back. 'I mean,' said Sheila, getting me to light a cigarette so she could concentrate on negotiating the vile middle-class streets, 'you sounded sincere when you said you hated the communists. I felt quite *threatened*. And then we were on the roof terrace, with that *carabinieri* helicopter hovering overhead . . . We might,' she said, turning back to Schulski and straying perilously across the white line, 'have been making love.'

'They live in hope,' grunted Schulski.

'Watch the road,' I snapped.

'Well,' said Sheila, getting back on course, '*you* may be indifferent to the *carabinieri* viewing *your* buttocks, but I am not. And to think of all that petrol being wasted when they should have been looking for poor Mr Moro.'

I checked the road map on my knee. We were diverting from the route to see the shrine to Moro's escort. I wiped my hands, suddenly sweaty, across my grey roll-top jersey as we turned into Via Strega and then into Via Mario Fani. The flower-seller was there and the back tyres on his *furgone* were new. He had trebled the size of his operation now. He had not only spring flowers but a lot of exotics from the market that must have cost him a pretty penny.

We got out. I put my hands behind my back and Schulski did the same. At the shrine there were photos of the four escorts and the secretary. Some red candles were still alight, other white candles had formed pools of grey wax. Bouquets of flowers had withered amongst the fresh offerings. Sheila bent and tidied up, pushing the debris to one side. None of us was sure if you should put dead flowers from a shrine in the gutter; no-one was sure of the etiquette. The official wreaths were withered too. Only the five faces of the dead looked vital.

'My God,' said Sheila, 'what a dreadful place to die in.'

'It would have been their heaven, if you'd given them an apartment here,' muttered Schulski.

We looked around at the grill gates, the vibropack brick walls in delicate baby-shit yellow, and up at the balconies on the apartments. They were too small — too small to dance on, eat on, make love on.

'I can just imagine what those places are like inside. All those tacky chairs and tacky tables and revolting paintings they go for,' said Sheila.

'And velvet curtains,' added Schulski.

Sheila went over and bought a bunch of violets and placed them under the photo of one of the young guards.

'You know, it's as if it hasn't happened,' I said. 'It could have happened if there were cobblestones, or real *palazzi*. You know, somewhere in the centre. But there's nothing here. Just these suburban apartments. It's — it's peculiar . . .'

We drove away.

'It's as if it hasn't happened,' echoed Sheila. 'Yet it has, so I guess we'll just have to get used to history happening on a street like this.'

We drove along Via Trionfale, quite close to where Eleonora Moro was holed up in an apartment not much different to those on Via Mario Fani. Only bigger, probably. How was she feeling in her citadel? Was she allowing herself to be advised, as the Queen of England is advised, or was she eking out the time walking through rooms, ringing friends, then walking to another room? I wondered if it helped to have Pope Paul ring and say he was praying for you. Did it help that he kept making public appeals for the life of his friend, Moro? Is your faith being tested, Mrs Moro? Do you feel the Grecian sense of fate, the earth gods acting for sacrifice and mutilation, and Pope Paul left on the sidelines clasping his hands in prayer to a deaf God? Do you wonder at ultimate goodness, when torture — drugs, light deprivation — must have been practised on your husband? Certainly you know that if he is killed, the body, apart from the bullet holes, will look immaculate. And he will probably be dressed in a smart suit. Certainly in this furious grief of seeing your husband broken, I suspect you may guess who is behind it. If you spoke out with your suspicions you would bring a government tumbling down. But you have children and we all know who are taken first in punishment by the dark forces in Italy. If you ever spoke the puppet masters would, eventually, arrange an accident. Not for you, but for one of your children: a fatal accident. And so you, a former school teacher, will say nothing.

At La Storta, where St George's school was located, the *carabinieri* were waiting to search cars. Everyone was used to this now. Machine guns on sandbags, submachine guns in hands, an officer saluting, the boot opened, ID checked. A wave and onto the next car. We arrived at Bracciano, Schulski having decided to drive after the stop at La Storta. We found a large empty house on the shore of the lake and picnicked in its rounds. Around the lake the sedge was green, the willows green, the daffodils yellow, the sky a warm spring blue. We had red wine from Gubbio, some bocconcini, ham, and tomatoes.

'It'll soon be summer,' I said.

'Yes,' said Sheila, 'Greece again.'

Schulski yawned. He was going to the States to see his family.

On May 10 I went out in the asthmatic school bus to teach for the day at St George's. We again followed the route down Via Strega and into Via Mario Fani. I looked out the window at the shrine, which was now decaying around some unlit candles. The *furgone* was there but the flower-seller had cut down on the exotics and was back to what was in season — spring flowers, with some daisies. No-one was placing fresh flowers at the shrine any more.

On the way back, after school, I got off close to Largo Argentina in the historic town centre, crossing it to join a large mob which had gathered at the far end. It was cold that afternoon and the post-siesta crowd were wearing coats. I pushed my way through and got close to a street everyone was focussed on. People were strangely separate, strangely within themselves. They were not like a football crowd or a riot crowd.

'What is it?' I asked an onlooker. 'What's going on?'

'They've found the body of Aldo Moro.'

I climbed up onto a window ledge; now I could see. There was a cherry-red Renault; men who presumably had been checking for bombs were standing back, and a priest was doing something. Around the car were some photographers.

'He is inside the boot,' I heard myself saying as the priest bent over the back of the car. 'The shits have killed him.' I got down and walked back to Largo Argentina and had a coffee and a double brandy, then I walked down Via Arenula back to Trastevere. At home, I got out my notes and decided I had material for a thriller. But it felt almost obscene to write it.

Aldo Moro was buried privately. There was, of course, a 'state' funeral but no-one in the family went, apart from the brother of Moro, and Pope Paul. At his real funeral, back in his town, no politicians were invited.

And to this day no one knows who killed Moro. But, as usual, the Left got it in the teeth. And those who really killed him will still be gorging on Italy's carcass as they always have and probably always will. But the lesson had been taught: Moro's body was found in a street equidistant from the headquarters of the Communist Party and the Christian Democrats. The historic compromise died too, as was intended by the puppet masters.

Later I published a thriller, *The Concert Masters*, which began with the kidnapping of Aldo Moro and correctly predicted the attempted assassination of John Paul II; except, in *The Concert Masters*, the plot against the Pope failed. It must be something about living in Rome that keeps the soul optimistic. Something about history and time.

III

FROM ROME TO GREECE

Legends of Greece and Rome, with love from Mother, May 30, 1951. This was little Johnny's seventh birthday present. He decided by the end of the book he would like Greece and like meeting people who had lived with gods. They would be more interesting. He might even find he was somewhat god-like himself, that is, with a bit of luck. So he dreamed of gods and himself becoming one and remembered a long time later and wrote a bad poem to remind himself how he had dreamed as a kid.

Dreaming the gods . . seagulls roosted on the sea's flat surface
as he was born from the sea.
The blinding hyacinth brightness of the sky
became his eyes, his soul the water he came from;
from the black rocks he rested on, jagged with life,
the air itself rose lighter.

GREECE, 1968

Well, it wasn't to be that way. At St John's Cambridge, 1967, ancient Greece was really just the romantic memories of costive students at the turn of the century. The sort who Virginia Woolf satirised as seeing all that ancient male beauty with their brains but feeling nothing with their guts. They didn't know loins and base and powered life came from the animal joys of strutting creation.

The Greeks still know that but, God, what had happened to the Greeks? Hardly a one looked like the Apollo Belvedere and hardly a woman looked like Irene Papas who I would one day see in Rome and admire from an adjacent table on Sunday morning in Piazza Santa Maria with her small court of devotees and friends. They were, on the whole, an ugly race — as if they'd got the worse of every rape from the fall of Greece to Rome. Maybe it was those recessive Turkish genes?

But the romance began anyway. It was in the beginning the colours of the Mediterranean; not the mucky North Sea or the dirty Channel where you waded through mud to reach the cold brown waters. Then the surprise of those ugly little Athenian airport guards with two days stubble on their faces . . . it seemed the Greek genes generally had mixed with the Turks, and been left in a printing shop, forgotten by history and growing rusted and out-of-shape for the romantic imagination. But the land gripped as did the light and sea and islands and hospitality. It was my first visit to Greece. My friend George's house in Piraeus had potholes on the street out the front from a shelling in the civil war.

George and I visit a monastery frequented by his brother, who has too much religion.

The abbot has fat under the skin in a thick soft layer, with his gold ring indenting his fat finger. It seems to me the fat has come from food and sitting around in a vacant state of inactivity called, probably, prayer.

The abbot wants news from the English traveller. He knows of the court of Canterbury and its Lambeth Palace, the palace of the archbishop. I tell him about the Lambeth Conference. 'The bishops are coming from all over the world.'

'Ah,' says the Abbot, folding his hands on his semi-pregnant stomach, eyes soft as a doe's and deceptively mild. He rattles in fast Greek to George.

'He says,' translates George, 'there are always problems with bishops in the modern world. They do not like obedience. The archbishop will, no doubt, have to discipline them.'

I wonder how. Maybe a bit of light spiritual S and M, maybe a sound lashing in front of the cross.

Greece is beginning to become a country. Not the land of the gods.

We discuss the last abbot who, by popular proclamation, is already a saint, having performed two heavy miracles. This is discussed as I stare at the white walls of the visitors' room and the shining black table. The abbot raises his voice and a moment later a brother enters with examples of the ikons they paint.

There is the last abbot, now a Byzantine saint in a long line of saints with his halo and a holy body that never felt an erection.

It is time for lunch and we must eat apart from the brothers. The lunch room is cool and, through a huge arch, we see the wisteria of the pergola under which the brothers are dining and gossiping like men in a pub. Food is brought by a brother servant. The soup has a thick layer of olive oil to honour us. George slurps his, I put mine aside — the stomach and bowels need training to accede to his honour. But the fresh squid is excellent, as is the salad and potatoes, washed down with a rough honest red wine.

I cannot yet understand history since I have none. I am simply drawn into an earth that has passions of the belly. It is still the land of gods.

Greece, 1974

On Crete I skulk a little. The colonels are still in power. I understand now the meaning of being free because I've known people who are not. That was the Greece of 1968, but I didn't understand that then. I am here again as a tourist. I've talked to my friend Amalia Fleming, the resistance heroine, in Rome and although there has been a tourist boycott by those committed to a free Greece, she says, 'Go.' I think she says 'Go' because she sees nothing changing. I haven't been for a few years. The last time, I'd been followed from Piraeus to Santorini by an old workman who wasn't that skilled as a secret police operative, revealing that he spoke fluent English and good French with some Italian. It wasn't very convincing, this poor workman from Piraeus with an astonishing interest in my opinions and welfare.

The regime, the military regime, seems cast in reinforced concrete and no-one talks publicly about freedom and justice and secret police, bastinado, torture, rape and resistance. Zoe, my friend, came ahead to Crete and she has found me a wonderful small house at a sea village. She stays up in the hills to get the right feeling of light for her sea paintings. She is American, and someone who has worked clandestinely. We talk together but never when anyone is around. Too many police spies, too many willing to curry favour.

The house is two bedrooms in concrete, with a terrace overlooking the bay, just around a corner from the village. There is an outside loo with shower rigged up from the roof. There is a tiny kitchen off the terrace. The village is called Plakias. It's on the coast facing Libya and the house is rented from granddaddy Baksivannis who lives in the village of Selia — Zoe and I had walked up there through the olive groves and granddaddy had come down on his donkey and we had agreed on thirty dollars a month.

The village has a few fishermen, two tavernas and around twenty visitors. Hara's is the best place to eat, although she is a sloppy cook, because she has the shepherds who come down in the evenings to dance to the lyre. The best dancer is Jannis. He is lithe with wild black hair and wild sloe eyes. In fact he's stepped out of those Disneyland frescoes of Knossos, restored into some Hollywood ideal of the lives and loves of the Cretans. Thank God at Hara's they still sweat as they dance to that monotonous Asia Minor lyre. It has to be a relic of Anatolia or Sardis in the days of archaic Greece; like Arabic music it wails and compels over a few notes.

Jannis prances, kicks, sidesteps like a fretting stallion waiting for the mares on the mountain pastures to go into spring heat. He throws his head back, wild sloe eyes glazed with the red wine of Mirtios up on the hillside where houses crouch in yellow and white amongst the myrtles. Tollis holds the handkerchief with

Jannis, which gives Jannis his balance and earthing in the wild feet movements of his soul.

Hara, fat, motherly and with the brown cow-eyes of Hera, the goddess, is frying and grilling fish. There's already some meat, which always tastes like marinated leather, in the oven. But she gathers cress from the stream and herbs from the groves and these she cannot spoil nor the grilled fish. Unlike Sophia's, around a corner on a flat space with tamarisks framing the sea and the fishing boats, Hara has no cash register in her head. She likes people to sit and enjoy and if they eat only a plate of chips, who cares?

Now she is moving from table to table, wiping up the spilt food and wine and cigarette ash. No-one here breaks plates because that has been forbidden by the colonels who rule in Athens and, frankly, I'm not sorry; Greeks breaking plates is one thing; tourists playing at breaking plates is another. Anyway, they can't stop Jannis dancing in his soul. At the end of the dance line the men smoke, talk to friends, as the snake's tail moves slowly around the taverna.

It is now June and my friends Tom and Julia arrive, and then Tom's brother arrives, and I take them to swim in a small bay held by rocks poured into smooth black bronze. It is a half-hour walk around goat tracks and past wild fig trees already bearing ripe fruit. Then a steep climb down through jagged upthrust of rocks and then the bay. The water is as clear as glass and the beach is formed from tiny polished stones; some in agate and beryl have faces of the gods worked by the sea. From the hill, breezes come to us with the perfume of wild thyme, and we swim away the days; to another island close to Lebanon and a spy post for the Israelis and Americans into the Arab lands, the junta sends in planeloads of Greek army officers. The island is called Cyprus and the colonels are playing their last card. If they achieve *eonosis*, union with the mainland, the Greeks may forgive their torture masters who may reign forever. True, there is a Turkish minority and an elected president, Archbishop Makarios, who does not have a layer of fat on the back of his hands and he has not invited them; but power is power and must be made eternal.

The plot comes unstuck, Turkey invades the island, Makarios flees, and suddenly Greece is on the edge of self-induced psychosis. Good and evil are polarised with all the flatulent emotions of patriotism, and the tribal fears of domination, rape and pillage raise their heads again. The shepherd dancers vanish from Hara's and the fishing boats are covered in canvas wraps on the pebble beach in front of Sophia's. Up in the hills, the army tanks are camouflaged with boughs of myrtle and oak; the soldiers are young and brown-skinned and determined. Over in a NATO base, rumour has it that a fighter plane has taken off, piloted by a Greek officer with live bombs or missiles to destroy Turks and that other NATO fighters have taken off after him. We listen to the BBC, as they once did in occupied Europe. Tourists on the mainland are fleeing Greece, but all the island boats are being used to ferry troops and I am running out of money since banking facilities have ground to a halt, as have telephone communications.

My friends, Tom and Julia, go over to Iraklion on the bus, past the tanks and the soldiers. They do some shopping, find they cannot get a ferry and are invited in by a hospitable family to take coffee and eat and talk. In the crowded sitting room everyone is convivial. The Archbishop of Crete, a venerable patriarch, is orating on television about orthodox truths and Cretans truths and Cretan history and everyone casually is eating and drinking. The women are either in black or floral, the men are dressed as they feel. Everyone is laughing about the Turks and my friends laugh too; then Cretan resistance songs are being sung on TV. My friends are still feeling joy in their bellies when they see that now everyone is crying. It strikes hard and they leave and get a bus back to Plakias. That night everyone but Hara is following the order for blackout, but Hara doesn't care. Said without saying is her contempt for the colonels and her belief no invasion will

happen. She cooks; she watches her daughter clean tables. Her daughter is still white of face and sickly from a bullet in the stomach she'd collected in November, 1973. Then, the Athens Polytechnic had revolted against the regime and the soldier conscripts had gone crazy shooting at anyone they fancied. She moves slowly from table to table and Hara, with her large brown eyes, watches carefully.

The *metemi* was blowing hard at Plakias the night before freedom; hard and hot and dry, bending the olives and myrtles and tamarisks and oaks as the sea grew black and scudded with waves.

In the morning I went to Sophia's for her coffee specialty, made with Nescafe and milk and honey. The priest, dressed formally, no undershirt showing, was there and was not talking and laughing. He was morose, sipping his Greek coffee. The large glass of water he usually drank with it was ignored. He was not looking for conversation, nor looking for respect, nor looking at the few tourists who had stayed.

Zoe, the Greek–American painter and worker for the Panhellenic Liberation Movement, arrived and ordered a coffee. She and the priest were friends, so she and I sat at his table and sat there and looked out beyond the tamarisk trees at the now still sea. Her coffee arrived and she sipped and put some sugar in and stirred it. I noticed Sophia was also not talking to anyone.

'What is it?' I asked, feeling the silence of Sophia as a portent of something big. She was never silent.

'It came over BBC World Service this morning,' muttered Zoe.

'What?'

'The regime has fallen. Karamanlis is flying back from Paris this morning to form an interim democratic government. It's the Americans. They've finally forced out the colonels. Cyprus has done it. They can't risk a war between NATO allies.'

I sit there, my stomach tight. 'Fallen?'

'We don't know,' says Zoe, 'but they said the regime had fallen.'

I stare at the pink flowers of the tamarisks and then at the milky sludge at the bottom of my cup. 'Let's wait,' I mutter.

Zoe shakes her head and I see she is crying. 'I heard it on the BBC and the priest has heard it through friends in Iraklion.'

I find I am crying too.

I think of Rome. It will be hot there, the tarseal wet in patches and the cicadas manic as they always are. Amalia Fleming, friend and mentor, will have heard the news too. A heroine might be returning to Athens. I stir at the sludge in the bottom of the coffee cup and look again at the sea. Nothing had ever had such clarity as that sea.

Later that morning I write a poem.

There is no word to improve that silence —
of the aftershock when the heart starts to breathe;
under the trees, by the boats on the water,
we first bled into the light and lost strength,
and then the arteries healed themselves
and free men raised their heads.

Hours passed quietly; they were hours of possible resurrection; a time for stepping quietly around the bed where the patient, against all expectations, has broken the death fever and is beginning to breathe less shallowly. They were hours for quiet, hesitant conversations, looking at people and finding people saying the truth. Then, over in Iraklion, the afternoon deluged into victory celebrations. Over the hills from Plakias in Rethymnon, American students were attacked by old peasants heaving stones at them, and all the Americans on Crete became Canadians, in a moment, in the twinkling of an eye. Apparently old illiterate peasants of both sexes knew who had kept the hated regime in power and knew who was really behind the concentration camps, the bastinado, the starvation and rape of the nation's soul.

I managed, the next day, to get a bus over the Rethymnon. We ploughed up the hill to Mirtios — what a beautiful name — and then on through the gorge with the driver honking at corners and, far below, the delicate blood tracery of oleanders following the vein of the stream.

I go to the telephone exchange to make a call to Katerina, Amalia's housekeeper, in Athens. I am looking at the world through dream eyes. I say, 'I want to make a phone call to Athens and I don't have the number.'

The telephonists, a woman and two men, smile, since my accent isn't American or Canadian.

'It's Lady Fleming's house. The address is Kolonaiki Square. I don't know the number.'

For a moment I feel ice in my soul as they look at me. The man, a Cretan male with the old bandit look of the freedom fighters, sizes me up casually. The woman and another man smile with their lips then, suddenly, they see it has happened, since I am ringing the number of an Athenian who was proclaimed by the regime propaganda as a national traitor and she's been that for a few years. I look at the blue-eyed woman at the switchboard. She seems to be trying to read my mind, to ask me deep questions she is holding in her. Suddenly the Cretan bandit laughs — it's a Zorba laugh and the woman and other man laugh too and the questions have gone and we are holding each other as friends.

The bandit pours coffee and the woman telephonist begins working the switchboard. Most of the lines are out or taken up with military business. She keeps trying and she gets through. This is a miracle; it's the first time all day she's found a line to Athens.

The Cretan bandit has some English and the woman some too

and together we make conversation in a polyglot of Greek and English with a few words of German.

We talk about the people coming home from exile although we still do not talk too loudly in case we bring bad luck, and tomorrow the soldiers are back in power. I hear about some policemen beaten up in Iraklion as regime stooges, and we all enjoy from our bellies the details of their humiliation. Then the line to Athens is open and the telephonists has a long animated conversation before she hands over to me. I take the phone. I know it is Katerina from her accent. She had come to Rome to deliver to Amalia a selection of her cats to keep her company. And had stayed on to keep house for a while and keep Amalia company too; she had been Amalia's helper for years.

I pick up enough to know Amalia is flying back very soon, maybe tomorrow. I hand back the telephone to the telephonist who gets precise details.

'Yes, your friend is flying home tomorrow with Olympic Air and *kyria* Katerina says to come at once, that all her friends are going to the airport to meet her.' They continue exchanging details of the situation in Athens and Crete and the prospects of a sudden peace. They get stuck into a bit of ordinary gossip while I drink my coffee and find again the heart taking over. I think of Amalia's apartment in new Trastevere and the cushions donated by Irene Papas, the bookcase made by my mate, Tolia, whose father is a general in the army.

I finish my coffee. The telephonist disconnects the plug. We talk about ferries and planes. They've heard one might leave this evening from Iraklion. We finish chatting and I go outside and find myself swaying as if drunk. I decide I'll try for the ferry. I'll miss the airport welcome for Amalia but I'll see Athens celebrating freedom.

It's a deck passage and I've queued for two hours to get a ticket. I doze on deck that evening, smelling the oil fumes and the

lavatories, like all Greek public lavatories, only two grades up from Indian. Thank God the sea is calm tonight and so no mixed smells of vomit and fumes, only the smell of tourist fear. I can't work out the reason for their fear; do they think they will be machine-gunned from the air or that paratroopers will parachute down to rape and pillage, bayonet and shoot? They are frightened because there might be war. But 'almost' declarations of war, like 'almost' declarations of love, should be treated with profound scepticism.

We dock at Piraeus around seven on a calm hot morning. My nerves are twanging with excitement. I stop at the port, buy a cup of coffee and a newspaper. The front page has a large photo of Amalia coming down the gangway of the plane. The banner headline reads *Amalia Demokratia*.

I get a bus into Athens and get off at Syntagma Square. I find the backpackers' street behind the square and get a room, take a shower and change. I walk back to Syntagma Square and buy an *International Herald-Tribune* to pick up the details. There'd been thousands in the square the night before, greeting Karamanlis who had been staying at the hotel across the way. The flash place.

I get directions to Kolonaiki Square — just up the side of the parliament and then a left across the road and you're practically there. I bought some red roses. This was a good gift for a woman of honour.

Kolonaiki Square looked like it belonged in one of those smart modern suburbs of Rome, nothing special but OK and very central to downtown. I walk across the square to where a few TV crews are hanging around. It is the right address. I push through into the foyer and get into the lift. My heart is pumping when I get out and go to the half-open door. I ring. Amalia comes into the passage. I notice the floor is made from honey marble and that we are holding each other . . .

'Have you eaten?' she asks me, when she hears I've come from Crete.

I glance at my watch and realise it's almost one o'clock. I'm not sure where the time has gone to. I realise, too, she is filled with a kind of sombre joy. How long can this last, is the unspoken question. How will Karamanlis, that right-wing dabbler with even further-right forces, play for democracy? How long before I'll be on a plane again or back in prison, maybe this time for good?

'Katerina has plenty of cooked food,' she says. 'Go and eat on the terrace. Tell her to bring you some wine. How is Crete? How are the people taking it? I'd give you a bed but Melina Mercouri has taken the bottom half of the duplex. I think Jules Dassin flies in today so no spare beds!'

I eat and Amalia finishes another TV interview. Then she comes out onto the flowering terrace and gazes at an old cat sulking. Katerina comes too. Katerina is ecstatic; all the cats will be flying from Rome in a few days. Amalia and she rattle through the names I've forgotten them all except Mous Mous. He, I remember, from Rome. Anyway, from Rome, many, many exiled cats will be returning to their homeland. Maybe Melina Mercouri's cats will be flying from Paris and, if Irene Papas has cats, they'll be flying in from Rome. Oh yes, the cats will again be in free Greece.

I ask about the old cat, sulking now under a tubbed lemon tree.

'He was left behind to look after my house and he is sulking. He is Taki. Come, *agapemou*, and see me,' entreats Amalia, like a young girl with her boyfriend.

Agapemou sulks even more deeply, turning his head away to glare at the wall. He was not included in the exile. He is not a hero, just a caretaker.

'He will take time to come around,' decides Katerina.

'He is very proud,' says Amalia, as if this is what is to be expected of any Greek male, 'even without his appurtenances.'

Taki knows he is being talked about. He twitches his motheaten tail disdainfully.

Another camera crew arrives, with someone famous from the BBC. Amalia takes her chair again in her sitting room and the TV lights are turned back on. Out on the terrace, the ever-disdainful Taki accepts a saucer of milk and a saucer of tinned tuna. He eats thoughtfully, finishes and decides to slouch towards the terrace door, then changes his mind and turns to stare at the wall again.

GREECE 1981

It's the tenth of June and a hot day in Athens. I eat inside. It's a good meal that Katerina prepares and Greece is still free. A portrait of Alexander Fleming is on the wall and what remains of the silver is out and polished. The cats are well but Taki has departed for the celestial fields, after some years of reconciliation with his mistress and being back in charge of the Rome cats with due rank observed and dishonour forgotten.

I am on my way to Lesbos and take it as a good sign the ship is called the *Sappho*, since I'm going to research the island landscape for a book on the ancient Greek poet, genius, sexual liberationist, political activist, spiritual genius and woman of style and substance.

Amalia is now a kind of pilgrimage point for those who love freedom. People she does not know well, if at all, come to ask her opinions. She has become a kind of lucid Delphic oracle. She pats my hand. I am a friend and welcome but she is tired of too much attention. She is part of the Greek delegation to the European Parliament. I gather over some coffee that she is not happy with Papandreou, but I've accepted that with her there must be discretion and do not ask for details. We talk about the past; those years in Rome when she had thought exile would last her life. But the power of those evil men still lives. Alekos Panagoulis, who had attempted to take the life of the colonel, Papadopoulos, is dead, murdered in Athens. The dictator himself is in prison and too well catered for. Probably, I think, just a little bit of precedent-setting in case the tables turn on Papandreou.

Amalia talks openly about Oriana Fallaci who, in *A Man*, wrote about her relationship with the hero. That was a book I'd read over a weekend in Rome, enthralled by the knowledge she had of Greece, of Panagoulis and the Greek mind. She reflected what I knew, but Amalia is critical, mostly, I suspect, of the woman, Fallaci.

'Some things were simply fabrications. She wanted, John, to see herself centre stage in his life. Tried to possess him. I knew them both in Rome. He was out of prison; he needed women and she needed him for her dreams. You know, in his coffin she placed a wedding ring on his finger. What can a dead man say to that? Nothing!'

I had researched and read about Panagoulis and would write a book about the evils of power he faced. I knew Oriana Fallaci had written the truth in essence, whether or not she loved him or they possessed each other, even if only in her mind. I decide on silence. I look at the remains of the lunch: a salad with shrimps, meat, chips, Greek salad and fruit and I look at Amalia. Rome is far away now for her and she has problems with her diabetes; a drug which worked for her has been withdrawn and she has trouble finding it; the hills are drawing her away; death is ahead. When? Who can know? Only this: her body is sicker and she is still full of female courage and endurance which will crack one day. Pole-axed by time. And I am still young and have a life to live.

Three o'clock comes and, filled up with wine and food from Amalia, I board the *Sappho* which is now supposed to leave. But it does not. It leaves at five. The trains are not running on time.

'You know,' Amalia had said at the door of her apartment, (the downstairs is now rented out to somebody but not Melina Mercouri), 'they want to do a film on Panagoulis. They asked me if I would permit myself to be in it, but I said no, I did not wish that. However Oriana Fallaci was very keen — she wanted to be played by some young woman and she is not that young. I think

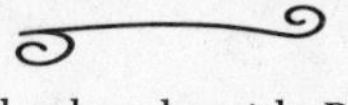

she wanted to run along the beach with Panagoulis and disappear into the sunset.' Amalia looked a little sad. Reality for Panagoulis and her was not a myth, it was simply vital life. She had gone to prison because she had attempted to free him from prison. She had seen people tortured because she had done it. She had been close to people tortured because, like Panagoulis, they had resisted. She was not a novelist or a journalist.

I think of her valiant soul as the *Sappho* pulls away from the wharf at Piraeus. The sea is wine-dark as Homer had seen it — a rich red loam of blackness and red.

'The isles of Greece, the isles of Greece! Where burning Sappho loved and sung . . .' So sang Byron, in the middle of his own pleasure in Greek boys' bums. Byron's Greece had to be as Ancient as his own pleasures! He died of fever, not having fired a shot, but the grateful Greeks took him over anyway — with his god-like proclivities for male sexual adventures, they probably felt quite at home with him.

The *Sappho* ploughs through the Aegean and the stars are bright and some kids play their guitars and a fat kid says, proudly, he wants to be a poet. In the morning, as we approach the island, I ask a distinguished-looking younger man about it. It's suddenly occurred to me that what I know of Lesbos is around two thousand three or four hundred years out of date. Jorgu, as he introduces himself, gazes at the shoreline visible to us. He knows about Lesbos because his family is from there; he did his doctorate on the hot springs of Greece and, close to Mythemna, there is a hot spring. He tells me the place to go is Mythemna, which I know is part of Sappho's heritage and now sometimes called Molyvos. We stare at the shore. We weigh anchor and are taken off by caique, along with a few crates of hysterical chooks and cartons of canned goods. There are not many tourists.

I spend the early morning walking the alleys, smelling baking bread, watching the women go with their cakes and bread and meat to be cooked in the bakery ovens; smell coffee and stare in a shop window at a copper bowl for which they want eighteen hundred drachmas.

Jorgu and I meet up again at the bus departure station and he draws me a map, while we wait, of the island — of Calloni, Thermi, the Gulf of Ghera — of Eressos which might have been Sappho's birthplace. We lurch off with the ikons of saints, plus Scrooge McDuck, Goofy and the Virgin screaming for attention above with dashboard.

The earth is denuded; the forests and wild deer and wolves have all long since died and sparse pine trees keep the hill slopes from total erosion. On high hills small chapels chart the ways of new heaven. Finally ahead, on a small jutting outhrust of rock, is Mythemna. We get out. A kid grabs my bag. We walk up to a street which is pouring green light through the pendant wisteria.

Jorgu knows a widow with rooms to rent at the top of the town, below the castle. The castle is probably Venetian, although the Genoese also had their imperial ambitions in this part of the world. Jorgu haggles for me. He will stay a couple of days, then visit relatives after resting.

The next morning I wake up early. Jorgu left last night. His relatives couldn't bear him having a rest alone. However, he will be back later in the day and we can walk to Eftalu where the hot springs are. I go to the window and then look at the blue-grey of the early morning sea and down at the lichen and moss-covered tiled roofs. Right below is the *kyria's* courtyard with a peach tree and old half kerosene tins painted white from which grow roses, lilies and purple convulvulus.

I walk down to the small port to have breakfast. Right there on the water, with water reflecting into the chapel, a gaggle of old ladies are at their religious duties; a stout motherly soul in rich black and with a rich contralto answers the priest's chant. The water ripples in light across the white walls and around the sparse ikons.

I return from coffee and fresh bread to find a farmer is at my end of the town with his donkey saddled with two wickerwork baskets. His scales stick out from one basket. The vegetables are not as beautiful as those you find at the Campo dei Fiori market in old Rome, but they are healthy and hard with the land.

I read, then snooze, and then walk down the weedy stone steps to the main street. There are a lot of women around with American accents — many seem preoccupied with deep problems. I find out a feminist congress has taken up roost because Sappho and Lesbos have drawn them here too.

Jorgu arrives at around four and we decide to walk to Eftalu. It is down a dusty road, but at the end there may be a house or a room to rent. This is the view of his relatives.

The land and road are still hot but a cool breeze moves through the air and the fields are carpeted in intense blue thyme. Everywhere too, there are birds; in Italy the birds are almost wiped out; hunters even kill sparrows to prove their virility; some say the size of their *uccelli* (the euphemism for the male organ) relates to the need to kill. But on the road to Eftalu, and at Eftalu itself, the virile Greeks have left the swallows, turtle doves, sparrows, blackbirds, finches, swifts, starling and pigeons to the air.

We walk down the steep hill with the sharp curves and down to the beach of Eftalu. There is one taverna facing the pebbled shore; there is one track to the right. We sit and order coffee and with it comes two glasses of cold fresh water a god would have taken pleasure in drinking. The taverna owner is a young man with black eyes and a strong body. He is also called Jorgu. He speaks some English but I leave him and Doctor Jorgu to discuss important matters of their world along with my need to rent something here, at Eftalu. Greeks speak from their bellies about life and so the dialogue is passionate and sharp and strong. After a bit Doctor Jorgu pays the bill since he is the host, this being his island, and we walk up the track to look at the few houses there. Obviously, in winter, the track is a cataract but now it is dried

out with one serpent sliding off into the thick undergrowth. Jorgu screeches. He doesn't like snakes. We reach, on the right, a small square house looking like a child's drawing. Standing over it is a mulberry tree, protective and full of female strength. It is shuddering with birds who move from branch to branch to eat its fruit.

'This place is perfect,' I tell Jorgu.

His grey eyes smile as he stops talking to me about spiritual matters that concern him. 'Yes,' he says. 'Usually the family comes down here in the summer but last year it was rented out. I think, maybe, we find for you this place.' That's what Jorgu tells me. 'The widow doesn't have anyone yet.'

We leave the house, walk down the track, round past the taverna and on along a track. Ahead is the whitewashed, beehive shape of the baths. I look at them, remembering the perfume of lemon vanilla in the child's house's garden borders.

'The widow's name,' says Jorgu, catching my lust for the house, 'is Virginia. She rents out rooms in Mythemna. I'll show it to you. I know the house.'

We reach the baths. 'It was built by the Turks,' Jorgu told me. 'Probably the local pasha. Turkish baths and all that.'

The entrance is like the vestry of a tiny church; it has a sombre, dark feeling broken by the sound of wings. Up in a corner, swallows have built a nest. They are safe, because to kill them brings certain bad luck. We leave the vestry and, half-bent over, shuffle down the two steps to the pool. The bath is dome shaped, about ten feet long and six feet wide. The brickwork of the dome is starting to crumble. There is ample room for the tallest man to stand. Perfect cubes of blue create the intended light and air vents, while where the mortar has crumbled, the sun throws speckles across the lime paint. The bath itself is whitewashed and in an embrasure stands a large terracotta water pot.

From the stone floor and through patches of sand, the spring water bubbles up. I put my finger in; the water is very, very hot

and floating around are wide, flat, cured seaweed grasses from the deep sea meadows, thrust through a gap in the sea wall during some winter storm.

I watch the bath water exit over pebbles and out to sea. We take off our clothes and carefully step in. Jorgu screeches in pain and pleasure, and delicately lowers his haunches in. I, like a gravid soul needing deep cleaning, sink into it and enjoy the purgatory as the heat eats deep into the nerves, skin and muscle. Five minutes later we step out; small pieces of seaweed clinging to pubic and chest hair so that both of us look like sea creatures. We leave the bathhouse and jump into the sea. The freezing water completes the ritual. We dry in the late sun, then dress and walk back along the road to Mythemna/Molyvos.

Jorgu leaves for Athens and I walk into Virginia's life.

It happens the next morning that I knock on *kyria* Virginia's door. It is a large house by Molyvos standards and I am invited in by Virginia with scarcely a word on the doorstep. First she insists on showing me the gorgeous rooms which she is in the mood to rent to me in Molyvos. After I gaze upon each spotless room, with vases of plastic flowers set tastefully on small occasional tables near the beds, the odd ikon and a few pictures, I am shown the spotless lavatory, the spotless bathroom and catch up on the main news that Virginia's daughter more or less heads the social circuit of Mitelene and that Virginia's husband has been dead sixteen years and that she, for three years, as a good woman unlike some women on the island, stayed in the house in Boston in full mourning, never stepping outside the door except for shopping, although she has been out of black now for quite a while.

Hearing the elaborations of these matters as we go downstairs, over the polished floor of the hall and into the marble-floored sitting room, I tell Virginia about my interest in the house at Eftalu. But Virginia, in a state nearing ecstasy, pours praise upon her house in Molyvos, the rooms, the convenience of the shops, the joy of the town, the pleasures of friendships and Virginia

being able to look after me with full and undivided attention. I start to get the picture — Virginia is hoping for a family down there of wealthy Swedes, like last year, or maybe even some wealthy Germans. However, she's made a tactical error.

But first we must be sociable and civilised so Virginia goes to prepare coffee for her new friend and returns five minutes later with it and some truly hideous-looking cakes of marzipan. I accept the coffee, decline the sugar and take a cake. It's time to exploit the tactical error. 'Now Virginia, although your rooms are truly charming and so clean and well kept, I am a writer who needs peace and quiet and inspiration, so I think I just might like your house at Eftalu. Of course, it is isolated, a fifty minute walk even to buy groceries and I don't think that the taverna would serve very good food — after all, who would even know it existed! It is so far away, as you say, *kyria* Virginia, from all the fun of the town and already it is June.'

The implication that she's missed out anyway on renting at her price is met with Virginia gazing piously at an ikon of the Virgin.

'But I might take your house at Eftalu since it has its charms — from the outside.'

Virginia sees the stage has been set and she has lost round one by too much enthusiasm for her unoccupied rooms in Molyvos.

'Who knows,' Virginia pours me some more coffee and offers again the hideous cakes of marzipan. 'It is a poor house.'

I shrug, grimace at the cake's sweetness and light up a cigarette. 'Maybe it is, but for a small rent I might take it.'

'Oooh,' says Virginia, 'eat up your cake, put on meat. Now, this is a very beautiful house in the country; a fridge even; peace and quiet and a nice beach.'

I smile at the ikon of the Virgin and at the photo of Virginia's husband who had a fatal heart attack at their steakhouse in downtown Boston sixteen years ago. I gaze at the photo of Virginia in widow's weeds, beside the cross and knowing it. Since those days of tragedy, Virginia has been solidly putting on weight.

'Why don't you answer?' asks Virginia, bosom beginning to heave slightly.

I shrug. 'Look, Virginia, you know this is a bad season, a terrible season. The tourists are not coming.' (This I underline with a soft confessional voice.) 'What month is it, Virginia?' I ask in a full brutal basso profundo.

'Last year,' prevaricates Virginia, hitching at the seams of her thick brown nylon stockings, 'I let the house at Eftalu to a lovely Norwegian man and his wife. And two beautiful children,' croons the voice, 'with hair like honey. Oh *kyrie* John . . .' Her rich contralto melts into butter drops, lavishes love around the memory, leaving even her husband's photo polished with Agape.

'Virginia,' I reply sternly, puffing deeply and *mafioso*-like on my ciggie, pulling in my belly, resisting the temptation to scratch my crotch and generally putting on an air of menace and terror, 'what month is it?' .

'Oooh, *kyrie* John, maybe I'll come down a drachma or two.'

Somewhere I lose the plot. 'No, Virginia,' I say quickly, checking my arithmetic and hoping I've got it right. 'I'm willing to pay you, Virginia, willing to pay you, not . . .' Then I realise Virginia hasn't mentioned the dirty number of drachmas. I pull back as Virgina's gaze of Agape dissolves into eros/money, with lust flickering as lightly and discreetly as sheet lightening around the beauty of her grandmother's face, followed in her eyes by the certain knowledge I have fallen into the trap.

'It is a bad season,' I say weakly.

'*Kyrie* John, you must eat and put on meat. Eat! Eat!' croons the voice as I take another marzipan cake.

'Now,' says Virginia, crooning hypnotically, 'I may rent the house at Eftalu, small though it is, for a man like you. But, I must say I think I will still find someone who will pay my price. And . . .'

'And your price?' I ask, *mafioso* to the fore, crotch bulging, Beretta sticking straight out at fat Virginia, who feigns not to notice it.

'My price is eight hundred drachmas a night.'

I smile to myself. I look at Virginia, soon to be taken to the madhouse with delusions of grandeur. *Eight hundred drachmas*, think I, *that is around eight dollars . . . Jesus, you old cow.*

'Dear Virginia,' I say, dropping *kyria* in this latest act of intimacy. 'You know the month is June, even becoming late in June. But, if the price is right, I will stay in your house at Eftalu for at least two months, O Virginia.

'And what is the price I will pay? I will pay four hundred drachmas a night.' *That is around four dollars*, I think. *OK, OK, try THAT one out, lady.*

Virginia goes into a coloratura wail of horror. 'How can I, a poor old woman, rent out my house for four hundred drachmas? What will I become?'

'It is guaranteed, Virginia, that I will pay you every week. Not every day but every week and I will not ask for any discount for the interest which will accrue!'

'OK,' says Virginia, pouring herself a new coffee, 'maybe we come to an arrangement. What about, John,' she says, in her Greek/Bostonian/Irish accent, 'that you give me seven hundred drachmas a night?'

The slightest of questions is in the voice. I shake my head. I finish my coffee. I stub out the second cigarette. I shrug my shoulders.

'OK, OK, John. Maybe I come down a bit. But for six hundred drachmas, you don't get the big front room. You get the back room with the pretty pashio and the trees and a view and the lavatory. You get use of the kitchen in the big room and also the fridge. But if I rent the big room we have to talk again.'

I know Virginia has hit rock bottom. To go further would be like ripping off her bloomers, defiling the Panaia, spitting on her husband's death photo, which I know I'm going to see.

'OK, *kyria* Virginia, for six hundred drachmas a night I will take the back room, the pashio, the lavatory, the view and the rest.'

'Paid weekly,' asks Virginia, looking hopeful.

'No! No! Virginia, I'll give you a better deal. I will pay you a month in advance, but for that I must have permanent right to the kitchen in the big room and use of the fridge. And, in return, you will clean the house and you will drive me down tomorrow with the groceries and vegies I buy, and the wine and my bag!'

I am magnanimous in my being.

Virginia wipes her forehead, in defeat before the male force. 'You bargain very hard, *kyrie* John,' she announces in a deep musical contralto, put on especially for the moment of submission. 'Very, very hard against a poor old widow who does a little business.'

Virginia leans back against the hideous purple plush armchair and eyes the hideous laminated furniture which puts her, more or less, at the head of the Molyvos/Mythemna social set. 'Now, *kyrie* John, we will have a glass of brandy to seal our agreement.'

Virginia is already on her feet and heading like *The Graf Spee* for the cocktail cabinet in laminated oak. 'And,' says Virginia, 'I will show you the photograph album. And, *kyrie* John, such lovely photos of my dear husband in his coffin and also my first grandchild's baptism. You know, John, he was christened by the archbishop. My daughter do so many good works he could not refuse!'

I hurriedly change my demeanour into respectful interest which, as it happens, is what I feel for Virginia. We definitely will get on well as tenant and landlady. But what I have not seen is that there is no cinema in Molyvos and Virginia, as a respectable widow, will not be kicking up her heels down at the beach disco. In fact, no Greek girl of respectable family will go down there and expect to find a husband worth his salt, for that is the playground for Greek riff raff and tourists and foreign girls with no mothers to keep them in order. Everyone knows the powers and passions aroused by the Beatles, the Everly Brothers, Nat King Cole, and Elvis Presley. So Virginia has no entertainment and Virginia owns

the main room at Eftalu and even the front patio. So what amusement can a respectable widow hope for but to observe her special foreigner, his habits, his conversation, his gossip and his scandals.

We leave for Eftalu around ten in the morning, myself arriving at Virgina's laden down with groceries and luggage and assisted by a village lad who finds everything highly amusing. Virginia loads aboard detergent, mops, buckets and a special picnic lunch prepared for both of us to enjoy after work is done.

Virginia's car is an American saloon of uncertain vintage, certainly post-Al Capone, black and highly polished and as I'm told at once, brought back from America sixteen years ago after the beloved passed away; brought back on the boat with the coffin, Virginia, her children and assorted grieving relatives.

Virginia is dressed today in a particularly loud festive floral, a design of hibiscus in radiant red with sun rays which have lost their direction. I'm wearing jeans, a T-shirt and sandals.

We climb into the car and I note that on the dashboard a few petulant saints are glaring out at the day with little appreciation of the journey upon us. Virginia looks for a while at the gears and the dashboard, then slips the key in and turns on the motor. We lurch and stop. Virginia looks perplexed. Virginia remembers the gears and puts the car into neutral. The engine coughs and I suggest some choke.

While the engine warms up, Virginia talks about her daughter, Elena, who has, as I say admiringly, an elegant Italian name. 'And,' says Virginia, 'my daughter just now is in Mitelene and she is very busy. She has afternoon teas for her girlfriends almost every day and also she gets her hair and nails done and she does a lot of work for the church. She is a very religious girl and this years she will present the horses with prizes at the races up at Stepsi. Her husband has three shops and . . .' The rest is lost in a

grinding of gears as we lurch kangaroo-fashion down a steep incline and almost turn towards the road to Eftalu. 'I cannot remember,' says Virginia, 'which is the thing which makes the gears go. And which makes the car stop.'

Palms now sweaty, I instruct.

'I am the first woman on the island to get my licence as a woman, but I have forgotten now,' announces Virginia complacently.

I give a fresh set of instructions, in a slow calm voice, to Virginia's feet and explain the gears again as we lurch off and in a sudden burst flee from Molyvos and take a corner.

I let our my breath as we slow and Virginia peers through the windshield and announces, 'I think I will hit this wall now.'

'Brakes,' I say in a terse voice.

Virginia tries the clutch and brake and just in time the right foot goes down on the brake pedal.

'Now,' I say, peering at the wall and noticing how well the stones are locked together into a very strong barrier, 'a tight turn and we'll be on the road for Eftalu.'

Virginia gives me an admiring look, then settles into deep concentration.

We are on the road and, God willing, it will not be the karma of some local to be driving today. As for a flock of sheep. Well, at least we will survive.

Virginia begins tooting the horn to warn the unwary.

We pass by the military camp and past the fields adjoining the sea which are still fenced off with notices warning against trespass. Mines are still laid, Virginia tells me, and occasionally a stray sheep gets blown up. I think of 1974 and Crete and Plakias that first morning of freedom.

Just across the waters that the mine fields abut is Turkey and the night winds bring the perfumes of rain from the Anatolian highlands. I don't ask how Virginia felt in those weeks of war scare since I can imagine that would be a long recital. But with freedom has come the old political chess game. Does Virginia,

as the innocent mother of two, follow the National Camp, the delightful name for the royalist and fascist party? Or, like half of Lesbos, is she still a Lesbian communist of the Stalinist persuasion? I don't feel intimate enough with her to ask her yet.

'Such nice girls have come this year to Molyvos,' says Virginia. 'They stay at the best hotel and also in a few houses. They are good girls. They do not allow our boys to chase them. And,' says Virginia, 'so fond of each other, just like Greek girls. They hold hands, they sometimes hug and kiss each other. Such nice girls.'

I assume this is the congress of American feminists but I decide to play for information. 'Oh, what are they here for, Virginia?'

'Oh, they are nice girls with class. They have been to university and they give talks to each other and also write poems to each other.' Of this Virginia approves. 'My daughter writes poems too and reads them to her girlfriends.'

We skirt a large bay and begin to climb a steep hill. From the top is the vista of Eftalu, the sea, the hot baths and further on the small white smudge of what must be a chapel. The road down is steep, with a nasty bend which we are approaching. There is a steep fall away into rocks and some scraggy bushes.

'Here,' says Virginia, taking one hand from the steering wheel and waving expansively towards the sharp curve, 'I go over the side a year ago. Down we go. Crash! Bang! I break a shoulder and they must get a truck from Mitelene to pull the car out. Jorgu at the taverna and a shepherd pulled me out and Jorgu gave me brandy and coffee. I was white. I was shaking. But now the car is as good as new.'

'Slowly,' I instruct Virginia, 'down into first gear; a little braking now. That's it, Virginia.'

We manage the corner and at a snail's pace Virginia, ever in obedience to the male force, lurches close to the taverna and applies the brakes with sudden ferocity.

From the taverna comes an ironic cheer. Jorgu is taking a coffee with some friends.

The house is still as beautiful; the rooms are simple and whitewashed. It is a triumph of economy and shows that Virginia considers herself as slumming at Eftalu — not one gilt mirror in sight, not even a single purple flock carpet. It's amazing. I've hit gold.

I sit on the front patio under the mulberry tree and smoke a cigarette while Virginia begins to clean the house in the time-honoured fashion of the Greek female. I listen to the whirring and peaceful shuddering and flapping of the birds eating the mulberry fruit; the branches are heavy with their bodies. I known I will loose potency in Virginia's eyes if I so much as lift a finger. Am I upset and feeling degraded? No!

Virginia finishes and then sets to with the simple lunch of homemade dolmathes, moussaka, some roasted chicken, fresh bread, olives cured by her sister-in-law, whom I'm promised a meeting with, as well as her daughter if she has time, and with other relatives who might be down one day or another.

We drink a little wine with the food and finished off with coffee and some new cakes which are sweet but not chillingly so.

Virginia would like to stay and keep me company for the rest of the afternoon but has things to do in Molyvos. Two girls off the bus that morning have taken a room and things must be checked since they arrive from the beach around four. They've left their bags in the hall but get no keys until payment is made.

I go back to the car with Virginia and offer fresh driving instructions. Virginia lurches off, head half out the window talking to Jorgu on some matter of national importance.

I return to the house. The back room is small and clean with two single beds which look unpromising, but there is a small table that I can write at.

The heat and dry of the summer catches me and I slow down. Across the fields a couple of Parisienne queens play opera in the early evenings — *La Traviata*, *Maria Stuarda*, *Aida*. I drink some wine, write and think of the sea and my evening meal. I walk often into Molyvos/Mythemna and stop thinking about Sappho, except as a dream — I do not know how to deal with her genius so instead I dream about her. In Molyvos I meet up with Sonia and Rachel who help run the congress. Sonia is blond-haired and romantic and has dreams of goddesses, with the occasional god allowed into the conversation. She also keeps gently correcting my masculist vocabulary and I have to think out every sentence in advance, as if I'm dealing with a benign inquisitor. God must be feminine or neutral and I am seeing the pain I must have caused existence by my unconscious masculist stereotyping. Still, I grow fond of them both and I like their knowledge and brain power. We mainly meet at Sophia's; she runs a good taverna and coffee shop with some brilliant cakes that put Virginia to shame. Several of the younger congress women have been rapping with Sophia in broken Greek. It seems they want to understand how she is but Sophia is too busy making money to think how she is and besides she has a bastard of a husband. However, the ladies persevere and it all appears to have to do with Sophia gaining consciousness through the missionaries. Sophia gets irritable at questions asked blandly and kindly. She has work to do.

A few weeks in, I suggest I should talk about Sappho to the women and then forget about it. It is Sonia who brings it up. Time is drawing to a close for the congress women, with a concert coming up to celebrate the last night.

'So,' says romantic Sonia who's been to the house for a drink, and seen me as naked as a young god from the sea after taking the hot baths, 'myself and Rachel would love you to speak on Sappho but most of the women feel that, as you are a man, it might somehow not be seemly.'

Sonia is fond of me and a trifle embarrassed while Rachel, who

is definitely in the style of Virginia Woolf, keeps a more aloof and well-bred distance from the subject. Inside me, the old John of the male persuasion says to himself, 'Fuck the lot of ya' while putting on a sweet mien and with many a cluck saying he understands.

'But,' says Sonia a couple of days later when I meet her in Sophia's, after finishing some shopping, 'Michelle thinks she has an answer to the problem.' Rachel comes in and Sonia repeats the statement. And Rachel, who has been dealing with the women, raises a weary eyebrow. I have the distinct impression Rachel is tired of the congress.

Michelle is a favourite of mine. She is butch Chinese from San Francisco. I have fantasies of Michelle chopping wood, swinging chains, dressed in leather jacket and trousers and dragging back to her den someone like Sonia who will be ravished, then set to work to cook and clean and sew. I know Michelle is one tough lady. She tells me about some street in San Francisco where these congress dames wouldn't last ten minutes. Oh yes, Michelle is one tough guy. On that street, the ladies live the Wild Wild West. It seems OK for Michelle to think of ravishing whoever she likes but I am not allowed to ravish anyone at the congress, since I am not Michelle.

Sophia is rushing around with her mannish face concentrated and irritable; her grey hair done in a bun. The view from the balcony is stupendous, down to the bay. Outside, the wisteria has stopped flowering and the street has become a cool, green passage. Sonia is talking about priestesses and the rest. I'm not convinced they were so ethereal, those old-time dames, but it is soothing.

My dream calm is broken as Michelle strides across the restaurant; jeans, brown short boots and a T-shirt in white which looks as if it needs a wash. Michelle sits down, lights a cigarette and sizes up the competition. 'Well,' she says, ordering from Sophia (who runs to do her bidding) a Coca-Cola and sandwich, 'why don't we make you a honorary woman?'

I interrupt, 'I've got a beard, Michelle.'

'Well,' says Michelle, 'the bearded lady. You can become, let's think . . . yeah, I've got it, Joanna Sligo. And that will really fuck up our congress ladies. Yeah, really fuck them up good.'

I laugh with Michelle. She's on my side but I can't use bad language unless the two of us are sinking a litre or two of wine and telling each other dirty jokes. Sonia accepts the verdict of Michelle with a tender, amused look. Rachael, looking lean and academic, preserves her silence, since tomorrow night is the final concert and after that she can finally speak her mind, if she feels like it.

'OK,' says Michelle, 'I'll tell them Joanna Sligo will talk on Sappho tonight.'

It takes place in a small room and five or six out of around one hundred turn up. Michelle has been too busy to come, undisclosed business being the reason. Afterwards I meet up with an army mate, Costas, who is doing his compulsory military service as an officer. We sink a couple of beers while he talks about the problems of the recruits — paid nothing, not even any decent food and half of them from the hills and without a clue as to what it's all about. I've seen them as I walk past the barracks on the way to Eftalu; kids smoking and bored; kids too poor to even buy a meal out.

The concert is up at the castle ruins. As evening comes in, we walk up the streets, climb the steps and trudge through the thistles and fallen masonry. The castle is a splendid ruin with what look like memories of the lions of St Mark, so is probably Venetian. People sit on camp chairs, on forms, on flat stones and on the remains of almost ground-level walls. Costas and I have bought some Coca-Cola and some Turkish Delight and baklava. We seat ourselves on two enormous stones, light up cigarettes and wait for things to begin.

Out front, the organisers are running around with the performers. Most of the ladies are dressed up, as if this is a

Sunday school concert — the air is all innocence with the almost full moon, the perfumes of thyme, and soft moths battering around. Perhaps this is how things are in a college sorority when they put on a concert for themselves.

A few of the village women arrive, seat themselves and get on with a good gossip and knitting. No-one knows what to expect and no-one cares — it's an occasion just sitting there. The village, anyway, has been agog with the subject of the ladies' purity, while the village boys are furious. Here is a whole bunch of Americans who should have kept their summers light and their loins pumping, and nothing at all has happened. Quite a few of the village boys arrive, respectful and disbelieving; maybe tonight the ladies' facades will crack and the held-back passions for their male beauty erupt. The boys sit together for company; they smoke, talk, scratch themselves and look mildly inane.

The compere, dressed in a pleasant flowery gown, walks forward and, in halting Greek and very poetic English, thanks the village women for their support and the mayor for his, and others for this and that. She talks about Sappho and Lesbos and love and it is very romantic with the bay way down there, the beach, the olive groves nearby, the silence of the evening. She finishes with a few sentences in Greek. The local women stop their quiet gossip and put down their knitting to applaud.

I suddenly realise that with Michelle, who's just joined us, I seem to put 'fuck' or 'shit' into almost every sentence I utter. I seem to have been driven to use these words. Some cosmic balance demands it, but I can feel the need flowing away. I pick some lemon vanilla and rub it in my hands as Berenice — who is from somewhere like Mississippi, dressed in dark blue and has some acne and is certainly wearing no make-up — reads the poems she's written in the poetry workshop. They are about her girlfriend Corinne, her sleepless nights, the ache in her heart for Corinne back in LA, who couldn't make it to the congress for undisclosed reasons.

The boys chew popcorn and size up Berenice and the village ladies smile and get on with their knitting.

Berenice finished ten minutes later with a long poem to Molyvos and what the congress has meant to her. I'm getting itchy just sitting. Costas half follows the meaning, his brown face and dark grey eyes intent. 'She has a girlfriend?' asks Costas, when Berenice finishes. I nod. 'Shit,' says Costas, 'this what they do here?' I shrug and swig some Coca-Cola as the next performer is announced by the compere. It seems Annabel has learned to express herself in dance on Lesbos and now we'll witness the results.

Annabel is a tall pre-Raphaelite woman and is dressed in long flowing gauzy drapes; she's like Vanessa Redgrave playing Isadore Duncan. Annabel explains, in a soft voice, that her girlfriend Margaret is down with a throat infection and therefore the free-play dance, to express their love for each other for the audience, cannot take place. Instead Annabel will dance a dance of she and Margaret in love.

Annabel stands still, looking fey and very Arthurian, as if waiting for some moment of magic. Apparently, unbeknownst to the audience, it arrives. The boys all sit up and gaze expectantly as she begins swaying while looking inwards. Then her long tendrilly white arms flap and quiver and begin to beat like a gosling's getting an idea about flight; then they are raised high as priestess's and suddenly she is ferociously leaping across the grass after the beloved. She is doe and hind, Arthur and Martha, and her face is anguished, tender, ecstatic, commanding and forgiving. 'What's she doing?' asks Costas, looking stunned.

'She's mind-fucking her lady,' says Michelle, chewing on some baklava in between swigs of retsina.

Costas concentrates hard in an effort to understand. Annabel stops. She's got a thistle in her foot but takes it out so artistically almost everyone assumes it's part of the ritual act of wounding.

Others follow with more poetry and by now Costas and I are sick of it and Michelle is morose but loyal. But we've got to sit it out and when it ends we've got to say how great it was. So I did the honours, while Costas holds back, still shaking his head as he works out the intellectual equation.

I finish our congratulations and refuse an invitation to join the girls for wine. I am bound for another party. We walk down the dusty road to Eftalu, the moon riding high and the ground silver-white. We argue about Marx and Freud. Such a bloody relief to be able to argue! Costas is communist with quite strong Stalinist leanings. I knew it was the red island, but even tonight could not grasp why Stalin and Russia were so attractive. Euro-communism? Berlinguer of Italy? Yes! But Josef Stalin? We argue theology down as far as the barracks: why does he want to turn the bad dreams of Greece into the nightmare of Stalin? Pointless to ask, as one aspect of the modern Greek male is a wild irrationality that has something to do with all that orthodox religious servitude — a kind of Dionysian refusal to accept orthodox reason on any level.

I tell Costas I've been invited for drinks to Pauline's place and Costas is anxious to size her up so, after shaking hands and saying good night outside the barracks, he decides to come on with me. Pauline is from Canada and is a nymphomaniac. She discovered Lesbos around seven years ago and most of all discovered there were two military barracks on the island with young raw recruits, whose only experience of sex was probably in the wild mountain pastures with the heavenly sheep. So, conveniently, the first year, Pauline's car broke down right at the barrack's gate, somewhere across the island. There apparently was a rapid conversion rate from a lower species to the human one and, as I tell Costas, she is performing good works in the orthodox sense of the word — saving bodies from bondage, converting them from bestiality, elevating their souls to the sphere of Eros from whence might flow Agape one day or another. Costas forgets being a Stalinist theologian and forgets about the congress women who perplex him. We link arms and stroll along together, talking about Ritsos, Theodorakis, Freud, wine, Lesbos and Pauline's so-Olympian exploits.

We climb a fence to shortcut to the house and come in from a field. Pauline is outside with two of her favourite new soldier friends (this year her car has broken down, more or less permanently, outside the Eftalu barracks) and one or two platonic friends. They've finished dinner and are all smoking reefers. Pauline listens with delight to my slightly exaggerated and scabrous account of the concert, embellished with many a lurid detail. Pauline is not a supporter of the gals and is prepared to believe any embroidery.

We sit down, Pauline pours wine and we pick at olives and feta and good crusty bread. There is a bowl of early cherries from a tree over against the fence.

Billy and Vassily from the barracks are both in jeans and cheap T-shirts, but both are wearing nice watches that Pauline has bought for them for service to the nation. Billy takes the reefer, draws in deep, holds his breath, lets it out and looks slightly stunned, then hands it on to me. I take a polite draw, not being a lover of the stuff, and Costas draws in deep to try it out.

A lot of restina later, we all decide to dance a bit — maybe some Greek dances, maybe just lurching around. Costas and I wander into the large open-space sitting area to find records. Billy and Vassily follow. Billy embraces Costas and myself and anyone else interested in making this into something deep and meaningful. I am not interested in some group grope, probably because of the pure influences emanating from Molyvos, and Costas as a good Stalinist officer. He is getting irritated by the decadence of the recruits, and now Pauline is too blown away to notice what might happen.

'You know, Costas,' I say, unwinding Greek statue Billy from around me as he declares eternal love, 'you shouldn't be so bloody moralistic. That's the problem with Stalinism, it's so bloody moralistic.' (I half realise I'm a little away from normal me, since this does not make sense.)

'No, no,' answers Costas who has also been drinking wine and smoking with the gang. 'It's just that I have a small problem at the moment. I have a fiancée and, besides, these people are decadent. I do not make love with decadents, I've decided.'

'Who do you make love with?'

'With people who are not decadents. I would make love with them.'

I realise we have all been dancing and are back in the sitting room looking for new records. I've unearthed some Rolling Stones, Aretha Franklin and Elvis Presley. I put on the Rolling Stones and set aside a Bob Dylan. I am again untwining Billy from me and telling him, since I can't speak much Greek, he should return to Pauline who doesn't care about language as a form of communication. Billy says he doesn't care and tried out his French: '*Je t'aime.*'

Costas interjects in a rapid staccato of Greek, as an officer and gentleman and Stalinist theologian. Billy comes to some sort of internal attention, salutes, and wanders in decreasing circles towards the door. Costas gives up with an exasperated sigh. 'Just look,' he says standing over the large, round oak dining room table. 'Just look!' I go over and Billy finds the door in front of him is open and lurches out towards the remains of the party around the outdoors table. 'Just look,' says Costas again. I do. I see a mass of signatures and dates. I am quite amazed by the brazen method of keeping track of time and lovers. I presume these signatures are those who provoked interest in one way or another. I start counting and give up. I look at dates and see the earliest go back to the first year Pauline's car broke down outside a barracks. 'Look,' says Costas again, 'Pauline does not just make love to a few, she makes love to whole mobs. Look !' I follow Costas's finger to the centrepiece of Pauline's triumph. I read out loud, believing every word of the declaration — 'Love from the Greek Army'.

Time marches on and over in London the Prince of Wales is soon to marry Diana someone or other. Most of the congress women have long gone and September approaches fast. The eggs laid by the swallows in the vestry of the hot baths have hatched and five junior swallows peer and wobble and look discerning over the edge of their nest, like a mob of daft Anglican clergymen about to give some recalcitrant villagers a piece of their minds. And, indeed, over the halcyon days and weeks I have become the beloved treasure of Virginia. We have gone into great detail concerning Elena's success over at Mitelene and the redecoration of the bathroom there which will be a paradise of gilt and marble and flock and is already the envy of her girlfriends. We have sat over coffee and cakes under the mulberry tree on the front patio while the birds followed their twelve-hour cycle of eating and shitting in an ecstasy of greed; but now, thank God, the mulberries are finished.

The matter of the moment is the coming festival of the Saint at Eftalu, when Elena may well come down with some fashionable friends. The policeman has already been down to warn the naked sybarites on the beach past the hot springs, that we must put on bathing suits for the festival, since respectable and religious people will be visiting. They'll also be taking the waters for kidney stones and arthritis and also gallstones, so we must not be naked there either. The sybarites yawn and agree to be respectable. Already the chapel beyond the bathhouse has been given a fresh coat of paint, as has the bathhouse; two new terracotta pots have been placed there for ladies who may wish to ablute discretely.

All this news is discussed and discussed. Today we eat moussaka and have followed this alarmingly light lunch with salad and fruit and cheese and then, in an arbitrary fashion, Virginia produces a pudding in the English style, the name of which she is uncertain. I tell her it is called trifle and should have some sherry in it. Virginia doesn't know what sherry is so I explain. Virginia decides we will have a go tomorrow or the next day and will put plenty of brandy in and we can both decide if we like it with this variation.

It is evening by now and the French queens are again listening to opera, and the stallion in the adjacent paddock is under his tree; a shiver of life hardens his piece but he hardly notices, so busy he is drowsing and flicking the evening flies from his rump. Virginia fetches coffee and some brandy for me. We sit and sip and admire each other and Virginia tells me again about the latest letter from the naval Charlie, her son, and the probable dates of his arrival in Lesbos which means he will not coincide with me. This year Charlie will come with his wife and three children and plenty of presents. Virginia likes the idea of the presents but most of all the grandchildren. They remind her of the tragedy she had averted in the Charlie's life when he wanted to be a submariner in the United States Navy. She mentions it, mulls, and heaves around her floral bulk to observe the scenery and look at the distant villa where the music comes from.

'I don't like that music,' says Virginia, 'too much noise. Maybe you should complain, John, that they disturb your peace.'

'Maybe,' says John, relishing Mimi in full screech.

'So, the Charlie! And you will be back in Rome having a nice time with your friends?'

I agree that this is probable.

'So,' says Virginia with impeccable logic, 'I must tell you about the time when I save him, the Charlie. He want to join the submarines when he is a young man, but I put him right.'

I sip the brandy, trying to imagine anyone not accepting that Virginia put them right. Certainly I have been put right.

While I consider this, Virginia settles back in the chair, summons Charlie into exact memory and tried out a few facial expressions ranging from maternal solicitude to maternal iron to maternal incomprehension. Suddenly, she is ready for the story.

'So I said, My son, come and sit here. Come sit beside your mother who loves you.

'My son, if you join the airforce and there is a war, you might be bombed.'

Bombed in a plane, I think. No wonder the Charlie had a fight on his hands, convincing Virginia of the reality of a man's work.

'What can happen?' Virginia waves her arms about, possibly simulating a fighter attack as seen on TV. 'It is a quick death. You explode and that is that. But where does your mother find your body? No body, Charlie! All blown to bits! No flowers from your mother. No tears from your mother on your grave!'

Obviously, to Virginia, this is a very telling point since she tanks up on a thimbleful of brandy. Obviously a telling point. But the lack of a grave is also, I gather, not the main point. Virginia is reserving the big guns for later.

'And then, if you join a ship and there is a war, and you are bombed, you will die in the water or maybe — ' her face scowls with distraught horror, 'you may be eaten by a shark living there.'

Virginia sees the ravenous jaws, the sharp white teeth, the mouth wide open approaching the terrified Charlie and with a largish bite he has ascended to heaven. Satisfied, Virginia crosses herself. 'Not nice,' she adds in an aside to me, 'but quick.'

Now she is back with the Charlie. He is now moving uneasily on his chair as he feels the matriarchal power in full focus on him.

'My son, why do you want to go the submarines . . . why do you want to go to the submarines, Charlie, my son?'

'He shrugs, John, he does not yet tell his mother.'

'Aah!' Virginia gazes lovingly at Charlie and wheels out the Big Bertha, guaranteed, in one shot, to knock Charlie flat. 'Do you want to break a mother's heart? If you go into the submarines you break your mother's heart. What will happen in a war? You will be bombed and sink to the bottom of the sea and no-one will find you.' Virginia makes a few subtle noises to indicate black horror and panic. 'And then, the food runs out and you boys will have to eat each other.'

Obviously, in this situation, as I already know, Charlie will be at particular disadvantage, being plump from Virginia's good cooking.

'And then there is no air. It is a slow death, Charlie. It is a

terrible death. You will gasp. You will lose control of your bowels. Your face will go black; it will take hours and hours. Oh Charlie!' Virginia breaks into a coloratura wail that even interests the sheep, 'Why do you do this against your mother? Why, John? Why do he do it?'

I am at a loss, which pleases Virginia.

'He say,' goes on Virginia, 'I want submarine, mamma, because the pay is better than the ship.'

Virginia smiles at such male wantonness. 'No, Charlie. No submarines. Maybe in ship you get saved and the shark does not get you. Maybe if a war come, you live to see your mother again.

'And,' says Virginia to me, 'he see reason. He says, OK Mama, I go in the boat.'

Satisfied, motherly duty done, Virginia wipes her brow. 'He come to Greece last year and stay in this house. So red-faced, so fat, so beautiful. And he come again this year to be with his mother and keep her company.'

I yawn, I'm hitching a ride back with Virginia into Molyvos/Mythemna to meet Costas and Michelle. Michelle has stayed on to get the congress out of her system.

The days of the Saint arrive and since Elena, her daughter, cannot get away from Mitelene, Virginia will leave in a couple of days, after the event, to give her some heavy company. And, as this is probably the last time she will see me, I must also be given some heavy company.

The foreigners at the nude beach and Eftalu baths are wearing bathing suits, as promised to the local fuzz, and a number of old ladies have been taking the waters. I find them black-skirted and white-legged, sitting on the edge of the pool and curing the ills in their feet. Michelle comes down to Eftalu for an evening meal once in a while, but Costas is off on army business. The two principal actors in Pauline's bedroom dramas have had some sort of retribution for their hubris . . . Billy has been seen weeping full of shame and sorrow, at the taverna, with several rellies sitting black-faced at the table with him.

Virginia descends on Eftalu with Takis, Elena's eldest child and her brother and sister-in-law. Dramas take place the first evening when an enormous spider arrives to attack Virginia. Virginia has screamed and screamed while brother-in-law killed it. Virginia is full of foreboding when I arrive home from Mythemna and have a late drink with them. 'I have killed the spider and now her husband come to make revenge. I know this, John. They live together and now the husband will come to find me. They are also poisonous. They come down because of fires in the hills.'

Virginia is struck by fatalism for an hour or two, but forgets it the following morning as we prepare to celebrate the eve of the Saint with a very long lunch.

The menu begins. Takis, Elena's blood offering to the feast, wants to be down on the beach with some boys he knows.

'Be a polite boy. Be a gentleman,' says Virginia in English to show the family her multi-cultural expertise. Takis smiles and sits on his hands.

'He is growing his manhood,' Virginia tells me, 'but he is still frightened of the sea. Last night he says to me, What if a big fish eats me up, grandmother? And noises at night: What is that, grandmother?'

Lunch is into its fourth hour and Virginia, the matriarch, has forgotten about the evil spider and the unpleasant intentions of its husband. She looks at the remains of lunch and observes a wasp crawling over the rind of the watermelon. 'He does not come to do us good.' Virginia's English slithers around when she is with just Greek speakers. Virginia gently squashes him. The wasp revives. Virginia looks compassionate and gentle and picks up a knife. 'He is still in life.' She cuts him in half and wraps him in a funeral pyre of salad remains, bread, dolmathes, garlic sauce, fish bones, lamb bones, potato salad, moussaka in a special festive recipe, meat balls, rice, melon rind.

'And tomorrow you will be in Mitelene for the tickets for the plane.'

I nod.

'And tomorrow we have a special feast but you, *kyrie* John, will not be able to enjoy us here?'

I admit I will not be able to enjoy them here and wonder just how much weight I've put on since becoming Virginia's favourite summer occupation.

Virginia looks around. The party is still fresh, so with coffee and *raki* and brandy and maybe some sweet wine for the English pudding we will enjoy another hour or two.

Virginia arranges things with her sister-in-law and settles down again. 'And such nice ladies this year,' she tells me. 'Those ladies are good ladies. They do not do bad to themselves with the boys. Like good Greek girls. Just like Elena.'

Virginia does a quick translation of her opinion to her sister-in-law who has dyed black hair and, like a Disneyland bride of Dracula, two solid gold teeth in the bottom choppers and two exactly above them in the top set. They gleam in the late evening sunlight. From such images, no doubt, Takis's sexual nightmares are born.

The sister-in-law chimes in and Virginia does a running translation. 'She thinks the American girls must be from very religious families since they are so good. She says she thinks many of them are married and they come to keep each other company on holiday. She says they are not like tourist girls at all.

'Aiiee, hmmmm.' Virginia feels revived with the trifle and now is starting into the coffee and some sweet wine. She feels like a bit of gossip. 'But last year and year before, not like these good girls. You go to see them, John. I hear a girl dance ancient Greek dance — just like a flower. And, they read out their poetry to their girlfriends and they have studied ancient Greek things. But last year not so. Last year I take more boarders — only ladies, not gentlemen. I will not often take gentlemen.' (This is a compliment

to me as someone who is perhaps more than a gentleman?) 'But I take a Swedish lady who is very nice and around thirty-five.

'And first night she stay I hear three, then four feets. Then I think. Ha! Aha! Not on house of Virginia does this thing happen!' Virginia fills up with some more wine and everyone follows suit. She does a rapid translation into Greek and on return her English is still slithering.

'I tell her when she is arriving, You do what you wants. You all have keys but no man in Virginia's house. You do it outside!' Virginia makes a large expansive gesture to include the long beach beneath Molyvos, the hills, the ruined castle, the nearest bush.

'So, I hear these feets and I get out of bed and creep up the stairs like a little mouse and I stand on the top stair and I say, Who is there?

'No-one. No-one, says the Swedish lady.

'Yes, there is someone there. I know. I hear feets.

'No, no-one, says the Swedish lady.'

Virginia casts a look of exaggerated irony around the table and translates quickly. 'So I go right to the door. I open it. I stand! He is there. Big boy with hair right to the shoulders. I say, Get out! What you do here? Out! Out!' The birds in the mulberry tree cackle softly in appreciation. 'You do it outside! You do it in the bushes! In the house of Virginia you do not do.

'We just talk, says Swedish lady.

'You talk?' The irony drips. 'At four in the morning?

'Yes, yes. We only talk!

'Out! Out! I say to boy and he say bad word to me and push past me and I am frightened like a mouse.'

Virginia pats her forehead with a new paper napkin and insists that I have just a small piece of melon, cut up just now and cold from the fridge. Virginia is pleased to be talking English and translating, which shows what a cultivated lady she is and most worthy of respect, not only for her business acumen but her general cultural sophistication.

'Then later, some days later I see from my bedroom she bring in a Greek.'

The story is of obvious interest and Virginia does a quick resume for the family who all nod approval, including little Takis.

'The Greek! He is married to a foreign girl! Two lovely children.' Virginia's voice drips honey. 'He is a big man, so from carpet on the stairs I take an iron rod and I say, Who is there? She say, Bla bla bla bla. I no understand!

'I open the door and hold tight the iron. I say, Shame on you, you Greek! You married with wife and childs! You think you do this in Virginia's house?'

Virginia's bosoms, two mighty hills, are heaving with emotion as she pours out her scorn.

'He says, We just talk. We don't do nothing.

'I say, You just talk at four in the mornings?

'She say nothuns. She don't understand us.'

Virginia, now in full flow, makes another quick translation back into Greek.

She turns back to me. 'I say — Shame on you. If I do not feel sorry for your wife and childs I send you straight to prison.'

Virginia is obviously feeling most omnipotent.

'He run away fast. He say, We do no bad thing to us.'

'You do no bad thing to you?' There is a rising crescendo of disbelief, followed by another quick translation for the rest of the audience, all of them, including Taki, riveted.

'Next day,' ends up Virginia complacently, 'he go to my sister-in-law and he say, Tell *kyria* Virginia she is wrong. We do no bad thing to us. You tell her not to be mad and not tell my wife.'

Dracula with the gold teeth stitches on a smile and so does Virginia.

'And,' says Virginia, 'when we walk last night we see you at taverna with a girl.' (I hadn't seen them but had found Michelle at the taverna and stopped off for a glass of wine with her.) 'We think, maybe John bring her back. We say, OK. We say no thing.

You see what good company we keep!'

I agree they keep very good company and I wonder what Chinese Michelle would make of Virginia's innuendo.

Anyway, it is time to go down to the beach and walk and have a swim and redirect my soul to Rome. I suddenly realise, that, what with the congress, Virginia and Eftalu and Molyvos, I've actually forgotten I came here to write. Greece does that to the soul. Living seems to be an intense experience of company.

IV
ROME AND THE EAST

Noni — That Summer

It felt as if things and time were standing still. I moped around the apartment as if it were some dying landscape. It probably had something to do with being thirty-three; long gone were the days of champagne and raspberries. Where *did* one go for something to happen?

There was a knock at the door, and books and wine and lovers and God — all mixed up in this apartment like some barmy washing machine I couldn't turn off — turned off, for a moment.

'*Chi e?*' I asked, wary, now that heroin was in Rome, of opening the door.

'*Sono io, stronso*,' said Noni gaily.

'I am not a shit,' I retorted, tetchy.

Noni sashayed in just the same, radiating Scorpio in some good conjunction according to that week's planetary observations in *Expresso* or *Paese Sera*. She smiled artfully at the priest's sideboard and the whisky on it. It was five o'clock.

'*Un wiskino, caro.*'

I got the whisky and poured for both of us.

'I feel as if life, society, myself, has its head on the block waiting for the axe,' I said, thinking this rather poetic.

'A little ice, darling,' replied Noni, not indulging me while there were still important matters to be settled.

'Yes, darling.' I went to the fridge in Freud's dream kitchen, returned with ice and settled down on the settee. Noni was already in the hand-covered armchair which I had found on the street; it was now in stripes of violet and mauve. It was truly hideous.

I glanced at the armchair, at the silver church lamp from Naples, the marble-topped priest's sideboard, the silver-painted candlestick from the eighteenth century. Nothing fitted. Noni sipped and observed me. She was a brilliant photographer, pounding with life, frailties, wishes, wills and desires — but at the stage at which one feels that one is caught in aspic. I mentioned aspic.

'More likely hen shit,' said Noni. 'I simply have to leave Cippa. How can I survive with him in that subterranean room?'

'I don't know,' I said, her companion of some adventures in the past. 'I don't know.'

We had another whisky.

'You know,' said Noni, 'my mother was in the chorus in some show touring Argentina and she tossed the coin whether to marry some Yussupov or my father. It was my father's luck. Then he invested in some caviar enterprise and it went broke and Vivian had to sell off her minks and go back to highkicking in the chorus.'

'How is Cippa?' I asked. Cippa was what Noni called a *burino*, which means, at its worst, a clodhopper, and at its warmest, said with the right inflection, a warm humble clodhopper. I eyed Noni. She was wearing smart black pants and a smart pullover. She always managed to look chic. I never looked chic, in the male sense of the word, and I was getting vague about my status in life, too.

'Cippa,' said Noni, rolling her eyes in exasperation at my interrupting her quick foray back into the past. 'He is as expected. He is as expected. I must move soon. Why I ever went back to him I don't know.'

I did, and I knew what was expected. 'It was after you finished with Rafaello.'

'You know,' Noni rolled her eyes, 'his wife brought around the *carabineri* to put me in prison as a wicked and depraved woman. Rafaello and I crept out of my bathroom window and over the roof. She was still screaming in the street when we were having coffee at Domiziano!

'And then we ran away to Caracas. We had an apartment and we used to make love on the *terrazzo* in the mornings, and after about two weeks I realised the building next door was not going straight. It was moving from left to right, and then it was moving sideways up to another storey. And then, I realised why — in the middle of our intimate caresses all the builders were watching us. Aaagh, the horror! But at least we have a monument to our love in Caracas, the most unbalanced building in the world. They should have asked us to open it. I should have thought of that, for I was still known, then, in Caracas. I was the first non-whore on Caracas television, and the first and only baroness; I had my clothes made by Dior. I had an hour on television: news, you know, some horrors — things like mothers eating their babies — some gossip, some interviews. The whores were furious. They had been flown over specially from Cuba, since before Noni it was thought in Caracas that only a whore would appear on TV. These whores used to supplement their income, when not doing the news and commercials, and demanded very, very high fees from their admirers since they were stars. But me? No-one — I was still a virgin!'

Noni's face grew pure, her high cheekbones defining the face of the Austro-Hungarian aristocrat. 'And they were so furious that everyone loved me, and that I would not compete for clients, that they sent me ju-ju dolls with pins stuck in them. I've still got one as a good-luck charm, somewhere around.'

I understood perfectly. When Noni had arrived in Europe she had stayed only at the best hotels, but her money had run out and this had meant decamping and leaving behind trunks and suitcases plastered with the labels of the continent's great ocean liners, hotels and barrage balloons.

'Our problem,' announced Noni, when we were securely into a new whisky, 'is that we were born at the wrong time. We should have been born before all this communism. So debilitating.'

'The problem isn't communism,' I said. 'It is that we don't know how to make money.'

Noni flicked a shoulder and looked arch. 'Perhaps we should

find a rich bourgeois wife for you, then we poison her and live happily ever after.'

'Why not? Or maybe for you some old millionaire. One who is very old.'

'And drops dead,' said Noni, 'before consummation. Oh, dear, dear, dear, what are we to do?'

'I don't know,' I said. 'I think I may go to India to visit this guru I've been reading about.'

'Why not,' said Noni, 'we all need a change from time to time.'

We had a cigarette.

'I thought we would have a very nice dinner,' said Noni. I hadn't noticed her shopping bag.

'We will have early flowers of zucchini stuffed with mozzarella and anchovies and then a special special steak with green peppercorns and cream and garlic and potatoes to die.'

'To die?' I, willing for anything.

'Yes, to die. Steamed, then basted in the best oil which you, *caro*, will go down and buy at the grocers, and with garlic and cooked and cooked,' her voice became dreamy, 'until brown and crisp. And a good bottle of red which you will also buy. Now it is too early for dinner. We will take a constitutional.' She picked up her black *carabiniere* cloak and she swung its heavy weight around her shoulders. 'Did I ever tell you how I got this cloak?'

We walked across Ponte Vittorio and on to Campo dei Fiori. Giordano Bruno's statue was there. He is a lesson. People who enter the inner path tend to get burned. Back there is San Pietro, beautifully preserved, full of old men in skirts, with limp balls and power written over every line of their faces. They copulate with it like dogs on heat, those Vatican priests in those cold dead bureaucratic men.

But who really cares about them? *That* is the amazing thing about Rome, old Rome, Queen of Heaven and Whores and Wives and Girls. Old Rome *does not* care. San Pietro is just another dick, sticking into the sky, which thinks it is immortal. Old Rome, in her deep humous, knows otherwise.

'Anyway, darling,' said Noni as we reached Piazza Navona, 'let's sit and smoke a cigarette and look at the world.'

The fountains were playing that cool March evening and there was a red glow from a brazier at the corner. I went and bought some chestnuts and when I returned Noni had ordered two black coffees and two wiskinos.

'Who do you fancy?' I asked, looking at the young crowd strolling around.

'Hmm,' said Noni. 'You know, darling, the trouble with us is we could not bear the indignity of some young thing of either sex on our arm. Much too demoralising, so obvious and vulgar. Rather sad, too.'

I looked at the fountain of the Four Rivers. I looked at San Agnese with its baroque facade. 'You mean, we are not young?'

Noni shrugged. 'No, darling, we are *just* on the other side of youngness.'

'I think I will definitely go to India to visit that guru,' I said, shivering with the cold wind of truth.

'Well, darling, why not. Maybe you'll find something. I mean, people like us always make the *best* converts. We don't have any inhibitions about telling God about ourselves. It's always the bourgeois who are terrified of that, never the sinners. We've done it all, one way or another, already.'

'In one form or another?' I suggested.

'Well, we know it leads nowhere. You know, we know about things, but as yet I am not going to enter the Carmelites.'

I sipped my whisky. 'I wonder what happens in India.'

'Oh, I daresay, vegetarianism, no sex, plenty of meditation, early morning walks, devotion, singing songs. I imagine that is what the guru is up to. Very pure, visions of paradise. Maybe you'll have an experience which will convert me. Maybe you'll come back and I'll be so inspired I'll enter the Carmelites for a life of bread and water. Oh God, but all those bags are so ugly. All those girls their fathers couldn't marry off!'

In my bedroom I convulsed again over the book of Shri Bagwan Rajneesh. It was called *The Book of Secrets* and was photocopied. It had arrived at Mercedes' place and I had collected it, read it and got very keen. Mercedes read it and got keen too because she knew, too, that it had *meaning*. I knew it was *actual*, and would be better than going to mass. I was a little tired of masticating Jesus Christ, who never seemed to be closer than a communion wafer; I wanted him here now.

The Book of Secrets had taste, elegance, style and wit. It had a sense of space and a sense of culture. It seemed to be written by a master craftsman, who therefore must be *that which arrives to fulfil humankind*. Mercedes thought so, too.

I found myself dreaming strange dreams and woke up and read again as, into chips of sapphire and flashes of gold, arose the internal moon, large and glowing: ready for anything. I slept again and grew uneasy, as does a dog when it smells scents of other alien beings blown across its territory. But I was ready to go to India.

Ah, woe! Living in Rome, I thought truth was only told fresh when it was truth. I had never heard of sects, gurus, New Age thinking, crystals (which came later), Shirley MacLaine (who also came later), and the lemmings-rush to truth when death is gnawing at the vitals of a culture. I didn't really, as it happened, know anything at all. But then, it is only the ignorant whose sails are filled by the winds of an unwise faith. And yet, without unwise faith, how do you make the journey? Only fools never try — and only the fool arrives — so they say!

An Indian Summer

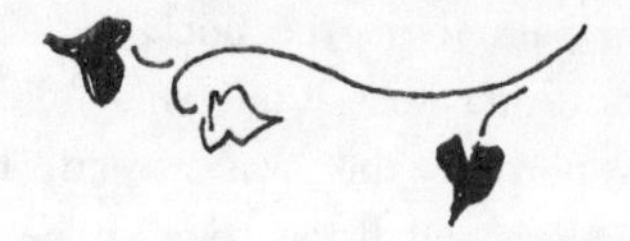

It was a hot June midday when I planed for India. Mercedes had left already, clasping books, her luggage minimal. She had had her health department injections. It was all stamped in her book: cholera, typhoid, paratyphoid, smallpox. But no reactions at all, for Mercedes had in fact gone along, paid for the inoculations, had them stamped in her book, joined the waiting mob and, when no-one was looking, slipped out. She did *not* believe in injections and would, by preference, take homeopathic remedies.

I had no idea what I was travelling to. I knew only that I wanted to take a journey, flirt with God maybe; I like flirting and I need a holiday. I sweated while the engines revved up and hoped Iraq Air had Allah on its side. By the look of the plane's interior they would need him.

We lifted off and I stopped praying for an easy death and settled into my first whisky. A lurching right-sliding wheel was the occasion for sweat to gather again around my groin and bead my back. I moaned quietly to myself, and sipped. Then we were above the sea and soon above buckled grasslands of the south, the sea placid-grey washing against the littoral and on to Greece and a swing again over Turkey.

And I was following, I realised, the routes of the mystery cults which had long ago arrived in Imperial Rome to tell it that its gods — with them its greatness — were falling. I dozed on and hours later we reached Baghdad. It was an easy descent; no-one much bothered to fasten their seatbelts and the smokers kept smoking.

I disembarked; we were to wait in Baghdad for three or four hours. Is Iraq what used to be called Syria? I couldn't remember, but anyway Iraq was probably Baathist. Depressing!

I had in fact had one or two too many whiskies. The waiting-room was long and bare of everything but rows and rows of plastic orange chairs parked on the pock-marked concrete. I had heard somewhere or other that Rajneesh's followers were called Orange People, so perhaps this was a sign. I imagined that I would speak to Rajneesh and listen to what he had to say; I had written to Rajneesh; I imagined a letter sent by Rajneesh, via his secretary, to be a personal invitation. I imagined it would be something like an audience with the Sufi master, Inayat Khan, to whom Mercedes was devoted: I would go into a room, I would be inflamed by Rajneesh's energy field; I would experience love, harmony and beauty and I would understand where I came from and why. I really was quite naive. I knew Christianity had become big business, just as communism had become big business and was usually run by executives who had gone from being the poor and oppressed to owners of dachas where they planned campaigns and made a better life for their wives and children. Why should this guru be any different? Maybe because Inayat Khan was different, the genuine article; but then, he was dead.

The Arabs whom I watched sitting in the orange plastic chairs looked to be from the mountains. With cruel predatory expressions, they had wrinkled dry skin and hard hooked noses. They hawked and spat, some of them, into blue squares of cloth. It was obvious they would all prefer to spit on the floor but it was not allowed. There were many notices in Arabic and some of them were bound to concern penalties for spitting on the floor. I wandered around thinking about first-cousin marriages in mountain villages, going on since the day the Prophet arrived at the door with the message of submission. Well, the genes, at least, were in total submission.

I tried to buy a Coca-Cola but the wayside stall didn't sell Coca-Cola, only an orange drink, and it was warm since the wayside stall didn't have a fridge. I smoked and fidgeted and other passengers wandered about smoking and drinking orange drink.

There was not food, not even a sandwich. Then, as I was thinking of trying to doze, some workers arrived and set up a screen at the front. One or two people turned towards it, as if this were lesson-time after playtime. There were even a few apple cores on the floor, thrown there by people who had flown Iraq Air before and had brought along their own supplies.

A technician arrived with two workers, who put down the projector and set it up and connected it. The screen blazed white.

The technician fiddled and fussed while a row of *chadors* turned to watch, forgetting for a moment their snotty-nosed kids and their packages and string-tied, old cardboard suitcases. The credits rolled. I smoked a cigarette. It was Doris Day and Gregory Peck in some comedy I had sat through around thirty years ago.

I half watched. Gregory might have been a history professor and Doris might have been a mature student of his, or else she was a professor, or perhaps they were neighbours. It was dubbed in Arabic and the story didn't give that much away. But it was progressing: lo and behold Doris and Gregory, the archetypal Barbie Dolls, moving up to a spectacular climax, their mouths pouting sweet nothings that came out in a stream of glottals. Gregory had a deep male Arabic voice, caressing as velvet on warm skin, while Doris sounded a trifle shrewish — the annoyed harem lady.

Doris had carmined lips, wore a blue twinset and pearls, sprouted blonde hair perfectly coiffured, and had a contrived virgin face — from the days when virginity was worth losing. The *chador* ladies knew, they really knew, that this Doris Day would get the better of Gregory, even though by their standards she was over the hill (below the hill is around fourteen and that Doris wasn't). Gregory was wearing tweeds, smoked a pipe and had warm brown eyes — less daring and hawk-eyed than the sheiks of Araby, but sufficient. He was wearing a red cravat. The men knew that Gregory was stirring, his loins pumping thick blood. He had her alone, and this American female, like the strumpet she was, had no husband to keep her in a *chador*. Gregory Peck was almost ready to force her down and have his will; the Arab men hoiked and spat with excitement. One forgot and expectorated on the floor, then rubbed it furtively into the thin film of dust over the concrete.

What would happen to Doris? I imagined her the terror of the Souk, no tame concubine but a Rudolph Valentino lady galloping across the sands and the terror of the unbelievers in the local supermarket. Outside the sand lapped and the wind howled through moon-struck distant mountains as the Arabs gathered into collective thought, which burned low like a town whose electrical generator was working with only half its turbines. Gregory moved in for the kill, sweatless, and an extra generator began a slow turn. The carmined lips of Doris the houri quivered, and layers of twinset and tweed clinched . . .

Blam! The screen blazed, as blank and white as the desert sun at midday; the town's electrical supply went from flicker to dead. Two technicians stood in a huddle with what looked to be two Baathist gorillas: they were tough, squat, and had hard black eyes that had seen plenty of people dancing on the end of a rope. The senior technician, hands raised and then down by his sides like a private on parade with the sergeant-major about to chew him to pieces, was explaining to the gorillas. He nodded, then minced across to the front of the classroom and raised his hands again. 'Government of Iraq doesn't want people to watch bad things. No more film.' The centre lights were switched off and on, and then there was a film about the achievements of Iraq from the day one of whatever revolution was being represented in the ascent towards the light of truth and humanity.

I supposed that the Doris Day and Gregory Peck film had somehow strayed from the pornography library and that the Baath party leaders might watch it on a blue Saturday night after mosque.

With the revolution ending in the triumph of a dam opened to loud Soviet orchestral accompaniment, the plane took off. I looked down on that ribbed, moonlit land, as harsh and earthless as those Arab faces with their Allah, who would have found little contention from humane gods for their minds and souls. India ahead, however, felt more omnipresent and more female and more *understanding* — or, perhaps, more amorphous.

Where do the Sufis, some of them the great poets, architects, kings, singers, fit into Islam? Allah, by the look of his modern-day descendants, must have found a lot of people who had a long history of first-cousin marriages. Islam is now an animal, to be *whipped into obedience*; it does not know good food, books, literature, fine paintings. Except Iran, once; except Islamic Spain, once; all a long time ago. Yet Islam is most certainly accurate in one matter — that Allah is the final revelation of the patriarchal God, and thank God for that!

I went to sleep. I felt myself landing and taking off, and again no-one bothered much with seatbelts. I had vague memories of oil wells, and of fires high in the air like acetylene torches as they burned off, somewhere, the gas. Oil was there, and fire and gas, but there was no reality except rock. It was a world for the mad, the disenchanted. It was a world that could be imposed on by the schoolboy mind of a T. E. Lawrence; it was the world of adolescence — of codes and truths systematised to conceal what it loved most, its own male power.

Through a doze, the captain's voice told me that the potential bird of death, the iron-clad bird whose wings might have been ill-fitted by an apprentice, had survived the winds of heaven and was descending on Bombay. It was now six o'clock in the morning, local time. Below were some ships, faded and grey, mottled as if with leprosy, limping through the grey, oily sea or lying comatose. The air, too, was grey as the sun started to burrow through the clouds. Below is the Arabian sea, announced the captain. And that sea, like the ships, was mucky and tired. One

imagined rivers bearing bloated corpses and many diseases; one imagined the rivers, weighed down by mud, reaching towards some crystal sea where the corpses would be given eternal life.

Maverick, I put on my safety belt. Most of the passengers seemed to be standing to get their luggage out of the overhead luggage compartments and some were lighting new, nervous cigarettes as the pilot levelled the craft down and it sank, swooped and shuddered and touched the runway at Bombay's Santa Cruz airport.

I knew the airport was pronounced Santa Cruth. This didn't help me as I sniffed in a grey sweat-smelling Turkish bath, overlaid with ancient memories of sewage and drying Bombay duck. Fat blowflies washed around the ceiling fan, too lazy to go to the lavatories which must have been nearby, for their smell beckoned imperatively.

I went easily through customs. It may be of interest to Freudians that I left my wallet on a shelf. It was retrieved by an honest Indian businessman. Had I been telling myself I was about to be robbed? I noted a few orange-clad people, with a seeming confidence in their saffron clothes. But I was otherwise immersed in the sweat pouring down my back and the problems of faces, endless faces, demanding, demanding.

Outside, the Sikh driver accepted my bags and stated his price. I could not work out the cost, and although a determined bargainer in Italy I allowed the rip-off. The luggage was hefted into the boot and children scrabbled at the window for some cash. On vacant land to the left, some women were working as labourers, their blue sweat-stained saris caked in dust. They were hard of face and gazed ahead out of large black eyes in an empty manner which encompassed all but registered nothing. They moved like ants, seemingly bound by some common will that lifted their feet, moving them towards a vast pile of grey dirt. They scooped it up and walked away to place it on another pile of grey dirt.

I, the visitor, did not exist, except for the beggar children who clawed enthusiastically at the closed window as the taxi began a gentle acceleration. The children's faces seemed imprinted on the glass; their fingers continued a ghostly clawing but the driver didn't notice. He lit up a biddi, blew moodily at a blowfly defecating on a picture of Ganesh the Elephant God, blew his horn a few times to test its resilience and swerved out into the fast lane, leaving far behind the bullock carts and bicycles. It was long and flat, the road, surrounded by humpies which stretched across broken ground to mangrove trees. There cardboard houses dripped in a monsoonal downpour.

The cab was smelling of cloves as it stopped under a fig tree at the spot where the taxis leave for the hill station of Poona. Three fat gentlemen dressed variously in brown and cream suits with brown and cream shoes and white shirts — a chorus line gone to seed — smiled and nodded at me and the fat on their necks rippled and jiggled. The film posters, I had already noticed, emphasised fat: fat young actors, pink of cheek, white of skin or, at the most, light brown; ladies in brilliant saris of green, vermilion and gold, spangled like the jewel boxes they kept in the bank, who camped it up with simpering lips and fat cheeks and large chest-of-drawer bosoms. The ideal was fat: looking at the gaunt-ribbed coolies dragging along carts piled high with furniture, vegetables and wood, you saw why. Fat was success; fat was status and money. I was fairly fat myself at the time and hummed to myself, 'Fat is beautiful'. I might even fall in love with a fat Indian film star in Bombay and live happily ever after.

The driver, wild of eye, ignored me and consulted with the three fat businessmen. It seemed we had a full complement for a trip to Poona. The driver hefted my luggage onto the roof rack and secured it with cords. He nudged his elbow towards the front seat.

'You go in there,' he muttered. At least, he muttered something, picking as he did so at his betel-juice-stained teeth, then hoiking and spitting onto the pavement, which looked like an advertisement for tubercular lungs.

'No, please,' I said, wishing to be the polite visitor, 'one of you take the front seat.' I was feeling acutely conscious of being taken for a sahib if I put a foot wrong. Cousins of my grandfather had arrived here with their lean white faces and in their fine military uniforms and always took the front seat.

The driver hoiked and spat some more.

'No, please,' I reiterated.

'Yes sir, yes sir, indeed.'

Fatty no.1 in cream seized good fortune and nimbly dived for the front door before the opposition was even at the get-ready. I climbed in the back door while Fatties no. 2 and 3 stood back. The I realised the other two's play, as they entered from opposite doors and forced me into the middle. Sweat flowed, fat flowed into fat, body odours exchanged telephone numbers, and deodorants sang songs of praise while the two Indian businessmen looked with tolerant amusement at my gaffe. They, after all, in the same situation would pull rank at once, and a sahib, a *real* sahib, would have no doubts that he belonged in the front seat.

We left town and its monotonous drab whites, broken-down-looking apartment buildings and wasteland. Life was on a low burner in dreary pastels and washed-out greys and yellows. Ahead were the Western Ghats and over a distant escarpment waters cascaded down in a white torrent. Close to it the land was a feverish green, trailing its colour like a green feather boa through the grey earth.

'And what are you doing in Poona?' asked Fatty no. 1, who was in the underwear trade.

I said I was going to an ashram. The taxi moved up onto a steep road and we were on the Ghats.

'Aaah. Aaah,' Fatty no. 2 breathed deep with interest, 'would that be the ashram of Shri Bhagwan Rajneesh?'

'Yes, it would actually,' I said, now bristling with sahib feelings at the natives' overfamiliarity. But the natives like details of your marital status, a small summary of religious faith, children, perversions and favourite cigarettes. 'Ah, yesss,' hissed Fatty no. 2, which had Fatty-in-the-front-seat trying, without success, to make a forty-degree turn of his head so that he could watch the drama unfolding. 'Ah, yesss,' he repeated. 'Rajneesh is a very strange man. He does a lot of strange things in Poona. The newspapers speak of him very much.'

'Oh yes,' Fatty 2 beamed. 'Now are you married?' I did not understand the conjunction of questions. I did not know that the ashram specialised in free or paid sex, in bacchanalian dancing, in groups which had arrived from California, and in enlightenment. I did not know that many Indians were raring to go there too — to get into touch-feely, multiple religious orgasms, and the excitement of devotion of Shri Bhagwan Rajneesh. But they didn't dare. What would mother say?

'Yess,' interrupted Fatty no. 1 who had ascertained that I was not married, 'it would be better for you to go to Sai Baba, who is traditional. He performs miracles. One maharanee got a tiara for her daughter for her wedding because maharanee is hard up these days. Also sacred ash comes from his fingertips, which is good for illness.'

'Ah yess,' affirmed Fatty 2, 'the travel people can tell you how to find Sai Baba.'

For some reason I was not that particularly impressed by a guru who apported objects, although I wouldn't have minded something really elegant and expensive, like a silver cross set with sapphires, to indicate my potentially holy state.

The road opened up onto the speedway. There were already plenty of victims: trucks lying rusted down steep banks; a truck lying on its side with the tribe of survivors sitting on it, bruised like fruit shaken from a tree but not too seriously hurt. The taxi driver honked the whole time and burst around blind corners overtaking. *Peep peep, don't go to sleep*, admonished one sign, but the driver probably couldn't read anyway. I tried to sleep, or at least close my eyes. This driving was like a never-ending take-off in an aircraft, my most hated feeling. Then sleep came, merciful, to waft me into oblivion.

Fatty no. 2 nudged me some time later. We had, presumably, arrived in Poona. Ahead was a statue of what had to be Queen Victoria, looking stout and disapproving while the imperial rabble milled around. 'This is Poona,' said Fatty no. 2. 'And sir, now that we have arrived, why do we not come to visit you? The races are on — we will all go to the races!'

I clambered out clumsily under the benign smiles of the three businessmen. I hailed a bemo, smiling profusely and saying how pleasant it would be to go to the races. As the bemo driver put my luggage onto the seat I found my Burberry had vanished — in a moment, in the twinkling of an eye. I emoted judgement.

We had hardly lurched off, and I had hardly had time to complete my invocation calling for retribution on the little shit who had stolen my coat; of punishment condign — terrible whippings, boiling oil, discharge from the mouth of a cannon — when the bemo pulled into a driveway. Ahead was a large, bleached wooden building with its first-floor balcony protruding solidly like the stomachs of my recent companions. Outside a number of young Indians, lean and handsome and dressed in freshly washed and ironed jeans, chatted on the stoop. I lumbered out, staring around. My luggage was placed on the doorstep and someone called Pratak — who, it transpired, was from Zambia, where he had been chased and fired on by a plane — helped me up the stairs.

The interior was pure Bournemouth. The stairs were wooden, washed and bleached, and on the landing at the top was an aged corgi called Roger, who hardly noticed me passing by. He was losing hair in eczema patches and was concentrating quite hard on breathing. We put down the bags. Next to the locked office, in a recess under the window, was an old chintz sofa with a youngish man on it, asleep. 'Who is he?' I asked.

'He is Harrison, the assistant manager,' said Pratak.

Harrison woke at the sound of our voices. He surveyed us, the brass tubs, the rattan chairs, the fan, and the dusty date-laden palms which clacked with a sudden short wind. He yawned and slowly moved from one dream to another, his white teeth gleaming in an almost black, pockmarked face. 'I am Harrison. I am the assistant manager. I study at the technical college. Mr Amrashram isn't here. He owns this. Welcome to the Ritz. We have a room for you in the backside of the house. Leave your wallet and passport for safekeeping in the safe, except it is locked up.' The eyes smiled indolently, their yellow glow reflecting the activity of parasites in the liver and guts, and other beasties who had found comfortable residence in his bloodstream.

'You are madam's friend? She tells me about you.'

'Madam?' I asked, unused to thinking of Mercedes as a madam.

'Madam, yes. Madam from Rome. Roman madam,' he elucidated further, relishing his sophisticated contacts. 'She has booked a room for you if you are her friend.'

'Yes, I am.'

'Madam,' he went on, delicately picking at an inflamed pimple lodged between two smallpox craters, 'is at the ashram meditating with herself. She says, "Do come on, if you can be bothered." And if you arrive, of course,' finished Harrison, to beget new clarity.

A servant in white cotton *kurta* and tight rousers arrived as Harrison was considering ringing the bell. Harrison languidly motioned to the luggage. The corgi heaved itself up with an asthmatic wheeze and waddled over to join the procession as it formed up. We set off through the dining room. Around the walls hung photos of old Indians with beards, who might have been saints or gurus or sages or someone's relatives picked up cheap at some local garage sale. A few potted plants lurched out from the wooden walls. At one of the tables which were laid with stained, starched white tablecloths, an old Indian sat sipping his post-siesta tea and adjusting his dhoti, which had got tangled at the bum. He hawked peevishly.

Roger lay down to rest and the procession moved around him and out onto an open verandah. To the right was an open kitchen with scoured pots and pans hanging from the wooden back wall and embers glowing in the iron range. Harrison opened a door and ushered me into a room painted in mud yellow, which had two beds, two wardrobes in plywood, and a view onto a wall thirty feet away which was growing green mould.

'Madam is next door,' Harrison announced chattily. 'She has a nice room with a double bed and a rural view from the bathroom.'

'Of what?' I asked.

'A tree and tiled roofs which remind madam of Rome. Same sort of tiles she tells me.'

I got down to costs and resurrected my bargaining persona. 'I think, since I will be staying here quite long, I should have a thirty-three per cent reduction in the tariff. After all, you save money by having a long-term guest.'

Harrison looked doubtful, then a conclusion presented itself. 'Maybe you share with Roman madam, she has a double bed.'

'No, I want my own room.'

'You come for Rajneesh too?'

'I *think* so.'

'They say bad things about him, but I don't see nothing yet.' Harrison sat himself down on one of the beds. 'I go to meditate at five-thirty this evening. Costs five rupees the *kundalini* meditation. Good for sex *chakra*. Lady before in present madam's room does *tantra* group three times.'

'*Tantra*?' I asked, sitting down too and lighting up a cigarette and feeling most bewildered.

'Yes, they go into a closed room and make sex all day. Former madam wants to understand sex and make different postures with lotsa people and she has book of *Karma Sutra*. She said I just know, honey, that Bhagwan Shri Rajneesh wants me to do it a lot.

'When she finishes *tantra* group she practises with me her favourite positions in the afternoons when the servants are down in the compound and at night when they go to bed.' Harrison fished for his wallet in the pocket of his pressed, thin, navy blue cotton trousers, which looked to have been stained and restained by many curries. He took out a tattered letter folded around a photograph and handed it to me reverently. 'She is in Los Angeles, America, and wrote me a letter of love. She gives me twenty dollars in it. She is a grandmother and very wealthy. She have lotsa fat,' said Harrison, lost in admiration for his former inamorata. 'But this madam is thin. I do not think she want to do *tantra* group, since when I ask her she say she is not interesting in such things and is grandmother. I tell her my beloved from LA is also grandmother but Roman madam still not become interested. And also, she is thin.' Harrison sighed at such a sad fate for a grandmother.

I relinquished the photo of Miss LA, bleached hair, bouncy boobs and a youthful seventy or eighty.

'Perhaps,' suggested Harrison with aplomb, 'this madam is your madam and wait to practice *tantra* with you?'

I considered elegant Mercedes of the Bloomsbury style and fine Spanish face. I thought of her waiting in passionate need for my arrival. 'No,' I said shortly, 'Roman madam is not my madam.'

'No?' Harrison looked surprised, lost in a cultural sea. 'She is your mother or your aunt?'

I stubbed out the cigarette in a saucer provided by Harrison.

'No, she is a close friend.'

'I'm a Catholic,' said Harrison, suddenly severe, 'and I mostly worship the Virgin Mary.'

Monsoon clouds were gathering, thick and greasy, down on the plateau near a huddle of ancient mountains as, two hours later, the bemo turned into a narrow road in a posh quarter of the city.

Poona had been the favoured retreat of the memsahibs and their imperial consorts. Some ageing memsahibs, being made of sterner stuff than the male, had survived the rigours of independence and apparently lived in some of the decaying villas we were passing by. A few 1940 Austins trundled out of drives, with the former ruling class looking distinctly frazzled.

Koregaon Park was an aristocratic quarter of the city and was once the retreat of the Mahastrian aristocracy, so Mercedes had disclosed in a quick letter to me in Rome. Some of the mansions in their seedy baroque curves or semi-Palladian graciousness were of the sort you might find in a town like New Orleans. In May, Mercedes had written, snakes died from sunstroke and general exhaustion, but now the land was green and cool. Innumerable small flowers had opened, birds flitted everywhere, small brown frogs had taken up residence in the puddles, butterflies moved from home to stately home. I was pleased, although surprised because I had expected something more rigorous.

On the road were women and men dressed in different shades of orange. I found it difficult to make the connection: I knew nothing about the New Age and gurus; I lived in provincial Rome where the tides of northern European disassociation had not yet reached the eternal city.

At the ashram there was a garish gate with guards on duty. I stared blankly. It was all a bit like being taken as a new boy to school and God knows what initiation ceremonies they would have here — being thrown naked before the guru, heads being plunged down the dunnies by the fourth-formers. I got out and paid the driver his few rupees, avoiding a beggar child with a baby. Inside the gates I found Mercedes walking towards me, definitely enjoying this new dispensation, and we embraced.

Further down a short stretch of path the sound of beating music issued from a building. 'It's the *kundalini* meditation,' said Mercedes. We walked to it and Mercedes decided to join in. I stood to watch for a moment — young half-naked bodies, guys in drawstring trousers, gals in dresses, all vital and vibrant, apparently celebrating. Mercedes was at the back of the hall where air could reach her and there she tentatively shook like some delicate sea flower feeling an energy swell which was not precisely hers. I joined in from the side amongst the young fellas and started to shake and fart too. Up on the stage were a couple of lines of go-go dancers, every move of unrepression as contrived as a classical ballet and every ego beaming a profoundly narcissistic harmony. Christ (which, according to Mercedes, was the name of the swami) was encouraging everyone.

I had not imagined them so young, half of them being around twenty or twenty-five. The dancing and shaking, mostly shaking, went on and on and on. Mercedes was as usual delicate and pensive, with a classical reserve as if she were tripping along the notes of a Mozart rondo. Others, impelled by their youthful energy, careered around the floor, swirling, smashing, stopping; aggression run rampant like a balloon with the string suddenly pulled free.

Another gong sounded. The pipes and an Indian harmonium combined to wheeze out tunes of peace; a sitar flurried across the evening. People lay down; the mosquitoes, waiting in ordered squadrons in the greenery, homed in for the kill.

Mercedes and I returned to the hotel and ate some light food in Mercedes' room, which may or may not have inclined Harrison to the view that Roman madam was indeed my madam.

I slept heavily and was awakened at 5.15 by the night watchman, a small sturdy man, who brought me a cup of sweet tea.

I showered and dressed and wrapped myself in a Peruvian *ruyana*. Mercedes, in a brilliant puce top and trousers, went ahead to call a bemo. It was damp and cold outside and she held a shawl across her mouth. Along the street families enacted their destiny with cardboard. A woman held a child close to her. I had already decided I could not afford to have any feeling, or I would be engulfed in a hopeless horror. Hindu theology had probably been created to allow better-class Indians not to feel either — karma, after all, has an ineluctable social logic.

The bemo arrived and we got in and scooted off for the morning meditation. At the ashram I gradually felt myself waking up. I cast a few glances at the neophytes, hard at it belting the air, punching Mum in the face, the whole world, their lusts, their angers — the Mongolian hordes awakened from sleep and streaming through the ether, swords raised, swords bloodied. Revenge was in the air, aggression was rampant and Mum was dead under the prancing dancing feet of the vital young — the future — killing the past, history and death. Some thrust semi-silent howls into the air, which seemed to lance a boil but really only inflamed it, I concluded, mentally consulting my psychoanalytical friends.

The music stopped and the howls with it, as if a sharp knife had done a fast clean job on the collective windpipe. Now we were jumping up and down on the spot to new music, thrusting down into the sex centre (I was breathless, anxious to hit it good and hard). From somewhere — low in the belly? — came the sound 'Hu'. Off I went, ankles and fallen arches protesting, belly blubber concentrating with sweat, heat and cold, sweat dribbling down my back, cock shrinking in protest at this rape of sound, balls tight to sustain the shock. Hu! Hu! Hu! HU! HU! HUUUUU! SHIIIIIT! HUU! HU! Hu! UUUUU! uuuuu! U? uuu?

Hu — Nothing exists but God alone.

How in God's name was Mercedes managing? This was not the world of our small meditation group in Rome, where we would contemplate, surrounded by vital colours, silks, beautiful things and children's drawings, with the lemon tree in flower on the terrace and the waters from the fountain a distant sound, a roar of water. This was a new world and I was left somewhat bemused, yet fascinated by its vigour. There was a certain animal charm about the experience — a dance to the lower cycles of existence, a dance of play. It was very attractive in its Hollywood technicolour.

Today, it seemed, God was angry with all the violence being released. While *Hu* expanded in angry waves, He thundered rain down on the tin roof, while dawn chased between the rain sheets.

I went to see Ma Yoga Laxmi, who turned out to be the company secretary rather than just an intimate disciple of Bhagwan. I waited in the office, the beehive buzzing around me. She was an attractive woman; a well-bred woman. I had questions I wanted to ask, but could not find the words.

Laxmi talked. She remembered that I had written; she just knew that Bhagwan had called me. All I knew was that I used deodorant, I smoked, I had not washed my hair in scentless shampoo but I was still given a *darshan* — a small group meeting — that evening, which was against the rules. Later I recalled this first meeting as the real power of the play. In front of us was the Master and all our energies focussed on and fed him. Each of us was thus gradually weakened by this spiritual cannibal: it was the great dance in reverse — Rajneesh gave nothing while we gave everything. He was the king at the centre of each soul.

That evening I sat on a log, just inside the inner compound where Rajneesh hung out with a secure buttress of ladies and gentlemen. Around twenty others waited with me. I stared at the fading scarlet and grey of the sky. It seemed that seeing the Master was like some sort of Sunday-school treat, permitted only to those who had done a Group (what was a Group?). I looked at a black woman sitting nearby. She could have come from one of those archetypal photos of blacks on a verandah somewhere in the American south, wearing thin cotton dresses and staring out into an expanse of trees and cotton fields and horizon which will never be theirs to own.

Just then the head prefect called the class to order and people began to line up, jostling to get near the front. The head prefect smiled at the black woman and an Aryan male who was dressed in planter's white and had a solid prosperous belly. Perhaps white was the colour of purity or perhaps this was simply his lightweight tropical garb. I did not like the prosperous Aryan and watched as he strode to where he clearly felt he belonged as of right, at the front of the queue. The black woman followed him with a natural diffidence.

The crocodile moved off. In some windows domestic scenes were taking place; beneath a yellow lightshade a black woman read a book.

I was directed to the second-last row. The greenery was lit with small lights and there was a tangible feeling of peace. People from the group came forward and discussed with a naive and refreshing frankness their problems, their sexuality. It was as if *pudeur* had not place, nor dignity either. Someone with a guitar sang a song and Rajneesh listened.

Eventually I was called forward. Rajneesh was like fine porcelain, like something rare with a magnetism like a vibrant green-dark glaze, and I became a tree or whatever he said I must become. I returned to my place swamped by Rajneesh's will to power; I looked at the name he had given me and I didn't like it. Pragosh. What would I be called: Gosh? Proggy? It meant divine declaration. Ho hum!

The black woman and her Aryan companion were called up. She moved with diffidence, as if she had been in the kitchen cooking, brushing flour off her hands. She sat with her great natural humility and dignity and looked up at Rajneesh (we were all on the floor before him) and smiled. Within her it seemed to have been a hard journey — I didn't know from where or what. Her companion, on the other hand, had always known his importance. He intruded like a bright hard light; like a busker at the circus fairground. Perhaps he was here to buy Rajneesh, for certainly he was into a sales spiel. He talked confidently about interface, love, human growth and many many other words that flowed by me, unrecognised. They were all words which, I found out later, had deep appeal for the Orange People, who were into non-language. The Aryan was full of authority; he knew he mattered. He was a true social construct and, as I listened, I imagined the people who had constructed him, without roots, without a past. It was as if he had, like a vacuum cleaner, run across the carpet and sucked up the pain and discomfort of life from which he had formulated a get-well plan.

Rajneesh did not like competition. He liked obedience, he wanted us to love him as Buddha. The Aryan did not notice his rather aloof reception. He was hearing, with rapt attention, his own interior music — a patchwork of notes from pop psychology mixed with a variety of assertions and dubious half-truths. Then he tired of it and the sales pitch finished, the lights went down and he returned with the black woman to his seat, satisfied he had made a big impression.

Sitting next to me was a young woman, dressed in orange and wearing a *mala*. She was filled with adolescent exultation, like a superstar's moll at a rock concert. She turned to me, her face lit up: 'That's Diana Ross and Werner Erhardt of EST,' she whispered. She murmured to me about how Bhagwan had drawn them here, in the twinkling of an eye, and how they wanted to fall captive to him.

Outside, when the audience had concluded, the air was warm — sultry, they would call it in romantic novels.

I wrote to Rajneesh. I received a reply, scribbled on my letter, to the effect that everything that happens is good. I kept seeing the beggar girl outside the ashram. She had an angry, intense face and held a mummified baby-thing, eyes half-open to the blinding sunlight, who may or may not have registered the flies drinking from its optic fluids. These two were condemned before they began, stepping out in a *danse macabre* between the swirling orange robes, the *biddi* smoke, the tea-sellers, the jugglers, the snake charmers. As a bemo arrived she thrust her hand at me, the new visitor, who was shamed into giving her a rupee or two. Then she sat and drank a cup of tea and the baby-thing was ignored — a mere prop in her theatre of need. For the amiable Italians who were arriving in droves for *tantra* and God and let-go, the beggar girl and others who rooted amongst the ashram garbage were taught phrases like *V'affan culo, figlio di mignotta, cazzo, testa di cazzo*. And the butterflies flew in swathes of colour, the frogs croaked in puddles. One day the baby-thing wasn't there. It must have eventually died, like the frogs and the butterflies of the ashram garden, which also had a short season.

I was to do a group. Oh heavens, said one part of me, while another part said, 'Yum-yum, time for *tantra*, sex and let-go and passion and all that lovely lower level activity so blessed by Bhagwan — who apparently, for all his sensual poetry, fucked with the expertise of a barnyard rooster.'

But it seemed that Bhagwan had decided I would involve myself rather in aesthetic and beautiful events. The group met one evening and walked across a bridge over a reed-covered pool, where a shepherd boy lay with his head resting on the flank of a white buffalo. We turned a corner and walked under huge interlocking trees which had linked stately home to stately home, like a series of marriage alliances. Once the Raj women walked on these still meticulously kept lawns amidst the carefully tended flowerbeds, and perhaps a cousin of my grandfather danced a courting dance.

The house we entered, however, had a drive which was pitted and weedy; the lawn, too, was pitted and overgrown. The house had fallen on hard times, which happens fast in India. Around the back were external stairs shaded by a large avocado tree. I climbed up with the other aspirants and left my sandals outside the door and walked into a spacious empty room. The room opened onto a terrace, where no doubt the evening once heard the clink of ice and the soft, seductive fizz of tonic settling into the gin.

People in the group now discovered each other and lay close together as night fell. As they settled down, lights out, some slept and some screwed and some, like me, listened peevishly to both.

Days passed in a blurr of meditations, relaxes and underground journeys. The group, which was made up of around ten people, was a soft group. Hypnotherapy was the apex of grouphood which would begin with enlightenment and end with dreams; those who needed to get rid of violence did so through *tantra* and other groups. I listened to their stories. It seemed that one young Spanish man in the group had done *tantra* but found it hard to get a hard-on and felt that the soft group might enable him to. Santosh, the group leader, looked around and asked if anyone would mind if the young gentleman wanted to masturbate. The young gentleman had dark curly hair and was very charming. Having lived in Franco's Spain, all this must have seemed to him like paradise regained. I had not done groups before and was unsure about what was allowed. Theoretically everything was allowed: we held each other naked and emotions became like honey, sweet and soft; we talked and talked. It was extraordinary to me that people were not at all frightened to say what they were thinking and feeling.

Marco, a Swiss Italian with long greasy blond hair, sat clutching the thin layer of fat on his belly. It was mid-afternoon and we had drunk lemon grass tea and were resting after an underground journey in search of treasure. 'So I have this dream. In first dream I am wiz muzzer and, man oh man, I want to fock wizz muzzer. But man oh man I cannot.'

Marco was something like a carpenter back in Switzerland. He had innocent blue eyes. He had no idea why he wanted to fock wizz muzzer and neither did anyone else.

'So what happens then?' asked Santosh, eyes twinkling. Santosh was a most pleasant person and had probably read Freud.

'Well, man oh man, I cannot get a hard-on. So I see ziz broom and I pick it up and fock mit muzzer who is a hairdresser with broom handle. And then in second dream I beg Mr Bhagwan to fock wizz me but he don't say Yes so instead I suck his cock and it is good, man, real good.'

Everyone agreed that this was an interesting sequence of dreams. I wore my polite analytical face and supposed that at the next *darshan* Marco would tell Mr Bhagwan all about his father fixations.

The underground journeys continued and sex alternately tightened and flowed free, like water going nowhere in particular. On the fourth day a big Australian girl called Pipassa, standing up, fell backwards. Bhagwan had told her to let herself fall. She was caught and held upright and then she rocked, tears streaming down her cheeks. She had that heaviness of build that comes from farming ancestors and mutton chops for breakfast over many generations; she was a Patrick White woman, Pipassa. She talked little, her doing was being: Mrs Godbold in orange, possessed of grief as ancient as womankind. This grief drew the others to seek comfort from her strength and, in an orange dress falling away from an ample belly she, in her ampleness, allowed them. Her face became icon-like in its abstraction, like della Francesca's *Mater Misericordiae* in San Sepulcro; then, too, the Virgin protected citizens from the plagues they carried with them.

Later the group lay down again, to listen to Jonathon Livingston Seagull. Yet another inner journey: my 'yum-yum' ideal about groups was evaporating and I felt irritable. I lay down with the *lunghi* over me, knowing I would hate every minute of it, Jonathan Livingston Seagull seeming to be a mixture of Jesus Christ and Peter Rabbit. But as the story unwound and the bird flew further away, an unwitting ripple of energy rode up my body from head to toe; I craved to be rid of my known self and never return. The waves moved higher and something flexed and strained to free me of this heavy mix of earth, like a clayey river in flood which was carving out channels to lift me towards the sea. Half beyond myself I have no name and the blessing of that limitation removed is as vast as the sky I struggle towards, my leaden wings flapping and beating, trying for a good run which will set me airborne, circling the high cliffs, soaring with the currents high towards the sun.

The group ended and most of the participants were already looking towards some other group experience. It was nine at night and I returned to the hotel and walked through the dining room to my room. In the kitchen, beside the garbage cans, sat a large, sleek rat, and frustrated by eternity, singing through my inner chaos, I decided on some non-touchy-feely action. I walked briskly back to the office, where Mr Amrashram was contemplating the price of gold in Bombay and matters such as Swiss bank accounts. (At least, this was Harrison's view of what Mr Amrashram did when he unlocked the safe and took out the safe box.) I knocked on the half-open door and interrupted Mr Amrashram viewing a pile of one hundred rupee notes.

'There is a rat in the kitchen,' I said, sahib to the fore.

This galvanised Mr Amrashram, who collected Harrison and two of the kitchen staff. They arrived at the rat hole in procession with Roger, the corgy. Mr Amrashram was now temporarily held in the sahib energy and was tut-tutting to the two kitchen staff who, wearing their off-duty dirty trousers and dirty floral shirts, crept forward at his request. Rat and men spent moments in communal loving interest.

'Well,' I said, 'it *is* a rat, isn't it?'

'Yes indeed, sahib,' said Mr Amrashram.

'And it *is* in the kitchen, isn't it?'

'Indeed, indeed sahib, it is in its hole in the kitchen. It likes

very much the scraps, particularly it likes the scraps of *masala dhosa* and the Sunday lunch scraps it is most happy with.'

I felt myself dissolving into radiant India, and concepts such as Rat, Kitchen and Hygiene dissolved into small letters and flowed away into the place where karma, dharma and who knows, bharma reside.

'And,' said Mr Amrashram, face lightening in comprehension, 'it is indeed a fine rat, sahib, and it is fat and well fed and will not trouble you. Oh no, no indeed, it is also vegetarian.'

Roger, the corgi sat down heavily, having performed his duty of observing, and began to concentrate on his once-a-minute yoga breathing to preserve life, *prana* and so forth.

'Well,' I said, illogically irritated, 'Roger is not looking too good.'

Roger was more ancient than the Ancient of Days, hatched ten diseases a week, was coated in fleas, had rotten teeth and stank and could hardly wag his tail. He needed a purge, vitamins or, most kindly, an injection to put him permanently to sleep.

Mr Amrashram saw things differently, however. He folded his hands on his belly and looked benignly down at Roger, who was deep in a yogic trance and close to final realisation. 'Ah, Roger is very happy. He lies about all day having a very nice time. He is so happy he does not *want* to leave his body. Oh, no sahib, not at all. He enjoys himself so much!' Mr Amrashram pointed a finger at Roger, who knew he had the best karma any Indian dog could hope for; not as good as the Queen's corgis, Mr Amrashram was willing to admit, but almost as good. Roger wheezed out agreement with these loyal sentiments and launched himself back into what I assumed was either a semi-coma or transcendental dog meditations.

The kitchen staff vanished with Mr Amrashram. It was bedtime. The monsoon heat was upon us and the clouds low and heavy.

I walked by the river at Poona with the Spanish businessman who had been in the group. The monsoon had begun and a few scraggy cows gathered at puddles to drink, while on the river fishermen from the houses nearby netted for fish. There were cobras around and we picked our way delicately, ready to levitate at the drop of a fang. Ahead were rows of houses constructed from bits and pieces of wood, plastic and tin, with strangely solid tiled roofs. Outside them women were sand-cleaning their copper cooking pots; spangled and lean chooks strutted around clumps of bright green grass; and small kids, also spangled and lean, played.

We arrived at the *ghats* and stopped on a bank above them. There, someone's life was on fire and a Hindu family was gathered around the cremation pit, which flamed and then died down suddenly into glowing ashes. The Indians stood like creatures of an alien dispensation. Ram! Ram! Ram! Like the soil, life is hectic yet shallow and then it leaves. The Indians seemed to struggle in thin air, like birds which had no current other than that blowing from a distant time and which now was hardly even a breeze.

The Spaniard and I wandered over to the Kali temple, bending low to enter through the door. The first room was sunk into the earth. In a niche was a photo of a benevolent old man, before him cracked vases holding marigolds. 'It is like a stable,' said Avigan, the Spanish businessman, sniffing up the earth and wood smell. To me it was a place to be if winter existed in this country. I imagined a clock ticking on the dresser, a coal stove burning and a fat marmalade cat asleep on the rocker. It had that good dense reliable comfort.

The Kali priest smiled. He was fat and wore white robes that could have done with a wash; he fitted well into the darkness in which he was sitting, on a stone next to the fire. The hearth was of earth, with a half-cracked open chimney to suck up the smoke, and over the fire was a tripod from which hung an old, smoke-blackened steel kettle. A copper teapot which was filled, indicated the Kali priest with a friendly wave of the hand, with warm tea, sat in the ashes. He poured it, after a pause, into two cracked railway cups with brown stains streaking the white. The tea was sweet and good, like the haloed dhoti-robed Indian in the pictures. The Kali priest glanced slowly around to him like any old wife receiving her visitors on behalf of the old man in the photos, her husband.

A female disciple of Rajneesh, who was also sitting in the darkness, glowed with orange.

The old man in the photo was the Kali priest's guru, she said. It seemed that in life the old man had despaired of the pomp and vanity of this wicked world, not to mention the sinful lusts of the flesh, and totally submerged himself in the nearby cooling river for days at a time. The Kali priest waved his hand towards the bridge. 'Yes, it happened out there,' said the Orange disciple, 'just by the bridge. He would be underwater for days at a time.' There, it would seem, he had happily spent his time amongst the dispassionate fish and other aquatic life forms. The Kali priest, who did not have this capacity and roosted where he was, in the earth, basked like any old wife revelling in her husband's glory.

Ram! Ram! Ram!

While I had been writing ecstatic letters about Poona to all my friends, inside something gentle nudged me towards myself. It is confusing for a spiritual aspirant, dying to lay his burden at someone's feet, to find that he ultimately prefers his own reality. The Poona ashram was a wonderful and complex web of desire, madness and collective possession, but that was beyond me just then and I knew it was time to get back to Rome.

It was seven in the morning. I got up and took a shower as the servants came up from the compound and raked out the ashes in the range. They placed a grate across the embers and while I dried myself the toast was browning and the tin kettle was coming to the boil on a single gas ring. I ate my breakfast and Harrison came on duty from somewhere in the bowels of the house. He had had some bad dreams, which he recounted, and was filled with anger at Mr Amrashram, who would not give him a raise. Harrison was also in a frenzy of envy of the two German male Rajneeshies who were visiting the two female hotel Rajneeshies — well, as much frenzy as he could raise, for like Roger the corgi, extremes of activity tended to get lost somewhere in the brain which, like Roman shops on official holidays but still trading, keep their shutters half down for the clientele.

'So these *mas* across the way do not want to do *tantra* with me. I miss very much Los Angeles madam and your madam, Roman madam, is also not interested in *tantra*. Also, Los Angeles madam says she will send more money but it doesn't come.'

'Maybe,' I said, 'she hasn't got your recent letters, Harrison. They say the post is terrible in Los Angeles.'

'Maybe,' said Harrison, moody, drawing back on the last of my Benson & Hedges. Next door Mercedes was listening to Mozart — Clara Haskill playing a piano concerto. I offered Harrison five rupees so he could do the *kundalini* meditation in the evening; not as good as *tantra* with Los Angeles madam, but plenty of exercise to sublimate the tantric needs. The tip cheered up Harrison, who had just failed his exams for the second time and was thinking of going to Kuwait to become an electrical engineer.

'Doing what?' I asked.

'Well,' said Harrison, 'I could clean the air conditioning. I could change light bulbs.'

I decided to change the subject. 'I must get some books; I've been through Roman madam's books.'

'Maybe you could ask her and she buy some more,' suggested Harrison.

I shook my head. 'Well,' said Harrison, 'I will lend you some books. Come and select from my library.'

'OK,' I said.

Mercedes called out through the wall and I went in.

Resplendent in a smart little number run up by one of the local tailors, she was resting with tea and toast and Clara Haskill.

'Don't forget,' Mercedes munched on some toast and put down a Bhagwan book she was reading, 'that the funeral procession is at six.' (That had been announced the day before — the baby of an American disciple had died.) 'And could you tell the servant to bring me a fresh pot of tea.'

Mercedes always looked mildly distracted in India, which she enjoyed.

'You know,' she said en passant, 'one of my great grandmothers was excommunicated by society for dancing with a maharaja at a ball. Isn't that extraordinary! Excommunicated! Although occasionally one can see why, now that one is in India. So different to the Indians one knew in one's youth.'

I left her to her book, ordered the tea via Harrison and followed him down the stairs past the room where the two young and buxom American sanyassins were no doubt considering, or in the middle of, *tantra* with a couple of blond Germanic swamis. Harrison was again emoting envy — not only were the swamis blond and tall with blue eyes but they felt no compunction in trespassing on Harrison's turf. Maybe the *mas* were not as good as Los Angeles madam, being naive and no doubt unskilled and lacking a grandmother's maturity, but still, they were on Harrison's territory.

Harrison was still complaining about this moral outrage when we reached the student quarters. The passage was dark and smelt of Dettol. It was cheerless, with its partitions rather resembling cubicles in brothels of the worst sort: a place Dante might have reserved for indigent whores who did not repent in time to elude his inferno.

Harrison took out a key, unlocked the padlock and ushered me in. The cubicle was too austere even for a whore flaunting herself in *Inferno*. High up was a small window curtained by a dirty polka-dot rag and thick dust on the pane allowed only a smidgin

of natural light to infiltrate. A truckle bed used up half the space, on it a dirty mattress and a dirty green sheet. Harrison had no library, nor did he have a wardrobe and nor did he need one, for his three shirts and two pairs of trousers were hanging from nails. Below them was a picture of a dotty Oriental dancing girl, all sloe-eyes, carmined lips, beguiling fat cheeks, fatter arms and fingers and very fat thighs. The carmined lips were formed into a simper of mystery. I presumed this was Harrison's erotic dream-girl for the lonely nights after Los Angeles madam left and Roman madam, in her prime as grandmother, proved uncooperative.

'This is my spiritual mother,' said Harrison, affecting a sigh.

I adopted a look of admiring interest and noticed the half-burned incense sticks and a small bowl of marigolds that seemed to have abandoned hope of brightening up the shrine.

'Who is it?' I asked. Some Hindu goddess or *dakini*, I presumed, or maybe Kali feeling happy about herself and willing for a bit of fun and games.

'Can't you guess?' asked Harrison flirtatiously, smoothing down a crease in the hanging trousers.

'Well, I did think you were Catholic, Harrison.'

'It is the Virgin Mary,' announced Harrison nonchalantly. 'I worship her and sometimes Kali and Shiva.'

'Well,' I smiled with determined interest. In the West the Virgin Mary was thought to demand exclusive rights over her devotees but here, apparently, she's lost the take-over bid.

'I love her like a mother,' said Harrison. 'After my mother die, she come to me and say she will be my mother.' He languidly flicked some dust balls off the shrine and onto the floor. 'She helps me a lot. She got me this job and she will get me work in Kuwait as an electrical engineer.'

'Well,' I asked cunningly, 'why doesn't she get Mr Amrashram to give you a raise?'

'Oh,' said Harrison, 'she wants me to learn humility. But she will show her greatness when I apply for work in Kuwait.'

That dancing girl, I huffed to myself. Disgusting! Everyone knows Mary is an Aryan, fair of skin and asexually holding an Easter lily. This one looked as if she might even have had an orgasm. Deesgusting.

Harrison ignored my reverie and dragged a box out from under the bed. He surfaced with two books. One cover bore a photo of an Indian saint who seemed, in his glare of irritation, to express a deep distaste for the photographer and for existence in general. The other was the biography of someone called Yogananda, a great enlightened being. It was typical.

Afternoon fell into evening and I thought of the baby who was to be cremated. The death of an European innocent has about it a terrible air. I thought of the old English graveyard in Poona I had visited when down with some monsoon fever which made me wan and melancholy. The graveyard was close to the ashram, with grass knee-high. The broken tombstones, mostly at a lean, read like a list from a *Who's Who* of minor gentry. John and Wendy and Clarissa and Peter had all died too, even at a hill station. It was, the place, like an Edgar Allan Poe set piece, gothic, rotting and revolting. The grass was too green and the empire was dead. I was pleased that this baby was being burned rather than buried in such sick earth.

I took a bemo down to the ashram around the time *kundalini* meditation ended. Mercedes was waiting for me inside the grounds. We talked for a moment and were joined by Avigan, the Spanish businessman.

We wandered out the main gate and encountered a group of musicians. Some were long-haired and hippy, the sort that were dying of hunger up in Kashmir or Khatmandu, clasping their copies of Rajneesh's easy Eastern guide to truth. Others, more virile in appearance, started tuning up. The colours they wore were deep orange and puce. As the sun began to go down, a man began the chant, *Shivam Devam*. Divine Shiva, King of Death, who in his cosmic dance had cast his shadow across the child and withdrawn its breath into his own lungs, the better to continue his dance.

The procession moved off, quietly and decently. The chanting spread and was haunting in its monotonous repetitions. Indian Gregorian. And the man who had begun the chanting had about him a sense of masculine depth and a good love.

Then more sanyassins arrived. They were mostly young people; curious Orange People, as we were curious Orange People, wondering what this funeral would be like, not really caring for the child, yet walking in procession — a pilgrimage towards the *ghats* and the idea of death.

Behind the walls of the large houses where the merchants and aristocrats live, servants gathered in small suspicious groups to watch. Bhagwan Rajneesh was not popular and these were servants of the upper classes. They reflected *their* disdain and that arrogance which all former colonial people feel when they see their masters showing their feebleness of being.

Finally the procession reached an arterial road. The large Orange group — now more like a crowd about to hear an opera or charge forward to get the best seats at a rock concert — broke and ran between trucks to reach the rich green grazing grounds of the riverside-dwellers' meadows. We followed, torches shining through the tracks which led to the *ghats*. The music faltered and broke and died and so did the chant, carried on by a few until they too were swept into incoherence and their voices broke off.

We streamed across the green grass, avoiding puddles and cow shit, torches flickering still to check for cobras. It was now a gay stream of orange, a Super-Orange cocktail party, fighting its way down the steps by the temple of the gentle Kali priest.

Ahead the pyre was waiting, around it grouped a few men and a few women in long gowns. They were contained in respect for

what must now happen to the baby.

Avigan and I climbed a bank as the darkness fell and the baby was shrouded in the baptismal flame. Mercedes wandered, tentative, bewildered, her face distracted, her antennae finely tuned to the resonance of Mozart of Piero Della Francesca, swaying with the gale of power sweeping around her.

They, the Orange People, were here to give themselves up to the joy promised by the most Supreme Master this world had seen since Buddha. He was also the body of Buddha (in time), and controller of all these souls who could not leave without his permission. He would conquer the world, and their small stream would be a mighty Ganges. All were chosen for his dance, this God of Life and Death.

They were, as he had told them, here-and-now Buddhas. It seems that Buddahood is that easy: just a few adjustments, a change of name and clothes, and All is Well. They danced on the wonderful wind of Bhagwan; a wind which blew up their anuses and distended them in some false pregnancy as they raced and danced and celebrated and whirled. Many faces assumed the vacancy of somnabulists as they rioted on the high. Others held hands. Some embraced in deeply felt let-go of emotion called love — love as they had been conditioned to see it by groups from California and the practitioners of that state-of-the-art culture.

Their hems touched the concrete, collected twigs; their sandals collected dog shit as they gyrated, pushed and shivered closer to the fire of the cremation pit. The flames, reaching insubstantial fats or kerosene, rose higher and the shadows cast by the cocktail celebrators gave them a strange appearance. In my throat is bile and also in the throat of Spanish Avigan as the Orange People dance their mass seizure. The shadow is with them and it is growing large. The jackboot is here, even though it has covered its leather with velvet. The camps of Nazi Germany are here, and the madness of those who cast themselves away to find meaning in whatever fills them with power.

Over it all was the sallow, power-filled head of Rajneesh. All this he had willed from the beginning. He was feeding from this frenzy. The little thing on the pyre, now nothing but blackened protein, had hardly taken its first breath; the few people who cared continued to offer that small soul, as a mother does her breast, their love.

Mercedes and Spanish Avigan and I pushed through the crowded theatre and out into the clean, night air.

Noni — That Winter

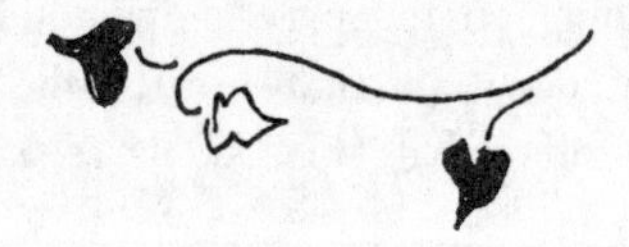

Back in Rome it is September and the dense heat of August has left for hints of autumn.

I settled back into my routine.

Colin, in no. 24 Penitence Alley, invites me to lunch. It is a ground-floor apartment with stone floors, one room devoted to Colin's sculptures and the other a solid harmony of kitchen things, paintings, a wooden table, carpets. Colin comes from New Zealand, loves the theatre of living and being father bountiful to his poorer friends. He is also devoted to Sarah Churchill, who sometimes had problems walking straight down Penitence Street. Colin listened to my story of my discovery of a Spiritual Master. 'I know,' he said over the pasta. 'When I was in Mexico this year I had this absolutely devastating thing with Gloria Swanson. We met over lunch at someone's house at Acapulco and we simply could read each other's thoughts. We simply excluded the other guests, it was so intense. We want to do something together, maybe working in New York on one of the TV channels — doing live sculpture. Anyone want some more pasta?'

I didn't like to say that my romance with Bhagwan was not quite the same as his momentous meeting with Gloria Swanson, although maybe there were elements in common.

I met Rosa, an Australian friend, up at her apartment on Via Luciano Manara for drinks. Rosa had, over one winter, specialised in listening to me and my troubles, cackling with glee as I sloshed

Spanish omelettes around the pan, egg flying onto the walls. 'Another gin please, Rosa.'

'Well, darling, let's get on with it,' said Rosa. We had met once since I had got back from India and I had explained the truths of Poona.

We went into a clinch at the door. 'Aaagh,' said Rosa with throaty glee, blonde hair waving in simulated passion. 'Deep genital contact, darling.'

The only 'That's what you've learned!' lasting lesson from Poona was that most people embrace from the chest up, bum stuck out and belly held in. 'Aaagh,' shrieked Rosa, still at it, 'do you think I've got it right, darling?'

Sheila became interested in the ashram but she saw that my sexual energies had changed for the meantime.

'You used to be such a wild lay,' she said with all the frankness of her Jewish American princess rank. 'Well, well,' (the patient resignation of Jewish mother) 'let's see what comes outa it, honey! Maybe I'll read something, but not that book he wrote on Christ!'

'So,' said Noni, having listened to the story, and being most sympathetic, 'do you think, darling, I could move into the spare room? Cippa is impossible. He spends all his money at the races and *expects* me to clean the house.'

'Deesgusting,' I agreed, 'of course you can.'

This happened as winter arrived and Noni was at her scorpion lowest, sting firmly in her own backside and too weak to pull it out.

Her whines preceeded her down the dark passage to my apartment as she arrived with countless pieces of luggage, surrounded by an entourage of young queens, who were all studying at the courturier school. They were Noni's latest interest; during winter in Rome one seizes diversions where one can.

They flickered and fluttered around her.

'Ma, sai Noni, carissima, mangiamo qualcose. Sai. Noni . . .'

'*Dio mio*,' I brooded, 'is the whole court moving in?'

They did. They came and went, dressed fashionably, talking about fashion and lovers and giving me the eye as a former lover of Noni. They all posed in bed together, surrounding the sick scorpion who was sick here, there, everywhere and could hardly move; might have been dying from the ennui of it all. Might not have been dying — perhaps it was just winter, that winter in Rome.

God! I thought, I truly hate you and your queens!

I went and sat on my vast *letto matrimoniale*, propped myself up with a couple of cushions since my back was playing up. I listened to the Emperor Concerto and prayed that Noni and the queens would leave forever — at least that the queens would leave forever. Yet it was all supposed to be entertaining.

Noni had said, 'Well, darling, we can work like buggery during the day and then have some drinks at six and discuss world affairs, local affairs and our own affairs. Then we can make some delicious little bits of food and soon it will be spring.'

'Aagh,' I moaned, 'it is all my fault, I am feeling so bored and miserable.'

Noni and I decided to hold a dinner party and invited a lot of people. I was in a deeply oral phase and eating too much. Noni accused me of eating most of the Hungarian goulash she has slaved over, before it was even on the guests' plates, and besides *no-one* paid her enough attention and nothing was fun and it was all my fault or maybe —

'Really,' said Noni, 'you will have to get India out of your system. It must be something you ate there and that guru is really too boring for words. You've become so disgustingly sincere! And who, anyway, said *you* had to take the weight of the world on your shoulders? Really, John!'

'I know, I know,' I moaned. 'I know that it is India. I've probably developed some disease of the brain.'

Noni looked medically expert for a moment, and we both knew it was better to leave things as they were — best friends who should not share houses.

'If only,' I moaned, 'we could afford a maid to clean up. If only we could go skiing. If only it wasn't winter.'

But winter was setting in and Noni decided it was all definitely my fault and we both froze, over a few days, into positive but well-mannered mutual loathing. With total good breeding Noni packed and with total bad breeding I pretended not to notice, in case my offers of assistance led to recriminations and tears and a fine golden sunset with us the best of friends again.

The queens were summoned and arrived fluttering, flexing their minimal muscles, and hoisted the luggage downstairs with many a plaintive cry. Noni, regal in her black *carabiniere* cloak and hip-hugging black slacks, hair immaculate, face immaculate, got ready to leave. I heard her feet, the feet of a baroness leaving with great good breeding. I ran to the window in the study, furtive, not wanting to be seen to be looking, and peered slyly from behind the white curtain. Outside in the deserted street was a blue Fiat 500 with, since the car was beetle size, all the luggage on top and the seats, leaving room only for the driver. The entourage obviously would have to walk down Penitence Street, down to the Via Lungara and on to Cippa's basement where Noni would stay for the winter.

I hung out the window now, unable to resist the spectacle as, with the most perfect timing, the sky opened above them with grey, heavy, splattering drops. Noni drew herself up. Behind her stood two ladies-in-waiting and behind them three more queens, as courtiers. But the driver wasn't sure where to go; he poked his head out the window and a discussion ensued. It seemed he had been recruited for the operation at the last minute, although Noni had had several days of councils of war, strategies and plans. These she had conducted in the bedroom, with the door shut, but with frequent sorties to the kitchen by a courtier for a coffee or a campari soda or a whisky, depending on the time of day.

Noni gave precise directions. The Fiat moved off, piled high with luggage plastered with the labels of the great European hotels, casinos, trains, planes and barrage balloons. A would-be courtier opened a large black umbrella and held it over Noni's head. She shrugged, and the courtier held it over his boyfriend instead. Noni preferred the rain, the dignity, the slow step to the scaffold.

By now I was almost falling out the window with the marvel of it all. Where was her missal? Where was her rosary, clasped in white bloodless hands? Where was her black veil? Ahead was the scaffold, in black crepe, the block in black crepe, the headsman giving a final sharpen to the blade. The Chopin 'Death March' struck up in my mind. I wished I had it on record so that I could put a speaker out the window. But there wasn't time to see if I had it, for Noni was now passing, at a slow walk, the rain soaking her hair, washing down onto her high Hungarian cheek bones, dribbling over her perfect false eyelashes and dripping discretely and lovingly over her lightly reddened lips.

They vanished around the corner into Via della Lungara into the worst rainstorm of the season.

Ho hum, I thought, smiling now. I wonder what I'll finally make of Rajneesh, Poona, truth and God. God knows. I returned to my desk and continued to chisel away at myself. Writing does have its use. And, anyway, Noni and I are friends for life and what is life without a few dramas. We'll roar with laughter over this debacle in a few months. Probably roar with laughter over Poona too.